Looking down at her as she knelt at my feet it was impossible for my eyes not to fall upon her delightfully shaped bosom, entirely exposed to view – a pair of breasts perfectly formed as to their profile, and while somewhat diminutive, charmingly globular, and with two enchanting tips of the most attractive pink colour.

The sight had an effect natural in a young man. Far from being offended, she smiled. I therefore drew her to her feet and pressed my kisses upon her breasts, whose elasticity was no less beguiling than I had supposed, and whose nipples, hardening between my lips, were sufficiently responsive to my caress to bring a gasp of delight from the young person's throat . . .

Also available from Headline Delta

Eros in the Country
Eros in Town
Eros on the Grand Tour
Eros in the New World
Eros in the Far East
The Eros Collection
Eros in High Places
Eros in Society
Eros off the Rails
The Ultimate Eros Collection
Eros Strikes Gold
Eros in Springtime
Eros in Summer
Eros in Autumn

Eros in Winter

Anonymous

HEADLINE DELTA

First published in paperback in 1996
by HEADLINE BOOK PUBLISHING

A HEADLINE DELTA paperback

10 9 8 7 6 5 4 3 2 1

ISBN 0 7472 5142 8

Phototypeset by Intype, London
Printed and bound in Great Britain by
Cox & Wyman Ltd, Reading, Berks.

HEADLINE BOOK PUBLISHING
A division of Hodder Headline PLC
338 Euston Road
London NW1 3BH

**For the convenience of the reader
we here record a note of
IMPORTANT PERSONS APPEARING IN
THE NARRATIVE
in the order of their appearance**

Andrew Archer Esq., our hero
Mrs Sophia Nelham, our heroine
Mr Fossgate, a gentleman's tailor
His female assistant
Ernest Simkin Esq., a bookseller
Mme Heloise le Brun, a dressmaker
Miss Prew, her assistant
M. Michel le Brun, her son
Harry, The Viscount Cricklewood
Devon, his servant
Margaret, Lady Cricklewood
Susan, her maid
Betsy, a maid
Mrs Spintwist, a bewildered mother
Robin Spintwist, her son
Meredith Whalley Esq., of the British Museum
Tom Fortescue Esq., RA, a sculptor
Joe, perhaps a costermonger
Bella, a wh*ore
M. Douclerc, a French consul
Mlle Douclerc, his daughter
Mr Trebetherick, a British consul
Mrs Trebetherick, his wife
Jack, a lad
Mrs Plumtre, a neighbour
Jessie, another wh*ore
Sir Franklin Franklyn, of Alcovary, in Hertfordshire

Chapter One

The Adventures of Andy

I have often been asked by friends to relate the events of the winter of 1818–19, but have hesitated for a number of reasons – the foremost one being that a protagonist, a gentleman of some position in society whose part in those events was scarcely creditable, has until recently still been alive. However, his death removes the chief obstacle to such a narrative, and I have now determined to set down the particulars of the occurrences which introduced me to London society.

Before embarking on this work, I naturally consulted my old friend Mrs Sophia Nelham, whose part in the chronicle is not negligible; she agreed for her part to transcribe her recollection of the events; and her acquiescence means that this book may take the form of those other memoirs so kindly received by a heterogeneity of readers over the past decade.

The reader will forgive me if I recapitulate some brief account of the circumstances which resulted in my arriving in London at the age of eighteen. I had (as readers of our first journal[1] will recall) spent the early part of my life first in domestic service and then as a member of a travelling

---

[1]*Eros in the Country*

theatrical company, when at last the elevation of my friend Frank to the peerage and the acquisition of a certain amount of money (which in due course I increased until it became a large fortune) enabled me to stand back and consider with care which direction my life should take. In the first instance Frank (better known as Sir Franklin Franklyn, Bart., of Alcovary in Hertfordshire), who had been my friend since childhood, kindly assured me that his good luck was my own, and that at least for the foreseeable future I need not concern myself with a need to make a living. The income he guaranteed enabled me to set about my adventures without the necessity of concern for money.

At the time of his elevation to the peerage and a financial security, my closest female friend, Frank's half-sister Sophie, had inherited almost as large a fortune through the death of her aged and excessively displeasing husband, a miser whose treatment of her was better after his death than before it – for though she had excusably deserted a husband so repugnant to her (and forced upon her by an unkind father), he had neglected to remove her name from his Will.

Those kind enough to purchase our second volume of memoirs[2] will recall that as it opened Frank and I rode into London in order to visit his town house in Brook Street, and discovered it to be let as a brothel – when through our own endeavours we transformed it from a somewhat sleazy establishment into the finest house of its kind in the kingdom. I fear that at the time of setting down that volume I allowed my readers to believe that this was my first visit to the capital, while my friend Sophie was similarly somewhat disingenuous in her narrative, omitting as I did the incidents which separated the autumn of our sudden enrichment from the spring of our beginning work on the two establishments, ours and Sophie's, the very

---

[2] *Eros in Town*

full and candid description of which has enlivened and delighted (I am pleased to say) those who have been kind enough to peruse it.

It will be no surprise to anyone that my first inclination, upon being granted a pension of considerable generosity, was to make for London – for having grown up in the country, I had always regarded the distant prospect of the capital as one desirable for any young chap wishing to make his fortune, or even to enjoy himself, for such tales as I had heard of the place described it as one likely to please me. Having privately reached that conclusion, my next inclination was to invite my friend Sophie to accompany me, and having settled upon my purpose, I rose one morning determined to put it into practice. I could see from the frost upon the window that it was a cold day, though my room was warm (the fire having been well kept in), so that I was able without any discomfort to step from my naked bed – a great pleasure to me, for until very recently my means had certainly not been such as to afford me the comfort of a warm bedroom (except were it warmed by the presence of some comfortable bedfellow, which I will admit was frequently the case).

Sophie lay in an adjoining chamber, and it was the work of but a moment to step through the door into her room, where I found her already awake, and just receiving a tray of chocolate from her maid – who, such were the known circumstances of our relationship, showed no surprise at my unclothed arrival in the bedroom. This was perhaps not quite as warm as mine, for Sophie preferred a some-what cooler atmosphere; and without waiting for an invi-tation, I slipped between the sheets and took a sip from her chocolate bowl.

'My dear Andy,' she said, laying a hand upon my breast, 'what a cool chap you are,' and setting the tray upon a bedside table, began warming me in the friendliest manner: that is, by laying her cosy body along my own and chafing

3

my flesh with her palms, which lacking that modesty which would have been false between us soon found their way to that part of my person which was perhaps least in need of chafing but most delighted by the action. It had of its own accord adopted a stance which declared itself ready for just the deed which my friend now proposed, and her attentions considerably advanced its eagerness, so that when my friend placed herself upon her back she had no need to coax me into such a position as enabled my prick to find its home.

I should perhaps, as an illustration of our characters, mention that Sophie and I – whose familiarity was complete – had enjoyed each other on the previous evening, and indeed had parted at eleven o'clock or so after celebrating the rites of Venus on two occasions. My relating the fact that scarce eight hours later we were once more engaged in the delightful game of one and one should not be regarded as boastfulness, but rather as a tribute to the liveliness of our natures and our affection for each other.

We needed no particular invention to set us on: while we were happy at other times to experiment with any attitude or gesture which seemed likely to make pleasure keener, the occasions on which we greeted each other by way of friendship were distinguished by the simplest of acts most simply performed, and while we did not hurry, the unadorned movement of my staff within her tight and lubricious pussy resulted in a charming paroxysm which both enlivened and quieted our emotions.

'And now,' said Sophie, when we had separated and she had been so kind as to wipe the juices from my slowly diminishing prick, 'do I take it that you have some announcement to make?'

Indeed I had, I replied, and disclosed my plan to her – which was that we should both, if she was willing, make our way to town, and spend the winter season exploring those pleasures which society might allow us to enjoy.

She was happy to agree, and to cut the story short, in three days we set off, and after one stop at an inn at Ware, arrived in London, where we put up at the Bell Inn in Holborn. As was usual with us, we shared a room, describing ourselves for the satisfaction of the landlord as 'Mr and Mrs'; though separate establishments were often desirable (both of us frequently wishing to entertain friends in our rooms if not our beds), on this occasion we meant immediately to search for our own accommodation, and so the convenience of a single room was natural.

Our immediate requirement, then, was to find an apartment or even a small house; why should we be restricted by the inconveniences of an inn? But, as Sophie pointed out, we first should bespeak some clothes, for those we wore had been bought in the country, and the acquisition of the best sort of town attire, in the latest fashion, would better equip us to deal with those from whom we might wish to lease a property, and who might regard country bumpkins with contempt.

Sophie therefore took herself off to discover a shop where the best gowns might be bought, while I made my way down that magnificent thoroughfare of Regent Street, recently built at the design of the great Mr Nash, and into Savile Row, not far beyond, where I had been advised by Frank that the finest men's tailors were to be found.

I found there a number of doors upon which were advertisements of tailors working within, and having no notion which might be the best, knocked upon one at the southern end of Savile Row, nearest to Piccadilly. It was opened to me by a young gentleman much of my own years, but of a quite remarkable fastidiousness, who upon setting eyes on me advised me, if I had some goods to deliver, to proceed to the back door – and on my explaining that I had rather come to commission some clothes, clearly disbelieved me: until, that is, I produced my bag of guineas, when his entire attitude changed, and he ushered me into a room upon the ground floor, comfortably carpeted and finely furnished with easy couches and chairs.

After but a few moments a gentleman appeared and announced himself as Mr Fossgate (of Fossgate and Crouch, tailors to the aristocracy) and engaged me in conversation. He clearly thought little of the clothing I was wearing (which was sturdy country stuff), and gave me a lecture upon the current fashion for gentlemen about town.

'English dress is now the best in the world,' he announced, 'thanks to the skill of our men in working in wool broadcloth, which can be stretched and moulded to the body. Yours, if I may say so, Mr Archer, is an example of British physique at its best: it will be a pleasure to suit you' (saying which, he laid his hand upon my shoulder in a manner which I found somewhat too familiar for my taste).

'I suggest a coat of plain cloth, without unnecessary embellishment, with a cutaway as worn by huntsmen (our dandies at present favour such a style, without necessarily indulging themselves in country pastimes). Mr Brummell has suggested dark blue, but there is no reason why we should not provide you with waistcoat and breeches of a different colour – for example, a crimson waistcoat and yellow breeches. As to the breeches, these must be close-fitting, so that not a wrinkle shows – they must fit your legs like a second skin. Perhaps,' he went on, producing a tape, 'you will permit me to take some measurements?' – saying which he laid his hand upon my waist in a manner which convinced me that the enthusiasm with which he would approach such a task might lead to familiarities I would not especially welcome.

He certainly sensed my reluctance, and with some hesitation immediately suggested that I might prefer a female assistant to note down the necessary figures. Somewhat confused at the recommendation, I was silent, which he took for acquiescence, and vanished. A few minutes later there was a knock, and a delightful, slim-built, dark young lady entered, attired in a simple straight dress which fell from her shoulders to the floor, and was low cut over a bosom which any man would have found attractive and which I, coming from the country (where it was still the fashion to be more completely covered), found positively inflaming.

The young lady stood for a moment regarding me, without (it seemed) finding the prospect positively alarming, and then approaching assisted me from my coat, which I permitted her to take. She then, somewhat to my surprise, also requested that I remove my shirt.

'It would be possible,' she said, 'to copy both it and that' – she gestured with disdain at my outer garment – 'that item, but neither is in the best of fashion, and we should prefer to begin afresh.'

Taking her tape, she began to run it over my upper body, measuring the length of my arms, the extent of my chest (both when I had inhaled and exhaled); then, taking the liberty (which I willingly afforded her) of loosening the band of my breeches, the circumference of my waist.

'As to underclothes,' she said, 'do you require drawers, and if so, are they to be short, or trouser drawers? We can make them of calico, cotton, worsted (either thick or extra thick) or even of white drill, though this is not convenient, being rather too bulky and unyielding. The latter will set you to the expense of one shilling and sixpence; we can provide two pairs of calico short drawers and the necessary buttons for one shilling and threepence, or a single pair for ninepence.'

I hesitated, not knowing how to explain that I had never worn drawers in my life, and was even in some doubt as to what purpose they served (the reader must remember that I was not much more than eighteen years of age). Happily, the quick young lady caught at my confusion, remarking that she supposed that in the country drawers were not yet worn.

'In town, sir, they are now considered in the fashion, for

like the shirt they prevent our outer clothing from being soiled. However, many young gentlemen eschew them, believing them unnecessary and even in some circumstances a hindrance to the prompt expression of those natural desires which insist upon satisfaction.'

She then stepped back, and looked critically at my knee-breeches.

'I am in some difficulty here,' she said, 'for as I believe Mr Fossgate has mentioned, breeches are at present close-fitting, while yours are (if you will forgive my pointing it out) in the fashion of some thirty years ago – which I know is still preferred in the country; that is to say your breeches are loose over your hips and upper legs, so that to take measurements over them would be impossible. Perhaps therefore you would not object . . .' And to my surprise, stepping forward, she completed the loosening of my waistband, and falling to her knees, in a moment had drawn them about my ankles, and was undoing my shoes preparatory to removing my nether garments altogether.

My feelings were extremely mixed. I had had dealings with the female sex for some years previous to the interview I describe, and as readers of my memoirs will acknowledge, was not of a shy nature where women were concerned. However, the young lady's self-possession had somewhat disarmed me, and this was the first occasion upon which my clothing had been removed by a female person without the act being obviously a preface to a carnal connection.

Yet the occasion was not devoid of lubricity, for now that she knelt before me, the young person's dress (which I have no doubt was in the best style – for I had already noted that a cardinal point of women's fashion in the capital was to wear as little as possible without positively offending decency) fell somewhat away from her body, so that looking down at her as she knelt at my feet it was impossible for my eyes not to fall upon a delightfully shaped bosom, entirely exposed to view – a pair of breasts perfectly formed as to their profile, and while somewhat diminutive, charmingly globular, and with two enchanting tips of the most attractive pink colour.

The sight had an effect natural in a young man, and my prick, which had been calmly folded away within my clothing, now – released into air and prompted by so inspiring a sight – began to stir, not growing indeed to an extent positively embarrassing, but certainly swelling sufficiently to be expressive of my admiration.

The young woman could scarcely have failed to notice this, her face being but a few inches from the phenomenon; but she took no notice, merely reaching for her tape and passing it first from my hip to my outer ankle, then about my calf, then (and at this point I attempted, not with entire success, to concentrate my mind upon the recent violent activities in Manchester, relative to the Reform Bill) threw it around my upper thigh, and finally with a cold hand inserted one end in the hollow between my cods and thigh, which naturally necessitated her cool hands brushing against my bollocks, the consequent sensation being so lively that despite my thoughts remaining determinedly political rather than carnal, my prick seemingly of its own volition swelled still further, and even began to rise.

The young woman still pretended not to observe this, and now enquired which side I dressed. I had no notion what she meant, whereupon without embarrassment she remarked that different gentlemen, when climbing into their breeches, disposed their masculinity to different sides, and that when tailoring breeches allowances must be made.

'In your case,' she went on to remark, 'it must certainly be the case that a substantial relaxation of material must be allowed for' – and she attempted to enclose my prick and cods between her hands, in order to dispose them to left or to right, thus demonstrating her meaning, for the former (though by no means fully extended) was now of a size which made it impossible for her small palms to contain it. Her action did not make the situation any less confusing to me, for my prick, tortured by so gallant an action, sprang now to its full size, bursting from her palms like a cannon through ramparts.

Far from being offended, she smiled – and I was persuaded by a saucy glance from a pair of sparkling black eyes, and the fact that she did not withdraw her hands, but rather now held my instrument as though about to measure it for a suit, that she would not be offended by my taking matters further. I therefore drew her to her feet, and with a roughness that I would not now employ but which was the natural accompaniment of youth (and no more I believe than she expected), tore her dress from her shoulders, and having rendered her upper body as bare as my own, pressed my kisses upon her breasts, whose elasticity was no less beguiling than I had supposed, and whose nipples, hardening between my lips, were sufficiently responsive to my caress to bring a gasp of delight from the young person's throat.

That my action gave no offence was clear not only from the unmistakable if muffled sounds of pleasure emanating from the young lady's throat, but from the freedom with which her hands now caressed my shoulders and back, now serving to pass over my breast and to reach down to my belly. Their progress there being arrested by our posture, I speedily corrected it by lifting my head from her breast, whereupon pausing only to place a swift kiss upon my mouth, she once more knelt before me and with every impression of pleasure, to my astonishment took my prick between her lips!

That this surprised me may be put down to my inexperience of the town. I had of course been caressed in this manner before, but had supposed that such rudeness must be a concomitant of country manners, for I could not believe that such an action, however delightful to the recipient and apparently inoffensive to the performer, could be proper in polite society. While it was true that the young lady whose lips were now moving up and down the column of my charmed tool was only a servant, it was also the case that she was clearly versed in proper behaviour – the establishment was, after all, respectable; and it delighted me to realise that there was apparently no social bar to the enjoyment of libidinous activity even in the most genteel society.

I admit that these thoughts were only registered in their roughest form, for my sensations were far too thoroughly engaged for rational deliberation to be possible: not only were the young lady's lips pressed about my aching flesh with an affectionate closeness, the skin now lubricated by the warm and slippery liquid of her saliva, but her fingers were meanwhile busy, moving with the lightest and most enchantingly ticklish motion over the cheeks of my arse, and persuading my thighs apart in order that they could the more freely range over my bollocks and the adjacent skin.

It speedily became clear to me that if I was to retain my manly powers for a longer period of time than the next fifty seconds, our attitude must be changed; and bending, I persuaded her to relinquish the titbit she apparently so enjoyed, and led her to a couch – the remains of her clothing falling away as we went. For a moment I stood and enjoyed the picture before me: she lay, one arm above her head, so that her right side was somewhat stretched, the relative bosom moderately raised, its tip now a darker red than when I had first observed it and drawn into a tight knot (equivalent in its appreciation of the circumstance, I supposed, to my own prick, which was now of the rigidity of iron, and stood up against my belly at an angle almost vertical).

She had thrown one leg out to the side, and it was now my pleasure to observe a small, curly black bush between her thighs which concealed without entirely obscuring a pair of entrancing lips, which as I bent to place a kiss upon them I saw enshrined a nub of flesh at their upper division which had the appearance of the tip of a little finger.

Unaware of the medical term for such a phenomenon, I was sufficiently educated in the manners of the bed-chamber to know that this was a part of the female anatomy which was capable of giving extreme pleasure to ladies, and kneeling at the side of the couch I bent over and placed the tip of my tongue upon it, gently agitating it. The result was a moan so loud that I feared that some attendant might appear to disturb us, and reaching up, placed my hand over the young lady's mouth to stifle further exclamations as I continued to stimulate the man in the boat (as it is sometimes called), the young person thrusting her loins upward in an attempt to encourage me to further efforts.

She seemed driven almost to distraction by my endeavours, and seizing my prick pulled so powerfully upon it that I was forced to throw myself upon the couch, when she wriggled into such a position that her head was inserted between my thighs, and I felt her lips once more close about my prick – not without some discomfort, for in order to do so she must prise it from its position into one somewhat unnatural: yet the pleasure of the sensation she conveyed negated any discomfort.

The intensity of her emotion was such that in a very short time her entire body convulsed, and a muffled cry indicated that she had reached the apogee of pleasure. The cry brought about my downfall (for it has ever been my weakness to be stirred by the enjoyment of others, as well as by my own); and I managed just in time to snatch my instrument from between her reluctant lips, discharging liberally over her bosom that liquid which is the sometimes inconvenient product of a gentleman's satisfaction.

We lay for a moment exhausted; but then I lifted myself from her body, and taking up my shirt – which was the most convenient piece of cloth – wiped from her person the evidence of my pleasure. She seemed touched by this, for she thanked me prettily, then invited me to remain while she fetched some refreshment. Dressing herself (and I was pleased to see that I had not considerably damaged her garment – the only covering she had), she left the room, returning shortly with some wine. I drank a glass with pleasure; whereupon she took her tape and completed her measurements – during which activity the door opened and without any fuss the gentleman who had received me entered, showing no surprise that his female attendant was at that moment passing a measuring instrument over the buttocks of an entirely unclad young gentleman, whose prick, however, showed no immediate evidence of interest – though for a reason I hoped he was unaware of.

Mr Fossgate next reappeared, bringing with him a small pile of garments, and when he had left, his assistant (whose name, alas, I never knew) took from it several under-garments which she invited me to try: these consisted of calico drawers, some of which were mere clouts, concealing prick and cods in a simple pouch, some of which covered the entire buttocks and upper thighs, and the most complete of which were virtually, themselves, breeches.

I was doubtful whether they were a necessary garment, and the young woman shared my view, though she did her best to make a sale, assisting me to try them on, and in the case of the more diminutive of them tucking the material about my person in a manner which certainly demonstrated the garment's worth, but also had an effect which was sufficiently marked to please her (as, I suppose, a renewed compliment to her charms). In those days I needed but a few minutes to recover sufficiently from one bout to essay another, and to cut the story short I was able to show her that my skill as a lover extended to a full demonstration of the carnal act, and that my prick was capable of satisfactory sheathing in that part of her person where convention encourages such penetration.

'I trust, sir, that you have found our service acceptable so far as you have experienced it?' said Mr Fossgate as I left.

'Indeed, sir,' I said – having placed a rather larger order than I had anticipated doing. 'I congratulate you upon the efficiency of your young lady assistant.'

'She is generally considered skilful,' Mr Fossgate asserted, 'though naturally we have young gentlemen happy to perform the same service, and should you request it, the fitting of your clothes, tomorrow, could be done by one of them?'

I hastily avouched that it would be quite acceptable for any fitting to be done at the hands of the young lady whose skills I admired; and indeed that I should look forward to such an event. I then returned to our inn, and on the following day at the appointed hour – for in those days it took no more than twenty and four hours for a suit of clothes to be made – returned to Savile Row, where indeed the young lady assisted me to try on the suit, though sadly in the presence of Mr Fossgate, who showed no signs of leaving us to ourselves, so that the possibility of a repetition of our enjoyable bout was denied us.

Instructing the tailor to destroy my old clothes, I left his premises elegantly garbed in a fine black coat with white waistcoat and sage-green breeches, making a fine figure – as I could see from my reflection in the windows of the shops as I walked down to Piccadilly and then along to the Haymarket, into which I turned.

It was now late evening, and at that time, when a dense throng of people crowd along London Bridge, Fleet Street, Cheapside, Holborn, Oxford Street and the Strand, perhaps no sight makes a more striking impression on the mind of a young man new to the scene than the brilliant gaiety of Regent Street and the Haymarket. It is not only the nobility of the buildings which affects one, but the brilliant illumination of the aristocratic shops in the neighbourhood, of the cafés, Turkish divans, assembly halls and concert rooms, and the troops of elegantly dressed women, rustling in silks and satins and waving in laces, promenading along these superb streets among throngs of fashionable people and persons of every order and pursuit, from the ragged crossing-sweeper and tattered shoe-black to the high-bred gentleman of fashion and scion of nobility.

At the north end of the Haymarket I stepped into a bookshop (such places being invariably attractive to me), and before I had picked up a single volume, my eye fell upon a discreet placard advertising the fact that rooms were available for letting to single gentlemen, in the premises above. Enquiring of a menial, I was directed to an office at the back of the shop, where the proprietor – a Mr Ernest Simkin, a man of middle years – informed me that indeed a set of rooms was free, and agreed to show them to me. They proved to comprise a small sitting room overlooking the Haymarket from a pretty curved window – a room sufficiently large to contain also a diminutive table for dining – and an adjoining bedroom with a quite sufficiently large bed, a cupboard and wardrobe. They would suit me admirably for a short season; and on discovering the sum asked was no larger than three shilling a week, I closed immediately with the amiable Simkin, and within two hours had paid my reckoning at the Holborn inn, left a message for Sophie with my address, and moved my small baggage into my new domicile.

It was a pleasure to me to sit in the window and watch the comings and goings in the street below – particularly the promenading of the ladies, of whom a great variety was to be seen, from those dressed in the highest style of fashion to humbler females. They appeared to be occupied merely in strolling, rather than to be about any business, for most of them I saw again and again, passing and re-passing below me; the street seemed to be one in which ladies and gentlemen commonly met in the way of friend-ship, for time and again I saw one of the young ladies greet a gentleman, who sometimes merely tipped his hat, sometimes ignored the greeting (a rudeness which seemed to me offensive), and sometimes after a brief conversation a pair would walk away together.

The truth is (and I blush to record it) that I was then so inexperienced as not to be capable of recognising women of pleasure when I saw them. I was fascinated when, upon venturing forth, I was stopped by five ladies within as many minutes, enquiring whether I was 'looking for business' or wanted 'a bout'.

As it happened, I was for that day satisfied – and might never have realised the truth had not one moderately handsome young woman assured me she only charged two shillings: whereupon the truth was suddenly born in upon me (the only loose women I had previously come across being either servants or their mistresses, neither of which desired any payment for indulging in a happy exchange of compliments in bed).

The following morning I spent in strolling about the streets, observing the fashionable and unfashionable – chiefly, I must confess, the latter, the lower orders being more prevalent about town before noon than their superiors, many of whom did not step from their beds until ten, and must then spend a couple of hours prettifying themselves and primping their persons.

Having dined off a pie and some ale in a public house in Covent Garden, I decided to walk to the Bell for a word with Sophie; but there discovered no sign of her, but only a letter addressed to me with the message that she was staying with a friend, the Viscount Cricklewood, at an address some miles away. She had lost no time, I thought, in ingratiating herself with the great; and I set out by carriage to discover her and enquire what adventure had resulted in her fetching up at such a place.

Chapter Two

Sophie's Story

I had no difficulty in falling in with Andy's plan for a leisurely winter in the metropolis, for although the experiences of my eighteen years had been sufficiently full and far-ranging to satisfy many people's curiosity about creation, I had never yet had the opportunity to take existence easily, and now determined to spend some months (with no necessity to earn a living) simply in observing my fellow creatures – and especially those who lived in society, for my time had chiefly been spent (apart from occasional meetings with the aristocracy) in the company of the more general class of beings – that is, what the Greeks called *hoi polloi*.

I therefore set out from the inn, on our first full day in London, to find lodgings in a civilised part of town – but before I had walked far along the Strand realised that before that, I must visit a dressmaker, for I found myself sadly out of fashion – not that there were not, about the street, persons dressed like myself; but these were clearly not ladies of society, for an occasional glimpse I had of such, as they climbed from their carriages to walk into this shop or that, showed them to be dressed in an entirely different mode to that which was being worn in the country (which is as a matter of course somewhat behind Town in these matters).

I therefore took myself to the Haymarket, and turned into the Royal Arcade, set up at the side of His Majesty's Theatre – a fine and elegant covered street or lane where a number of refined shops are to be found, several of them setting themselves up to clothe ladies in the latest style, as advertised by exquisite drawings of the latest fashions displayed in their windows.

At the bottom of the arcade was a shop with a plain front, a simply and beautifully calligraphed sign announcing it as the domicile of Mme le Brun, *couturière*. Having no means of distinguishing one such place from another, I entered it, to be greeted by a young person to whom I signified my desire to consult Mme le Brun. She looked somewhat askance at me, clearly unimpressed by my present mode of dress, but after some hesitation disappeared, to return with a handsome middle-aged woman, dark and of somewhat sallow complexion, who introduced herself as the proprietor of the place, and enquired how she could help me

I wished (I said) to acquire a small wardrobe of the most exquisite and refined gowns for wearing during the coming season.

'As you see, madam,' I said, 'I come from the country, and readily observe that the style to which we are accustomed there is no longer being worn in Town . . .'

'Indeed, madam,' she replied, 'but you need not rebuke yourself on that score, for had you come into London only a few months ago you would yourself by no means have been out of the fashion. However, the heavier clothing of the past decade has now been rejected, and even the *robe de chemise*, with its high waist, is somewhat *démodée*; we now go so far as to recommend a dampening of the material so that it clings tightly to the form – for bosoms are being worn this season, and those fortunate enough to possess figures of classic proportions are advised to disclose their fetching symmetry with as much frankness as is concomitant with decency – and sometimes, indeed, to go so far as to pass beyond those bounds, even in the best society. Within the past few weeks the newest French fashion has reached us, and shows a considerable transformation from what we have been used to – that is to say, the height of fashion is now the lightest possible muslin cambric or calico gown, with an extreme *décolleté* even in the daytime, though sometimes the use of a shawl – in cashmere, of course – is called into play to cover those bosoms which either through shyness or an acknowledgement of their imperfection must be concealed. But perhaps you would care to cast your eye over some examples?'

On my expressing myself as entirely willing, she instructed the young person, her assistant, to lock up the shop – for, she said, she only dealt with one customer at a time; and then escorted me into a room at the back of the building, which was somewhat larger than the shop – consisting as I suspected of two rooms made one by the demolition of a wall. At one end of this chamber was a small platform, at the other, two chairs, into one of which she seated me, while taking her own place in the other. Picking up a small silver bell from a nearby table, she then rang it – on which a young gentleman, of perhaps twenty and five years, appeared, and was introduced as M. le Brun, and the proprietor's son. He was a good-looking young chap, who – his mother explained to my surprise – had made a career in Paris as a designer of clothes for ladies; this apparently is a profession which in France is not considered improper for one of the male sex, though in Britain such an interest would be considered unmanly.

Michel le Brun (for such was his name) stood at our side, and the bell was once more rung, when the curtains behind the platform stirred, and a handsome young woman appeared, clad in what I took to be a gown of the most modern and fashionable appearance. This hung from the wearer's shoulders with the utmost simplicity, its line undis-

turbed by any furbelows, so that the contours of her body
were perfectly displayed. It was however caught in at the
waist, a phenomenon upon which I could not but comment.

'This,' said M. le Brun, 'is now the rage. As you will see,
the gown is of the utmost simplicity; a consequence of
which is that the style best suits the young, or those ladies
whose figures have been well preserved despite the passing
of the years. Waists are once more where they should be
– that is, where they naturally are, rather than just below
the bosom. Those without the necessary narrow waists
must necessarily make use of the corset – a facility which
will not in your case be necessary' – and he favoured me
with a smile in which I seemed to discern something of
admiration. 'This gown is in cotton, but of course any
material can be made up into a comparable style.'

He rang the bell again, and a second young woman
appeared in a similar gown, but this time made up in
cambric, which if anything clung even more revealingly to
the figure.

'I see,' I remarked, 'that what you say is no more than
the truth: and if I am not mistaken, this is a fashion which
must have its effect upon the diet of the wearers!'

'Indeed that is the case with some matrons, but you need
not concern yourself,' said M. Michel generously; 'nor, if I
read you aright, need another proclivity of the new fashion
– which is that for evening wear at any event, one's clothing
must be as light as possible . . . Indeed, some ladies prefer
the thinnest obtainable material.'

At another ring of the bell, the first girl reappeared in
a dress the style of which was much like that of the first,
but which was made in a material so sheer that the outline
of her breasts could clearly be seen, their tips shown not
only by the emphasis of the nipples, but by their colour,
clearly discernible through the white chiffon (as it is
called); while below, the mark at which most men would
aim their eyes was equally clearly distinguishable.

'And you mean,' I said, 'that such a garment is now worn in polite society?'

'That is so,' was the reply, 'and at court, even – for we are told that the Prince of Wales is an admirer of the style, which has been worn by that excellent woman Mrs Fitzherbert. It is a fashion which, I need not say, must commend itself to those gentlemen who are admirers of the sex.'

'Then,' I said, 'perhaps you would supply me with, say, four such dresses, two for daytime wear and two for the evening?'

'Certainly,' said Madame. 'We have a number of gowns which have already been placed before the public, and copies of which have been sold to ladies of fashion; or if you wish, my son will be happy to design especially for you?'

I expressed the hope that he would do so, for individuality is (as I have always held) the mark of the successful woman.

M. le Brun seemed particularly pleased at my decision, and producing a tape from his pocket invited me to step into his measuring room – a small chamber next to the larger one. 'If you wish, I will remain with you while Michel completes his measurements,' said Madame, 'for some ladies have an objection to such a necessarily intimate connection with a gentleman . . .'

I naturally replied that I had no such objection, whereupon she left. Rather than beginning his work, however, M. le Brun stood as though perplexed; and when I asked whether there was any difficulty, replied that the new fashions were such that a close measurement of the body was necessary, which would be difficult to obtain in view of the somewhat cumbrous nature of my present attire.

I laughed at this, and said the situation was easily remedied, without further ado removing my dress – which the young gentleman took and carefully laid over a chair. He then took his tape, and inviting me to turn around, passed it about my upper body, holding the ends just above my breasts: his fingers necessarily brushed my nipples, which, in that reaction which the most reticent lady would not be able to prevent under such circumstances, gathered themselves into tight knots. I fancied that I felt his hands tremble a little – though it might, I thought, have been my imagination, for he must by now be accustomed to just this situation.

He passed the tape now to my shoulders, then carefully measured my arms – both from shoulder to wrist, and from the inside of the wrist to that cavity beneath my arms, which he approached with great delicacy (for, he said, many ladies were thrown into easy hysterics by the slightest touch in that sensitive area of the body).

He now took the measurement about my waist, once more congratulating me upon its slimness, and excusing the pressure with which he laid his hands upon the mound of my belly – for, he said, this was perhaps the most important area of the body where the present fashion was concerned; to be able to discern the dint of the navel through the material of the gown was a mark of the finest design.

At just that moment, the end of the tape escaped from his fingers, and in reaching forward to catch at it, he necessarily pressed his body against my back – at which I was amused and complimented to feel the unmistakable pressure of an extended male member against a cheek of my arse.

I am sure that had I been able to see his face, I would have discerned a blush; though perhaps this would not have been the case, for no doubt realising that I could not but be aware of his condition, he apologised with great sang-froid: 'Although it is the fact that almost every day I find myself in the closest connection with ladies in a sometimes extreme state of undress, I have not yet been able to school my senses to ignore such beauty as your own, if I do not offend you by such an admission.'

I assured him that I was not in the least offended; and that he was indeed an admirer of mine became clearer when he stepped around to measure the space between my breasts, for I could not but observe that at that point where his breeches, apparently as closely cut as my own dress, closed over the upper part of his legs, the elongated swelling lying upon his right thigh seemed somewhat to enlarge as he looked at me.

Kneeling before me he now placed the tape about my calf, then my lower, and finally my upper thigh – which entailed his placing one hand in such a position that those soft hairs which decorate the centre of my being brushed against the back of it; at this, in an action so swift that it would have been impossible for me to resist even had I wished to do so, he leaned forward and pressed his own lips to my lower ones.

He immediately recovered himself, and rising (somewhat uncomfortably) to his feet, apologised for the offence.

'I fear madam,' he said, 'that your beauty is irresistible to me. For your own safety, perhaps I should summon Miss Prew, who will complete the measurements . . .'

'Don't be a fool, sir!' I said, and taking him by the shoulders, planted a kiss upon his lips so enthusiastic as to assure him that I was neither offended by his action nor disposed to insist upon his retiring.

I should perhaps in a brief digression point out that I was at the time a young woman of some years fewer than twenty; formerly married to an ancient idiot of a husband, who had fortunately passed out of this life before forcing me to cohabit with him; and that my experience of the male sex had been upon the whole confined to rough fellows – countrymen, gypsies, and the like; those gentlemen with which I had had to do were also of the squirearchy rather than of true aristocratic birth, and sensitivity, either corporeal or intellectual, was not marked in any of those with whom I had had the opportunity of intimate alliance.

I cannot deny that almost from the moment I had set eyes upon M. le Brun, I had been curious as to his nature: slim almost to effeminacy, his whole manner was very different from that which I had been used to – even in my dear friend Andy, who had not by any means at that time had that experience or learned those manners which were later to make him the most distinguished of men. If I am to be completely frank – and that must always be the aspiration of these memoirs – from the moment I had set eyes upon the *monsieur* I had wondered about the configuration of the body beneath the clothes; and it was most agreeable to me that it should be made clear that I would not longer be forced to remain curious!

'Please make yourself comfortable!' said I; and he required no prompting, immediately throwing off his shirt and trousers and (what was surprising to me) a garment resembling pantaloons made out of white cotton, and cut off above the knee: a French fashion which was not to become common in England for another ten years or more.

The body thus revealed was by no means disappointing to the female senses: though he immediately made to step forward and embrace me, I held out my hand and persuaded him to pause for a moment, in order to inspect it: an instruction he was happy to obey, for he possessed a sense of pride in his appearance which was by no means offensive, but showed merely a proper judgment of the importance of the visual sense where appreciation of the opposite sex is concerned.

His body was neither offensively effete nor particularly muscular, resembling more than anything those ancient marble statues of naked athletes so beloved of the ancient Greeks: a breast entirely hairless, its flatness relieved by the most elegant swellings about his paps, the gentle rosiness of which presented them like two delightfully tinted flowers. This breast was broad enough to be manly, yet narrowed to a waist almost slim enough to be a girl's, below which a tight, smooth belly had none of the protuberance all too often marked in those gentlemen too given to the delights of the table or the bottle. Two finely shaped thighs were, like his arms, perfectly in proportion – while between them was set a machine which demonstrated his masculinity with an assertion unmistakable enough to reassure any woman who by his profession and polite manners might have been placed in doubt of it, for above two shapely cods rose a third leg as sturdy as the others, and apparently as muscular, drawn up at an angle which almost laid it against his belly, its base surrounded by a little mass of tight, black curls – the only hair to be found upon his body, except of course that his buttocks might, as is often the case, be dusted with a light fuzz.

A simple gesture of mine persuaded him to turn – his eyes already glinting in acknowledgement of my approval of his person. I was pleased to find his back as shapely as his front: his shoulders broad, and the flesh beneath them marked by muscles sufficiently prominent to announce a healthy strength, without being so noticeable as to be offensively prominent. Below his waist hung a pair of cheeks whose round firmness and plumpness could scarcely have been more attractive: bare as billiard balls, they positively demanded a caress – and throwing myself on to my knees I could not resist showering them with kisses (for, like almost every lady with whom I have discussed the matter frankly, a brave backside can bring me on more speedily than the sight of the most outstanding prick!).

At the touch of my lips – to say nothing of my hands, which I placed first upon his hips, but which then almost of their own accord inevitably strayed around so that their fingertips began to feel the springy wires of those curls which so charmingly decorated the lower reaches of his abdomen – M. le Brun, or Michel as I should perhaps now call him, could no longer restrain a shudder of pleasure, and in one movement turned, bent, lifted me to my feet, and laid me upon the convenient couch (which I could not but suspect must previously have been used for just such a purpose as this, for this was not a gentleman whose charms could have always been resisted by his female customers – even if some may have preferred men of a more massive frame).

The sensitivity which no doubt he employed in his work was wonderfully well displayed in the passage which followed, for there was none of the rampant carnality about him which results in what amounts to rape: rather, there was a sympathetic tenderness which slowly built towards passion – a lovemaking which began with the softest possible caress of lips upon lips, and progressed to an equally delicate nuzzling of my breasts (the tip of his tongue approaching my nipples with the sensitivity of a bird feeding from the hands); meanwhile his palms stroked my sides and thighs with a sensitivity too rarely experienced from a lover, and finally fell upon my puss to pet it as one might pet a butterfly or a moth – the touch so light that that whole part of my person began to glow and tingle, and by the time his lips approached was longing for their caress – which when it came consisted first of a stroking with the tongue, then of a gentle sucking which seemed to draw out my soul; and indeed without the slightest roughness he raised me to a first paroxysm with only the most delicate approach.

My panting cry of pleasure pleased him; raising his head, he smiled, and hoped I had been gratified! My reply was to draw his body on top of my own, and throwing my legs about him, positively to invite him to that conventional congress which must please even the most sensitive of men – for although some (and Michel was just such a one) obtain great pleasure from pleasing a mistress, and are happy to give and receive the most recondite of caresses, I have yet to find many to whom the practice of thrusting their essential instrument into the body of their mistress does not represent the primary satisfaction.

That this was so in Michel's case was plain, for the position in which he now found himself immediately persuaded him to eschew the delicacy of approach which he had formerly displayed, and he began a motion as virile and positive as that of the least gentlemanly country fellow – the bones of his hips striking against my own, his belly smacking mine, and that charming arse (to which I must confess I should have liked to have given more attention) rising and falling with a motion as spirited as that to be welcomed from any man.

It is sometimes sadly the case that the more sensitive the lover, the shorter the period of his lovemaking, for I have observed that just those gentlemen who most completely understand the means of raising the female spirits are least capable of staying the pace for any length of time. Happily, Michel was an exception, for though it was as clear from his expression as from the sounds emitted from between his gasping lips that his enjoyment of the act was considerable, there was no sign that that enjoyment might be prematurely ended: indeed, his spirited motion had an inevitability more like that of a machine than a man. Once more, an expression of pleasure must have made it clear that I had experienced a pinnacle of bliss; and opening eyes which had been tightly screwed shut, he gave me a somewhat tormented smile and paused for a moment to enquire whether I was happy still to continue – to which I replied in the affirmative.

At this, he continued his motion, but now lifted himself and supported only by his hands and feet so positioned himself that the point of contact between us (now that I threw my legs wider apart) was his prick, which, looking down, we beheld entering and leaving my body like a piston, its length glistening with those mutual exhalations which were the signal of our pleasure. It was a charming picture, which I believe gave him as much satisfaction as it gave me; so much the case indeed that I could not resist reaching down and allowing my fingers to add to his pleasure by playing about the instrument. The pleasure however was now too great: for with a cry he once more closely embraced me with a violence which brought me off once more, before withdrawing himself to expel upon my belly the scalding evidence of his own satisfaction, within the puddle of which his prick for a few moments slithered before lying still and almost immediately beginning to relax.

After we had recovered ourselves, and Michel had opened a side cupboard to discover a bowl of water and some cloths with which he had cleansed my body (a convenience which suggested that the incident which had just occurred was not entirely uncommon), he picked up my dress with the aim of assisting me into it – but looking at it with some disdain, asked whether I would not prefer him to provide me with a somewhat more fashionable robe to wear until – in two days' time – my own would be ready. I was happy to acquiesce, and excusing himself (and first taking the precaution of resuming his own clothing) he left the cabinet, and in a short time returned with a handsome dress in lilac silk, into which he assisted me; it fitted me perfectly, something in which he took a pride (for, he said, the measuring of female customers in general only confirmed those dimensions of which observation had already assured him). He also kindly presented me with a fine velvet cloak, for – he said – my new dress being considerably more delicate than that to which I was accustomed, I might find the autumn air a little chill.

He then kissed my hand, and escorted me to the door.

I strode back along the Strand, and turned into a narrow

street which led north, towards the Bell Inn, where we had taken a room. Ahead of me strode a superior-looking gentleman in a cloak and tall hat – and soon I noticed that behind him lurked a young man of perhaps fifteen or sixteen years of age, dressed in an old ragged coat much too large for him, hanging over his back in tatters with a string to fasten it round his waist, and a pair of old trousers and a grey cap. He had the air of an old man as he sauntered along, keeping always a yard or so behind the other. As we reached a dark part of the passage or lane, he suddenly threw himself forward, precipitated his victim to the ground, snatched a purse, and turning ran straight towards me – of whose presence I believe he had been unaware.

Without wishing to throw myself into a situation where violence might do me an injury, I was (as always) indignant at such open thieving, and as the boy ran past me threw out a foot and tripped him to the ground. The gentleman, who had regained his feet, was already running towards us – and my victim rapidly sprang to his feet, with a quick motion threw the purse towards him, and made off, inadvertently (as I suppose) striking me to the ground with the speed of his movement.

The gentleman raised me solicitously to my feet, and enquired whether I was hurt. On my promising him that I was not, he was nevertheless most ardent in his desire to assure himself of the fact, and insisted on my taking his arm.

'It is sadly the fact,' he said, 'that one can no longer walk with absolute safety in some quarters of London – which was not so in my father's day; indeed, madam, if I may say so the streets to the north of the Strand are notoriously unsafe, and I do implore you not to take to them if it is possible to avoid it.'

I replied that I was making my way to the Bell – upon hearing which, he expressed some surprise that a lady of my breeding and nicety of manner should be staying in such a place.

'I assure you, sir, that it will be but for a few days,' I said, 'until I can take rooms for myself in some decent quarters.'

'My dear madam,' was his immediate response, 'I beg that you will allow me to place accommodation in my house at your disposal! There are rooms which stand ready, always, for my guests, and in view of your assistance to me, the provision of safe shelter can only be small reward.'

I hesitated somewhat, for though he seemed highly respectable – and his clothes certainly proclaimed a gentleman of means – he was entirely unknown to me.

Seeing my hesitation, he was quick to add that his wife would also be happy to welcome me; and the words proclaiming his respectability, I was happy to concur in his suggestion, whereupon he introduced himself as Harry, Viscount Cricklewood – and, our now coming in sight of the inn, commissioned a cab and within the half-hour carried me and my few belongings to a fine house in the country south of Hyde Park and west of Knights Bridge, on the way to the village of Chelsea.

Cricklewood House has now long been demolished in the rush to provide accommodation for the middle classes; in those days it was one of several great mansions, the only remaining one of which is Holland House, some miles further west. We drove, upon approaching, up a fine short avenue of beech trees, and were set down at the foot of a little set of marble steps which led to a door flung open upon his lordship's approach by a figure which struck me with astonishment – for the footman was the first black man upon whom I ever set eyes: his jet face surmounted and made to seem the darker by a powdered wig, and his clothing and white gloves entirely concealing the rest of his body, so that he gave the somewhat ludicrous impression (certainly to one unaccustomed to his race) of a white man who had covered his face with blacking. Devon, however (for that was his somewhat curious name), greeted us with a broad smile in which a set of brilliant teeth shone like ivory, and immediately escorting us into the hall accepted his master's instructions to order my luggage taken up to 'the rooms in the east wing', while Cricklewood brought me to his wife, sitting over a dish of tea in a pretty room upon the ground floor, from which she could look out upon the carriages making to and from the Park.

My new friend was quick to explain to Margaret (for so she subsequently begged me to call her) the circumstances of our meeting, and as he had supposed, she was quick to applaud his bringing me there, begged me to stay as long as was convenient to me, and assured me of her assistance in finding rooms in town – for, she said, while this living in the country was pleasing enough, for someone new to the pleasures of London accommodation in the heart of a respectable quarter would be the best introduction to society.

My rooms were capacious and comfortable, consisting of my own sitting room and bedroom, with a small room beyond with all the appurtenances necessary to comfort, including a larger closet for clothes than I could fill, and a bath which would be supplied at my command (I was told) with hot water with which to bathe myself. A maid was also placed at my disposal – Susan, whose tones suggested that she had been born not a hundred miles from the Bow bells, and who was immediately disposed to be friendly and confidential, assuring me that her master and mistress were the kindest of employers, and that I should not be alarmed by the presence of the 'darky' (as she called her fellow servant), for Lord Cricklewood was much interested in the race, and did much work in ensuring that those inhabitants of Africa who for whatever reason found themselves in these cold climes were not abused by bad masters and mistresses.

I took dinner alone with the Cricklewoods, when Devon

waited upon us. We sat for a while over our wine, but after the candles had been burning an hour I took my leave; and my lord and my lady walked up the staircase with me, assuring me that it was their habit to retire at about that time (though it was scarcely ten o'clock).

I had removed my clothing and was ready for my bed when I realised that I must have left my reticule in the dining room below; while I did not need it in particular, it contained some items of small value, and rather than ring for a servant, I threw on my gown once more and determined to descend and fetch it. It lay in fact upon a side table where the servants no doubt had placed it; and picking it up, I retraced my steps up the stairs. I must pass my lord's and my lady's bedroom doors on the way to my own; one of which stood slightly ajar, suggesting that someone had entered or left it without securing it. I approached with a view to quietly doing so – but on coming near heard the unmistakable sounds of congress from the bedroom; my lord and my lady were no doubt enjoying the pleasures of their nuptial bed!

It seemed to me the more important quietly to secure the door, lest some inquisitive servant should be so impertinent as to place an eye to the crack. As I stretched out my hand to the handle, my own eye could not but glance into the room – where to my astonishment I saw a pair of black limbs stretched upon the white sheets of the bed; and looking more closely (my readers will not I trust suppose that I displayed mere curiosity, only wishing to assure myself that no one was taking advantage of my hosts' absence from their chamber) confirmed that the nether limbs were those of the footman Devon, and that from their bifurcation rose a prick larger than any other which at that time I had ever set eyes upon.

This was not all: for above the servant, her knees straddling his waist, crouched Margaret, Lady Cricklewood, with some care impaling herself upon that astonishing limb which bade fair to split her open – but which before my eyes vanished between her thighs and, from her expression, not without giving her some sensual satisfaction. She now slowly began to rise and fall, her expression if anything yet more expressive of pleasure; but needless to say I did not stay further to observe her action, but very gently closing the door made my way past the unfortunate cuckolded Viscount's bedroom door, reached my own, and not without some difficulty (for the sight had been an interesting one) fell at last to sleep.

Chapter Three

The Adventures of Andy

My journey from town to the address left by Sophie was an interesting one, for I could now see how relatively small was that part of London where the best people lived: scarcely had I turned the corner westward from the Haymarket and passed the end of Albemarle Street than I met with a selection of building sites where splendid houses were being erected which no doubt would one day form the homes of the great and good; then in what seemed only a space of about a hundred yards found myself virtually in the country, only the park upon my left, towards Kensington Palace on the eastern side of that charming village, retaining a semblance of landscaping; the lane down which we turned just past the stream at Knight's Bridge, leading towards the village of Chelsea, soon passing between fields where cattle grazed. Within half a mile the coachman paused at a pair of imposing gates and enquired whether I wished him to drive up to the door of Cricklewood House.

I saw no reason why not; but on his setting me down instructed him to wait, for I could not say what my reception would be should my friend not be at home – which indeed proved to be the case, for on the door being opened (by an attractive blackamoor, a phenomenon sufficiently rare to be interesting) and my enquiring for Mrs Nelham, I was informed that she had gone upon a jaunt with Lady Cricklewood; but that he was sure that his employer would be glad to meet me – and ushered me into a handsome hall, whose marble floor and columns were impressive enough to encourage me to believe that Cricklewood was a man of means.

He was also a handsome gentleman some years older than myself, clad in a very fine embroidered waistcoat which must have cost the half of my present annual income! His bearing however was admirably friendly and his manners impeccable: upon my announcing that I was a friend of Mrs Nelham's he immediately invited me to wait for her return, for (he said) she and Lady Cricklewood had only ventured into Chelsea upon an afternoon's excursion; perhaps, indeed, I would care to dine with them? Or was I expected in town?

I replied, of course, that I was not; and during the course of casual conversation in a while revealed that Sophie and I were about to spend our first season in the city, and had as yet no firm plans.

In return, Cricklewood narrated the circumstances under which he had met Sophie, who he described as a spirited young woman – an impression I was happy to confirm.

'You have an understanding?'

No, I replied; or rather, only to some extent. We did from time to time exchange favours – but were more like brother and sister occasionally indulging in incest than man and mistress continually indulging in strife. He laughed a great deal at this, and remarked that he therefore supposed that I would not repine should he describe the lady as particularly attractive. Certainly not, I agreed.

He sighed.

'I sometimes wish,' he said, 'that I did not find so many of the sex so uncommonly fascinating; what with the time spent in pursuing some ladies and the time spent in attempting to please those who have allowed themselves to be captured, there is little enough left for those other pleasures to which you will no doubt shortly be addressing yourselves: the plays, the concerts, the balls, the dinners . . .'

His words interested me, for he was the first man of consequence who had openly spoken of traffic with women as a diversion which properly occupied a considerable period of daily life. He was, it is true, of an advanced age – perhaps being as old as twenty-seven or eight – and might have been expected to have run the gamut of such desires; I, at barely eighteen, was still of an age when the blood was hot, and was pleased to hear that it was both permissible and socially correct to spend a considerable part of the day in pursuit of the fair.

But I was a young man of small fortune; could I really expect ladies of fashion and family to permit me to make addresses? And if so, was there some real promise of acceptance?

Cricklewood looked astonished that I should doubt it.

'My dear Andy,' he said, 'if you will allow me to be so familiar: I have in my time perhaps twice been repelled upon attempting to board a lively frigate; on one occasion because the lady concerned was genuinely devoted to another, and on the second because . . . well, the lady is now my wife; but a rehearsal of how that came to be must wait until another time. You,' (and he looked me keenly up and down), 'may lack a fortune, but you have every other element to make you attractive to the sex – allow me to compliment you, by the way, upon your dress, which is admirably in fashion; you also have a certain natural style – and you will find these to be advantages so great where polite society is concerned that even the possession of wealth scarcely outweighs them. It is also the case, if I may be so personal as to remark upon it, that your face and figure are such as will likely be your passport into any bed upon which you may wish to recline.'

I was sufficiently unsure of myself to be both surprised and complimented by his statement; but cannot have seemed confident, for Cricklewood asked whether I had doubts upon the subject.

'I confess, my lord,' I remarked, 'that I have had little experience in society, and . . .'

''Sdeath!' he replied. 'You will find experience entirely unnecessary in the preliminaries, though certainly of some importance in the consequence. I trust you have some experience in swordsmanship?'

I did not fence, I replied; whereupon he laughed to burst, and explained that the sword of which he spoke was . . . and on my still not catching on, made a gesture which while vulgar was explicit. I believe I may have blushed, for he smiled – though not unkindly – and walking to a bookcase took from it a large volume containing a profligacy of illustrations which on my examining them convinced me that indeed I had something to learn – and that if any society woman I took to bed expected manoeuvres of that kind from me, she would at present be sadly disappointed.

'My dear Andy,' said Cricklewood, 'I show you this only as an example of the lengths to which some ladies and gentlemen will go when experience dulls the effect of those more natural postures with which we pleasure ourselves and each other. When one is as young and – forgive me – as inexperienced as yourself, a reliance upon the natural instincts will serve more than your turn: a simple performance of those gestures which come naturally will be sufficient to satisfy any partner – and even the most experienced woman would be so pleased to have such an article as yourself in her bed that she would forgive any lack of sophistication in your behaviour! In any event, you will find experience a great instructor; take it from an expert in the field (if I may be so bold): practice is the greatest teacher.'

He set the album upon a table with a sigh.

'I wish that book did not always make me so uncommonly randified. And you, I see . . .' Indeed, my state was such as could not have been disguised by trousers far less closely cut than those fashionable togs in which I was now uncomfortably clad.

'Well,' said my new friend, laying a hand upon my thigh, 'I must not be inhospitable. Let me offer you a bed and company!' – and rising to his feet he took me by the arm.

My experiences with gentlemen whose fondness was for their own sex had not been such as to render the activity positively nauseating to me; but I was surprised to find a gentleman so devoted to the ladies to be so ready to entertain a young man. I allowed him to lead me out of the drawing room in which we had been talking, up a fine set of stairs, and into a handsome bedroom. On his closing the door, I placed myself upon the other side of a table, and began to think of excuses for what he was about to suggest – which my expression must have betrayed, for once more he smiled and assured me that I had nothing to worry about, for (he said) he was not a buggeranto – though unless I was partial to the activity, he would advise me to keep my back to the wall in some company, for the present fashion set off so handsome an arse as mine to such advantage that certain gentlemen would find it impossible to keep their hands from it, let alone another portion of their anatomy.

To my irritation, I once more felt myself blushing, and told myself that I really must become accustomed to the loose talk which clearly was a feature of the aristocratic life.

Cricklewood now turned to a bell pull, and sent a signal from the room to some other part of the house.

'It is the time at which I usually recreate myself in the company of a delightful domestic whose services I am as happy as no doubt she will be to offer you,' he said; and inviting me to prepare myself, adding that he trusted that

41

I would find his hospitality satisfactory, he opened the door just as a maidservant approached it: to whom he said a few words in a low voice, then closed the door behind her as she entered.

The young woman, neatly dressed, was as white as the footman who had first greeted me was black. She dropped a curtsy, and taking a step or two into the room stopped and stood silently waiting.

I had no idea what my action should be. Had Cricklewood really meant to offer me her services in the way of copulation? Or was she simply to serve me by taking my clothes and performing the polite offices usually to be expected of a servant? If I mistook, I would give great offence not only to the young woman, which was perhaps unimportant, but also to my host. Yet might he not be even more offended should I mistakenly spurn his hospitality?

I coughed, and stood up; at which the young woman took a step forward, then again stood still. I enquired her name, to which she replied that she was called Betsy, and added an enquiry whether she could assist me from my coat.

Here was an invitation which could safely be accepted, surely? I therefore rounded the table, at which she approached me and helped me from my coat; but then placing it upon a chair, without my making any further enquiry unbuttoned my waistcoat, removed it, and made a start upon the buttons of my shirt.

This assured me of my situation, and without further hesitation I placed a kiss upon her neck, and then loosened the bow at the neck of her dress, revealing upon parting it a pair of pert breasts, pale as ivory, with nipples both large and handsomely formed.

The sight set me aflame, and the passage of only a moment saw us both entirely unclothed (she being no slower to remove her clothing than I) and upon Cricklewood's handsome bed, where I was able sufficiently to control my lust to spend a few minutes inspecting my prize, who was happy to recline and display herself in order that I might enjoy that pleasure.

Neither over-plump nor over-thin, Betsy was of such a form as any woman might desire: indeed, many women of great wealth and social position would I believe have killed to possess so handsome a figure. She lay, her hands linked above her head, a pair of chubby breasts thrown into prominence by the posture, slightly parted, the upstanding nipples thus pointing a little away from each other; below them, slender ribs could be seen beneath the satin skin, and the firm, pale roundel of her stomach was marked only by the dark shadow of her deep belly button, set only just below the line of a slim waist.

Eschewing the wanton gesture of throwing her legs apart, she lay instead with them crossed at the knee, the line of her thighs therefore beautifully delineated – and the mark between them enchantingly half-concealed, though perfectly indicated by a downward arrow of curly black hair, the sight of which so enthralled me that I could not but bend to place a kiss upon it – the wiriness of the hairs surprising me by their prickly nature – at which she did not hesitate to separate those handsome thighs in order that I could more thoroughly explore with my tongue the cave which I trusted would shortly welcome another part of my anatomy.

It may surprise the reader, especially in view of my former remarks, that a young man from the country should have sufficient self-possession and indeed enough experience to begin wooing a woman in such a manner. Well, it is a mistake to believe that the experience of countrymen and women is confined to a quick tumble behind the cowshed: this may be the case at fourteen or fifteen (a rural education begins early), but a lad very soon learns what best pleases a maid, and even if we do not comprehend every posture suggested by Aretine or the other dexterous

lovers of antiquity, or of modern society, we do well enough
– and that my tongue had learned some skill was soon
evidenced by the happy writhing of the young lady, whose
most sensitive spot I was complimenting.

In a while indeed I believe she feared exhaustion, for
by simple force she raised my head from her lap, and
planting a kiss upon my lips tumbled me backwards, placed
her hands upon my hips, and for a moment examined my
person with such evident satisfaction that I began to suspect the truth of Cricklewood's compliments. Here after
all was a girl who must (I supposed), by the nature of
her obviously interesting position in the household, have
observed the persons of a great number of her master's
male guests, yet who clearly considered the body stretched
out beneath her own (for she now sat or rather crouched
astride my knees) not unworthy of admiration.

She now proceeded to flatter it by the caresses of her
hands – much softer and gentler than those of any house-
maid (which again made me suspect that her position in
the establishment was a special one). Her touch was quite
remarkably silky and inspiriting: the effect of her fingertips
grazing the raised protuberances of my nipples, somewhere
between a tickle and a flick, was wonderfully thrilling; and
when, passing downward, her entire palms spread out to
smooth the surface of my lower breast and belly I began
to palpitate with a heavenly warmth!

Her bending forward now to press a kiss upon my bosom
brought her breasts into such a juxtaposition with my body
that my prick fell clear between them – a coincidence of
which she took advantage by closing them upon it with
her hands, a delightfully mischievous smile playing over her
face as, gently swaying, she imparted a sensation which
sent a spasm of pleasure through my entire body sufficiently keen to be almost fatal.

She must have seen my teeth close upon my lower lip
in order to restrain my emotions from overflowing, for she

released my blow stick, and instead, wriggling lower upon the bed, began to nibble at my cods. This was however just as deadly to my senses as her former action, for the sensation of her tongue playing about me, darting now and then below my accoutrements to play about that small area of skin between them and my bum-hole, was sufficiently keen to do my business! I could not resist a groan of disappointment as that sensation which is the reward of amorous play gathered itself and exploded, a gushing fountain leaping from my painfully distended prick to fall thickly upon my belly and chest.

Betsy's face was a study in concern, regret and mischief as she saw the effect of her play: but sensing my own misery – comprising shame at my sudden collapse, dismay at having failed my companion, and disappointment that our business was so soon done – she smiled, and kissing me whispered that I should not distress myself, for she was at my disposal for as long as I wished; and rising, fetched from behind a screen a bowl and some cloths, and first wiping away the evidence of my premature and exasperated eruption bathed my heated limbs with the utmost tenderness and affection. She then lay down beside me, turned upon her stomach and laying her arm over my waist disposed herself to sleep, proposing that we take a few minutes' rest, after which, she was confident I would be sufficiently recovered to (as she said) try it again.

At first I did half-doze; but then the surprising nature of my situation once more came over me. I opened my eyes. A black, curly head lay upon the pillow at my side, eyes closed and lashes of astonishing length lying upon each cheek. A slender body was stretched beside my own, the plump roundels of her backside seeming all the whiter by contrast with the swarthiness of my skin – for in the usual course of events I entirely discarded my clothing, when that was possible without impertinence, and allowed the sun to burn me as brown as it could; the past summer had been a fine one, and my back was only slightly more pale than my buttocks, upon which the lighter hairs were thrown into prominence by the darkness of the skin upon which they grew in what was for my taste too great a profusion – though many of my female admirers congratulated me upon this.

As a result of my contemplation of the scene before, or rather beside me, my prick stirred beneath my palm (for I had dozed in that position), and I did not resist the temptation to transfer it – my hand, I mean – to one of those captivating spheres of hers. The flesh was warm, and firm almost to hardness: even if I closed my fingers slightly, they no more than dented the surface (whereas with many of our young ladies the flesh is soft and pliable, so that one's fingers almost sink into it). I slid my fingers into the crack which separated the two halves of that peach-like rump, my forefingers nudging (more by accident than design) into an orifice which must have been peculiarly tender, for Betsy's head now stirred upon the pillow, was lifted, and a pair of black eyes found my own just as her hand found that part of me that was now in such a condition as to signal that I was beginning to recover from my recent exhaustion (oh that now, at the advanced age of . . . too many decades, I could so quickly recover my spirits!).

Sitting, the girl looked me up and down with renewed approval (as I believed), and testing my prick with her fingers evidently concluded that a little more encouragement was required before our affections could be fully proved, for lowering her head she placed her full, smooth and warmly moist lips about the masthead and with the gentlest and most affectionate motion slid them over the cap, then began to suck gently upon it as though less to extract the marrow of my being (which she nevertheless bade fair to do) than to test the texture of the skin and the rigidity of the rapidly strengthening flesh beneath it.

That I was enraptured goes without saying – yet at the same time appalled that I must lie back and do nothing; for I had had little to do with young ladies so particularly trained to give rather than receive pleasure, and had been used to more participation in the act than I was at the moment permitted – though I was certainly able to stroke Betsy's body with my hands, one of which I now allowed to stray along the length of a thigh, its tips winding their way into that thicket which protected the cave where ...

At this moment she realised, I believe, that should the situation long continue, so young a man as myself would inevitably once more relapse; and raising herself, threw a leg across me, for a moment kneeling upright before my enthralled eyes. Now, I could not fail to observe that I had had at least something of the same effect upon her as she had had upon me: the signs are of course never as strong, but a single glance revealed that where formerly the tight black curls between her thighs had betrayed no trace of the cavity beyond, now sensual pleasure had so distended her lower lips that they positively stood out, thrusting the mane aside to show within the cavern a glimpse of light purple skin, while at the apex of the aperture there stood out a little imitation prick, no larger than my thumb – but still more pronounced than I had ever seen in a woman: and so charming that I could not resist reaching out and placing a finger upon it, at which a positive wail came from between the young lady's lips, and opening those fleshy lower lips yet further with her fingers, she so placed herself that apparently of its own volition the tip of my prick found its way between them. So slippery were we through the vigorous flow of our love juices that had my eyes not confirmed the fact I would scarcely have believed that my prick was vanishing into her entrails as she lowered herself upon me, the warm and liquid embrace involving a sensation so delicate that had my spirits not been so roused I would scarcely have felt it. Indeed, so excited was I by her (to me) unusual charms, that the very sight of her livid flesh engulfing my own was almost enough to set me off.

I knew that should she begin to rise and fall upon me, the business would be concluded; but I could not stop her – and though she controlled her movements so that they were as leisurely as could be contrived, only two or three rocking motions of her body once more brought me off. I might have been more distressed at the fact had I not observed (ignorant of the fact that I should have performed the task which she took upon herself) that my companion, vigorously rubbing that nub of flesh which stood so prominently from the apex of her cunny (and with which my prick thus failed to make contact), brought herself off at the very moment of my own keenest satisfaction – her eyes turning upward so that a flash of white could be seen between the lids, her head thrown back, her hands clutching at my sides.

After only a moment's pause, catching each other's eyes, we collapsed together upon the bed, all pleasure and laughter!

What was my amazement to hear a muffled cry of approval from the direction of the bed-head! – and in a moment, what had seemed an innocent panel of tapestry at the side of the room opened, and in strode Cricklewood, bare as a bodkin, in a very obvious state of carnal excitement, his cock (not especially impressive as to dimensions, I cannot but recall) standing out before him like the figurehead of a frigate. Without the slightest embarrassment, he sat down upon the side of the bed and placed a hand upon Betsy's rump (who was still lying face downward half across my body).

I cannot, I believe, have disguised some repugnance at this sudden interruption – for I could not doubt that by some means my host had been observing all that had passed between his servant and myself. I was not at that time familiar with the predilection some ladies and gentlemen have for observing others in the act – indeed, a number of them seem scarcely able to function without that stimulus, and when Frank and I ran our celebrated nugging house in Brook Street[3] we found it necessary to provide an observation room for just that purpose, beyond which two of our young women (not averse to such an activity) would pleasure each other, or one of them would be pleasured by a young gentleman procured for the purpose from Sophie's establishment for the satisfaction of women, then situated in Chiswick. I myself have never been either averse to nor captivated by the sight of others engaged in copulation; where those concerned are both young and handsome the spectacle is certainly not unpleasing, and can be inspiriting; in cases where both are particularly experienced it can be educational. Otherwise, however, I do not concern myself with it.

In the instance I describe, I had found myself unwillingly the object of Cricklewood's observation, and I believe he saw that I disliked it, for he made a handsome apology.

'Remember, my dear chap,' he said, 'that I am some years older than yourself, and my senses are somewhat dissipated and need more arousal than your young spirits! I hope you will forgive me!'

I immediately did so – he had been so pleasant that I could scarcely do otherwise; besides, it was clear that Betsy did not disapprove (indeed, I suspect had known of her master's presence close by, for I have no doubt that this was not the first time he had observed her at work), so who was I to make myself unpleasant?

That Betsy's afternoon employment was not yet over now became clear to me through the manner in which her master was stroking her arse; for changing her position

---

[3]Fully, indeed elaborately, described in the volume entitled *Eros in Town.*

only slightly – that is, with her head still remaining on my breast, she raised her lower body so as to present Cricklewood with access to that part of her which could best comfort his present state, and standing and taking himself in hand he presented himself at the portal and in a moment was engaged in vigorous action.

This too was a surprise to me: I was still too young to suppose that any gentleman would wish to possess, within a few minutes, a lady with whom a friend had just been familiar – a practice known to the vulgar as 'having a buttered bun' – but any conception that the thought might deter Cricklewood could not be entertained, for he had not for a second hesitated. Nor could I believe that Betsy found it repulsive to divert him, for her face, within inches of my own, showed nothing but excited pleasure – her breath came pantingly, her eyes again rolled, and she displayed every sign of satisfaction with the situation.

More self-controlled (through age and experience) than I, Cricklewood was able to continue to plumb for some time. Betsy had (as I now realise) not been entirely satisfied by my activities – and had perhaps even counterfeited the pleasure she had shown – for her exhilaration continued to mount until, desperate to express it while in a posture which made it impossible for her to reach any part of her master's body other than his cods (which she mumbled busily with the fingers of one hand), she found my sadly devitalised prick, closed her lips once more upon it, and began to milk it with such assiduity and almost violence, that in only a short time (remember, I was barely eighteen!) it had again reached its fully expanded dimensions, and my spirits were once more so inflated that at just the time when Cricklewood with a shout reached his goal, an almost painful spasm released that tiny drizzle which was the only possible evidence of my third crisis!

So exhausted was I that I could think of nothing but sleep, and within a few moments – almost unconscious of the fact that Cricklewood and Betsy made somewhat strange companions for an afternoon's snooze – I had lost consciousness.

There was no reason for me to be embarrassed upon waking in that situation: neither my host nor his servant were by now entirely strangers. However, I must confess that I felt in a slight fluster when, some noise awakening me, I found an entirely strange lady standing at the foot of the bed, regarding us with an expression which while by no means hostile was not without an interrogative tone. Beside her, Sophie wore a look less of indignation or surprise than of humour.

'Harry, my dear,' said the lady, 'won't you introduce me to this gentleman?'

Cricklewood stirred lazily.

'Ah, m'dear – may I present Mr Andrew Archer? – a friend, I believe, of Mrs Nelham. Andy, this is m'wife!' – and he nuzzled his head into Betsy's side, who meanwhile made no attempt to move or in any other way acknowledge her mistress's presence. I, meanwhile, made some attempt to cover my nakedness, but found that no part of the bedclothes within my reach was sufficiently loose to be so employed.

'Please, Mr Archer, do not concern yourself!' said Lady Cricklewood. 'The landscape is at all events too charming to require any cover!' – and indeed she allowed her eyes to survey my person with a frankness in which admiration was clearly to be discerned – not that, at such a tender age, I was inclined to be any the less embarrassed by that fact, and indeed my embarrassment was not diminished either by the fact that the obvious esteem of so handsome a woman (though considerably older than myself) had had an effect upon my prick which was only slightly mitigated by the afternoon's activities (yes, reader, you may admire and envy the speed of recuperation enjoyed by that limb – as I admire and envy it, too many years later!).

'My dear,' said the lady to my friend, 'let us retire and allow the gentlemen to perform their toilet. We shall meet, no doubt, at dinner. In the mean time, I am charmed to have met you, Mr Archer, and look forward to a closer acquaintance.'

With which she turned and led the way from the bedroom – Sophie following her after pausing only to raise an eyebrow at me, commenting no doubt not only upon my present situation, but upon the equivocal aspiration just expressed by her new acquaintance.

Chapter Four

Sophie's Story

I was awakened next morning at Cricklewood House by the curtains being drawn by Devon, that very footman whom I had seen attending to Lady Cricklewood's needs late the previous evening. His exertions had clearly not too greatly fatigued him, for he looked perfectly spry, and greeted me with a charming smile as he placed upon the side table a tray bearing a jug of hot chocolate, then asking if there was any other service he could perform for me.

I replied that there was none, though with a certain melancholy, for I must confess that in those days unless I had had a companion during the hours of darkness I frequently awoke with my blood to some extent heated, and it was impossible for me, looking at the gentleman who stood before me, not to recall the last occasion upon which I had seen him, and the dimensions of that vigorous instrument upon which my hostess had spitted herself. Though it might be that Devon would be happy to afford me those courtesies which he had extended to his employer – indeed, the appreciative glance which he gave my unveiled bosom as I raised myself suggested that that would almost certainly be the case – I could not take such a saucy advantage of my hostess's kind hospitality.

However at that moment, Lady Cricklewood's voice

came from behind her servant, and on his moving to the side I saw her standing in the doorway in an engaging négligée which emphasised her charms.

'My dear Sophie,' she said, 'if I discern in your tones a note of lamentation, please do not hesitate to put aside any hesitation you may have in making use to the full of Devon's services; he is a young man of considerable energy, and is always delighted to accommodate the whim of any female guest, and in whatever way they wish – indeed, he is extremely versatile in the assistance he can offer.'

Saying which, she entered the room, and sitting upon the bed threw back the bedclothes, entirely disclosing my person, which was naturally wholly unclothed.

If I was somewhat surprised at her action, it did not distress me, who was never timid, and even in my youth was sufficiently confident of my beauty not to be ashamed to display it even in the presence of strangers. My hostess clearly found the sight now before her a pleasant one, and from the manner in which she laid a hand upon my breast seemed to me not to be entirely devoid of that fervour which is more usually directed by ladies towards gentle-men; however, her action appeared to be for my own benefit, for touching my rigid nipple with her forefinger, she exclaimed: 'My dear, it is clear that the attentions of a brawny gentleman is what you desire! Devon . . .!'

At her word, her servant without further ado thrust off his uniform – which consisted simply of a jacket buttoned to the neck and a pair of close-fitting pantaloons, and was therefore set aside with a minimum of delay, and indeed removed with a facility and speed which must surely be the consequence of frequent rehearsal. The machine disclosed comprised an element which, though relaxed and hanging between his thighs, could have been no less than ten inches in length, and appeared almost the thickness of my wrist – though most apparently of Lady Cricklewood's wrist, for she now took hold of it and lifting it so that it lay upon her palm offered it, as it were, for my inspection, while Devon grinned broadly, congratulated by her action and cheered by my own evident admiration.

I must by an involuntary gesture have betrayed my concern at so uncommon and to me unusual an instrument: it was not only its colour – a sort of dull matt, almost purple – which interested me, but the fact that although of dimensions quite extraordinary, it seemed not to be of a sufficient rigidity to perform that feat required of it. Of such proportions in repose, what in the name of Eros could it be like when extended? I could not but express a certain nervousness, for to be candid I was not at all sure that the application of so large an implement to my most tender part would not be painful. Lady C. must have divined my apprehension, for she smiled:

'My dear,' said she, 'do not be nervous: women's parts are by no means so delicate as we believe when we are young: otherwise, how could we give birth? Moreover, it is the case with Devon, as with brethren of the African race, that this delicious plug-tail is the same size when awakened and ready for action as it appears when in a comatose state. If I may . . .' – and taking my hand she laid it upon the object in question, which indeed proved warmly yielding, yet as I explored it with my fingers it stiffened until its inflexibility was all that could be desired by the most critical of ladies.

Lady Cricklewood now laid her palm upon my nether regions.

'Ah,' she said, 'it is clear that you are in such a happy state of anticipation that your natural liquidity will make the way easy. And further to ease the way . . .'

Leaning her head, she parted her lips, and first drawing the skin back from the fine domed head of Devon's cock, slipped them over it, then gently moved them to and fro and up and down upon the shaft (to the extent that she could compass so tall an edifice). On her removing them, the dark skin of the pole shone with saliva, and (on my taking hold of it) was conveniently slippery to the touch.

Devon now, after giving me a smile perhaps more tender than had previously been the case (when anticipation had sharpened it to a grin), gently knelt between my thighs and lowering himself presented the ramrod to the cannon's mouth. I cannot deny that there was a moment if not of pain at least of slight discomfort as that superior crown passed between my nether lips; but it was accompanied by a keen pang of pleasure, and upon his beginning a gentle motion (he was, I suppose, fully apprehensive of the damage he could do with his weapon should he lose control of his emotions), a fever of delight began to run through my body, conveyed not only by the physical pleasure I enjoyed, but by the very sight of that remarkable article, its surface now resembling shining black ebony, first sinking into and then withdrawing from the root of my belly, the black and crinkly bristles which lay at the base of the object once and again meeting my own fair locks.

It may appear to some sophisticates that the simplicity of the operation now under way might be less than exciting: and indeed it would have lacked novelty had my partner been less interesting – while any emotion that might have been raised by a more experimental or active docking was entirely compensated by the regularity, the confidence and the vigour of the gentleman's motions, so that in a relatively short time my spirits were raised to a remarkable degree, and tears started to my eyes at the sheer elation which was conveyed to my nether regions by his action.

Lady Cricklewood smiled to see my pleasure. She continued all this time to sit at my side, unembarrassed by a situation which a lesser woman might have found disconcerting; occasionally she laid a hand upon one of the cheeks of Devon's arse, permitting it to slide over a skin now beginning to shine with perspiration, while with her other hand she was good enough to pass a handkerchief over my forehead, similarly bedewed with the exhalation produced by pleasure.

At last, I could no longer deny my delight its natural culmination, and was unable to prevent a cry of pleasure breaking from my lips as a great wave of elation shook my person. At this, Devon's moments were immediately curbed, and after one or two more thrusts of his person, more tender than provocative, he withdrew his sword from the scabbard and lifted his body from between my thighs.

I was about to protest, for it was clear that he had not reached that natural culmination which satisfies a gentleman under those circumstances I have described, and I did not wish to deny him the pleasure he had given me; but Lady Cricklewood, divining my purpose, remarked that I should not concern myself, for (she said) Devon was remarkably long-winded, sometimes taking as lengthy a period as half an hour to reach discharge; and in any event he would without doubt have the opportunity later in the day to bring himself off – 'and if his cannon was discharged at every battle, there would be precious little shot left!'

I was not entirely convinced by this, for although the servant (who had now, with I suspect some difficulty, once more concealed his artillery piece within his footman's breeches) showed no disappointment, I could not but suppose that his feelings must be incomplete. However, it was not for me to protest on his behalf; all I could do was thank him, which I did with as much warmth as might be proper between a lady and a domestic; whereupon he drew himself up, bowed – again with that broad smile almost to be described as a grin – and left the room.

'My dear,' said my hostess, 'I trust that you will claim Devon's services whenever you require them: his capacity for passion appears to be insatiable (certainly, he has yet to disappoint me), and I am happy to place him entirely at your disposal. And now, it is eleven o'clock; if you would care to break your fast, may I invite you to accompany me upon a visit I have to make which I think would interest you?'

I was happy to acquiesce, and having enjoyed some chocolate, eaten some bread and clothed myself I descended the stairs, where I found Lady Cricklewood in the drawing room, whence she escorted me to her carriage. We set out towards town, and shortly after crossing the old bridge over the river Westbourne came to a little row of houses – those of a blindmaker, a carpenter, et cetera – in the midst of which stood a public house, the White Hart, outside which Lady Cricklewood ordered her coachman to stop. We descended, and my friend led me into the public house by a side door which gave directly on to a staircase, leading to a large room upon the first floor which was remarkably handsomely furnished for such a place.

'We meet here for convenience,' said my lady – who I shall henceforth refer to as Margaret, that being her forename – 'it sometimes being necessary to disguise from certain persons the purpose of the small association of ladies who make use of the place.'

One gentlewoman, much of Margaret's age, was already at the meeting place, and four others arrived shortly afterwards, the last of whom was in a state of some distress, and taking my friend by the arm removed her to a corner of the room, where she conversed with her in some agitation. My friend too looked grave, and taking from her bosom a small watch, consulted it, shaking her head the while. Then she placed a hand upon her companion's arm, as though to calm her, and came towards me.

'My dear Sophie,' she said, 'I must throw myself upon your mercy. We must all do so.'

Taking me aside, she explained that the small association of ladies and gentlemen of which this party formed the female component had been established for the education of the young – and especially those about to marry.

'It has long seemed to us to be the case that our young

people are thrust into matrimony without the slightest notion of how to behave – I mean,' she added hastily, 'not that they lack the social graces, but they have no notion how to behave to each other in those intimate circumstances which so swiftly follow upon the blessing of their union: that is, in matters of the bedroom.

'A small number of us therefore decided some little time ago that our sons and daughters should not be thrust into marriage in complete ignorance of those charming intimacies which can make or mar companionship between a young lady and her lover; and, in short, declared that a proper demonstration of what is required of both sexes should follow upon any understanding between our young people and their future spouses.

'The son of my friend Mrs Spintwist' – and she indicated the agitated lady who now watched us with some anxiety – 'was to have been introduced to the skills of lovemaking this morning by a young lady whose services we commissioned – but who now sends a message that she is incommoded by a fever, and cannot wait upon us. But the young man's intended is at this moment being educated at the hands of a young gentleman produced for the purpose by our husbands, who meet half a mile away at the Fox and Greengage inn; the wedding is announced for the day after tomorrow – and in short . . .'

'You are in some difficulty,' I said.

'Indeed. My dear young friend, would it be too much to ask if you . . .? I am aware that you have a natural enjoyment of the act, and suspect a natural talent for expressing yourself in it. If you would not object? The young gentleman is, I assure you, though entirely innocent, by no means ill-natured or unhandsome, and . . .'

'I am at all times happy to be of service to my friends,' I replied; 'but it should be said that I am not greatly experienced in . . . that is to say, while I have enjoyed numerous amorous adventures, I would not set myself up

59

as an expert in those skills which the experienced practise . . .'

'Dear friend!' said Margaret. 'I knew that I could count upon you!' – and immediately informed her confederates that their difficulty was resolved. She then assured me that everything would be conducted with the most careful modesty: the young man's mother would of course not be present, and while the other ladies would remain, the circumstances would be as little embarrassing as contrivance could ensure.

She then lifted aside a hanging cloth, to disclose a large bed, properly dressed with immaculate linen, above which hung a lamp. When this was lit, and the shutters drawn upon the room beyond, those disposed upon the mattress could clearly be seen by observers beyond the gauze, whose presence (I was now informed) was merely to ensure that the young woman engaged for the education of the subject properly carried out her task.

'Naturally, this will not be necessary in your case,' Margaret said generously; 'but for the form of it . . .'

My suspicion was that the ladies were set to observe what took place less for their information than their pleasure.

'I shall be happy to assist you,' I said; 'but I must ask for privacy. While I can see that under other circumstances you must necessarily ensure yourself that the instruction has been properly carried out, you may (as you have generously conceded) have no concern in this case; and it is not my habit to engage in so intimate an activity under the eyes of others.'

'But you had no objection to my presence earlier today?' said my friend.

'Indeed,' I replied; 'but the circumstances were somewhat different. You were my hostess, and it would have been churlish of me to object to your presence, especially when you were offering me such generous hospitality. This, however, is a different situation.'

I believe that my friend understood my objection; or at least conveyed it convincingly to her companions, who though with some reluctance concurred: what else could they do?

But now the door opened, and a diffident young man was led into the room. The ladies greeted him by his forename – which was Robin – and he was presented to me, making a polite bow. His mother then, planting a kiss upon his cheek, withdrew, and the ladies bustled around him, relieving him of his topcoat, cheering him as best they might – but without a great deal of success, for he was understandably nervous. I was pleased that I had made the point of privacy, for it occurred to me that it would have been an exacting task to bring him to the jump should he have to perform beneath the eyes of these inquisitive women, who now – again with some reluctance – withdrew, leaving us alone.

It was not an easy matter to start things off, and indeed we were reduced to the ridiculous pretence of discussing the weather. I then asked whether he had an occupation, to which he replied that he had just joined the Royal Horse Guards. Then surely, I said, his companions must already have introduced him to those delights which were supposed to be demonstrated to him upon the present occasion?

He blushed (he could have been scarcely more than eighteen years of age – that is, of my own years) and replied that he was not altogether in ignorance of the act (which he termed 'rantam scantam'), but that upon the three or four occasions upon which he had performed it his partner had been a 'public ledger' – that is, a woman 'open to public inspection', or a common wh*re! – and inferred that the copulation (or jigging) had been nasty, brutish and short, and not such as he would expect to please his wife-to-be – a refined girl to whom he must behave with the utmost gentility.

'Let me disabuse you, sir!' I said. 'To address your wife with gentility would be to open the door to discontent. Nor is it true that nothing is to be learned from common prostitutes; indeed, an experienced whore is perhaps the best teacher of all, provided that she enjoys the game and is willing to take time to convey all the expertise of which she is in command. You could certainly learn more from one such than you will learn from me, who is a mere substitute!'

'But I thought . . .'

'No, sir,' I said; I could not rebuke him for his mistake, for no one had explained to him the substitution which had taken place. I now did so; and immediately wished that I had not, for I could see from his expression that he regarded me as being quite as 'genteel' as his affianced. I must disabuse him.

'Let us unrig ourselves,' I proposed, and rising to my feet without further ado disrobed. At this he cheered up somewhat, and though with some becoming reluctance (I do believe he feared to offend me by the sight of his unclothed body!) reduced himself to that same state of nature, whereupon I took him by the hand and led him to the bed.

I do not claim to be the greatest beauty in the land, but the compliments of those gentlemen whose opinions I respect had convinced me that my person was not altogether repulsive, and I was not complimented by the fact that the young man's dangler remained just that – and indeed was not much over the size of an acorn. My first action was therefore to rouse it, which I did by the common practice of sucking upon it – an action which however seemed to dumbfound the young gentleman, who had clearly never experienced such an activity before. His surprise at my action was such that for a moment or two his prick remained soft and limber; but then began to swell until in a short time it was transformed into a blowing stick of a very respectable size and obduracy, whereupon I now drew myself up against him, only permitting a hand to remain upon his prick lest lack of attention should result in its diminishment.

'Should nervousness appear likely to prevent this admirable device from attaining a proper station,' I said, 'you may expect your wife to warm you as I have just done. I cannot suppose that the gentleman at present educating her as I have been engaged to educate you will neglect to inform her of the procedure. But now that you are ready, what is your next step?'

In answer to the question, he rudely thrust me down upon the bed, and inserting his hand between my thighs, attempted to open them.

'Oh, my dear sir!' I said. 'By no means! Nothing so prevents a lady's happy acquiescence to the act than such suddenness. Have you never heard of the art of wooing?'

But of course he had not: was it not what I was there to teach him?

First of all, I remarked, he should remember that the sense of touch was not the only one to be involved in these circumstances. Did he not appreciate the sense of sight? Did he not find it pleasant to look upon the person of a handsome female?

The idea had clearly not occurred to him, and I therefore encouraged him to kneel upon the mattress and consider the lineaments of my body – and was amused to see the effect this had upon him. I suppose that any connection he had previously had had by no means involved such contemplation – nor did I suppose that if it had occurred, the persons of the Covent Garden nuns with whom he had probably been familiar would necessarily involve much beauty (which is not to say that there are no handsome bawds in London – merely that they do not usually sell their services to impecunious members of the horse guards).

'You should also take note of the fact, sir,' I then said,

'that we ladies are by no means impervious to the sight of a handsome fellow; and you should allow any partner the pleasure of regarding your own person.'

His eyebrows rose at this; and he preened himself a little, pulling in a stomach which was by no means in any event globular (being so young a chap). I needed to make no pretence of my interest in looking over his person, I may say, for he was by no means unhandsome. He had now sat back upon his heels, his hands upon his thighs; his yellow hair, caught by the lamplight, shone like gold, and at the base of his prick (which stood valiantly to attention) more spun gold shone. Upon his breast, which was broad, only a sprig or two stood about the paps, while skeins grew with somewhat more fullness upon his belly.

After a pause, he stretched out a hand and placed it upon my breast, finger and thumb upon a nipple, whereupon I smiled.

'You are right, sir,' I said; 'such an attention is always pleasant – but perhaps more keenly so when the lips or tongue are employed.'

At this (he was quick to learn, and I had some hopes of him) he bent and applied his lips, and in a moment I felt that charming tickling which is only conveyed by an active tongue. In the mean time he did not restrain his hands from wandering about the surface of the rest of my body – nor did I dissuade him, for he was now tender rather than rough, and his explorations were as sensitive as any lady could require.

I was interested to know whether he would by a natural progression advance his lips to other areas of my person: and this was indeed the case – though I was touched to note that he transferred them first to my own lips, upon which he planted the most tender of kisses before he permitted them to compliment my neck, shoulders, sides ... On reaching my belly, he raised his head for a moment to glance up at me: I favoured him with a smile, and gently reassured him that there was no part of the female form which was not properly complimented by a kiss – whereupon he resumed his journey, and upon my parting my thighs (as, I confess, a form of encouragement) was delighted to examine that part of the female form which (I dared guess) he might have penetrated but would certainly never closely have observed.

It has ever been my experience that a gentleman of normal intelligence, when properly directed, may trust his instinct in matters of the bedroom – though sometimes he must at first be guided by his companion. Robin showed an immediate instinct for pleasing a lady, and no sooner discerned what gave most pleasure than he was happy to experiment in how to make that pleasure keener. His natural genius led him speedily to the centre of enjoyment, when his stroking and flicking the bud so delighted me that in a very short time I was unable not to betray by a gasp the extent to which his ministrations satisfied me. At the first exhalation of breath, he showed concern lest he had in some way hurt me: at which I was glad to persuade him to pause in his attentions so that I might explain that this was by no means the case.

'But you, sir!' I said. 'Are you not ready for a more active display of passion?'

'If you wish it, ma'am,' he replied; 'but I must confess that your enjoyment in itself gives me great pleasure – perhaps because I have not hitherto been encouraged to believe that a female is capable of that sensual satisfaction which we men take in the act.'

I was glad to hear those words, for they indicated that no lady fortunate enough to lie with him would do so without some degree of satisfaction. I therefore concluded that it was indeed time to progress to the next lesson, and enquired in which posture he wished to enjoy me.

As I had suspected, the question puzzled him. Was there, he enquired, a choice? – and clearly was aware only of that attitude most commonly adopted by the meanest *amorosa*: that is, of lying face down upon her! I must therefore explain that between two agile and ingenious lovers anything was possible which the intelligence could devise and the body perform. But perhaps he would permit me to demonstrate the simplest and most elementary attitudes? For instance, from within the position which he had proposed to take, others could follow. If he would be so good . . .?

Without further encouragement he slipped between my legs and eagerly placed his trumpet in that position which would enable him to sound a simple tune – indeed, he began to do so, but I beseeched him if he could to contain himself for a few moments longer, while I demonstrated those postures of which I had spoken. I then lifted my legs and closed them about his waist, locking my ankles first behind his thighs, then raising them so that they locked over his arse, my heels tucked into the nook behind his cods – which made him smile with pleasure; then slipped them up the length of his body until I was able to throw them over his shoulders.

'You will find, sir, that in this posture almost any movement of your body pleases a lady – while it is also perfectly possible for both parties to observe the motion of the gentleman's prick as it enters and leaves the lady's commodity – a facility which often commends itself.'

He glanced down, and beginning that motion which enabled the observation of which I had spoken, was evidently pleased by the phenomenon – and indeed the conjunction was agreeable to sight as to sensation.

However, I was forced once more to invite him to pause. There were (I said) a number of other possibilities which could be tried with the lady reclining upon her back: but had he never conjectured that another posture entirely could be attempted? On his shaking his head, I threw a leg across his head and while keeping our private parts in close conjunction contrived to turn upon my face, where-upon he discovered for the first time the possibility of what is vulgarly called the 'back skuttle'. I was able to point out that here was another posture which a lady would find particularly inspiring, for it brought the lower side of the gentleman's prick into a close and rewarding connection with the boy in the boat or button – that little nub of female flesh so receptive to agitation, and which his kissing had recently complimented. Moreover (I continued) by raising herself upon her knees – which I now did – the gentleman was given the freedom of caressing the whole of the front of the lady's body, including those breasts which were often so highly regarded.

Once more, Robin began those motions which would have rendered further experiment nugatory – and once more I had to invite him to desist: and indeed moved away from him, leaving him crestfallen as to expression, though far from fallen in any other regard. I had one more import-ant posture to demonstrate, I remarked, inviting him to lie upon his back. He did so, though with an expression so puzzled that it made me laugh. Could he not understand how copulation could occur in such a situation? I enquired – at which he shook his head; but upon my bestriding him, of course he immediately comprehended, and taking his cock (which was standing so firmly against his belly that otherwise the exercise would have been impossible!) lifted it into such a position that I could sink upon it – an exercise which appeared to give him, if his expression was to be trusted, considerable pleasure, which was not decreased by my gently rising and falling upon his body, while at the same time (passing my hand behind me) gently fondling his cods.

As I have remarked, I had no doubt that I gave him pleasure; yet after a while, in a voice which was perhaps somewhat unsteady, he asked whether it would offend me if he requested a deviation of posture, for he found the present situation one which . . . and he paused, as though embarrassed.

I assured him that I entirely understood: some men (I explained) liked to be ridden – but others (perhaps the more manly, I added – in order to encourage him) preferred those attitudes in which they were more obviously in command; and invited him to choose which posture most pleased him, whereupon he persuaded me to rise and to stand with my hands upon the bed, and thus bent over before him, whereupon he plunged his dibble into the ground with a single determined thrust, and in a moment was at work with all the vigour to be expected of a young gentleman who had spent half an hour in receipt of the demonstration of delights he had not been permitted to enjoy. The consummation was not to be long delayed, and if he was unable to restrain a whoop of pleasure at its intensity, he immediately and politely apologised should he have been premature in reaching that point from which he could not be expected to continue.

Clearly, those belly-pieces with whom he had previously consorted had permitted only a single completion; persuading him to lie upon the bed, I applied myself, after a brief pause, to recovering him – something not at all difficult, for those means employed were new to him (being for instance entirely ignorant how keenly the compliments paid by a lady to a gentleman's backside may revive his spirits) and therefore were particularly acute. Within a quarter of an hour he was capable of a second bout, during which with some intelligence he chose to adopt a number of those attitudes I had demonstrated, in order to prove himself master of them. He then professed himself extremely grateful to me, dressed and took his leave; upon which my Lady Cricklewood and her friends soon appeared, among them young Robin's mother, Mrs Spintwist, who expressed a gratitude only second in intensity to that of her son, and spoke too on behalf of his affianced

– a young lady who she was sure would have much to thank me for! My friend and I then once more entered her carriage, and returned to Cricklewood House – where on my hostess wishing to introduce her husband found him abed with Andy and a young lady who appeared to be familiar to both of them: a situation which was interesting without being altogether surprising, my friend's appetite for amusement being sufficiently keen to deprive me of incredulity in whatever circumstances I found him.

Chapter Five

The Adventures of Andy

Cricklewood having wrapped a sheet about himself and followed his wife from the room, I rose from bed, and having thanked Betsy for the pleasure of her company made my toilet and in an hour presented myself at dinner, where the conversation was all of the delights of town, to which the Cricklewoods looked forward to entertaining us.

Upon our retiring, Sophie came to my room not to indulge in those pleasures with which we had often brought a happy day to a happy end, but to retail the adventures which she has set out in the last chapter – a narration perhaps rather more interesting than my own, which followed. We agreed that the household into which we had so unexpectedly been accepted was a somewhat curious one. The kindness of my lord and my lady must be appreciated, but Sophie shared my doubts whether we wished to place ourselves entirely in their hands during our sojourn in the metropolis. It was not that we disliked either of them, nor (certainly) that we were uneasy at the extent of their hospitality; but that, being considerably younger, we wished to explore the possibilities of the megalopolis for ourselves – personal experience being ever the best tutor.

Next morning at breakfast, which we took at ten o'clock,

Cricklewood and his lady proposed escorting us into town – himself suggesting that he should accompany me to the Zoological Society's exhibition, of which he was an honorary official, while Lady C. and Sophie should visit the British Museum. Neither of these places sounded to any degree remarkably exhilarating, but we nevertheless concurred, secretly determining to escape as soon as we might and return to my rooms, then finding (as we had at first proposed) a set nearby in which Sophie could establish herself.

As we rode into town, I suppose that our demeanour betrayed some slight discontent with the plans for the day, for Cricklewood invited us to 'cheer up' – for, he said, it might be that neither the Zoological Gardens nor the Museum would be as dull as we perhaps supposed.

At Oxford Street we set down Lady Cricklewood and Sophie, the carriage then making its way for some time to the north to Regent's Park, where the Zoological Gardens lay. Their establishment (my friend suggested) had been a source of great and rational recreation to the world of London. Indeed, the success of the institution had abundantly proved how essential to the enjoyment of Londoners was a place combining much natural beauty with a great deal of what was curious, rare and instructive in animated nature.

I was pleased at the opportunity of passing through Regent's Park on the way to the 'zoo' (as Harry called the Society's exhibition). Although the newest of London's parks, even in its present immature state it is the most beautiful, and will certainly become more and more so every succeeding year. By far the most extensive and varied view within the limits of this delightful retreat is that from the rising ground immediately above the master's lodge of St Catherine's Hospital, embracing to the northward the gentle rise of Primrose Hill, and behind it, thickly wooded Hampstead and its sister hill.

Its most beautiful part is that towards the north, which is hardly interfered with by the hand of art, and where the natural disposition of the ground has scope to show itself; wherever the hand of Mr John Nash is manifest (except in that remarkable success, his re-designing of Regent Street) beauty is at once exchanged for artificial littleness, as in his greater and his lesser circuses, his ornamental bridges over puddles four feet wide, his Swiss cottages and his terraces crowned with cupolas that convey to the mind of the spectator the idea of a grotesque giant in his dressing gown and nightcap. Sadly, our modern architects have not the grace, wit and elegance of those of former years.

As we rode steadily through the park, at length a babel of inarticulate sounds greeted our ears, announcing the imminence of that modern ark of Noah, the Zoological Gardens! The strange and exotic animals we were to see, Cricklewood proposed, were so many lively aids to the imagination, and our walk certainly disclosed many of them.

'Regard the giraffe, for instance,' he remarked; 'looking at him one sees much more than a creature with a fine small head, elongated tongue, swan-like neck, long fore and shorter hind legs. One sees in him a map, as it were, of the countries he inhabits. His organisation is geographical; he is a delegate sent among us to describe the peculiarities in the botany and geology of the deserts of southern central Africa! His hoofs inform one as distinctly as if one had seen them that those deserts are sandy and sterile; his very body expounds, as plainly as if the animal spoke Arabic, that his food is derived from palms and such other trees as have high-branching leaves abounding in inter-tropical regions!

'Again, the monkeys fascinate by their shockingly human jealousies, thefts, over-reaching, battles, tricks and schemes – their anatomical structure so marvellously similar to our own that one might almost believe we were related! Then, look at the elephant marching about with his trunk reverted and his gulf-mouth gaping for apples or biscuits! Is he not a history of India in one volume folio, bound in leather?'

I could only agree. An hour's stroll about the place had, however, the effect of informing me somewhat too fully about the world of nature, and I began to wonder once more what fascination with the subject had persuaded Harry Cricklewood that it would be of engrossing interest to me. Observing, as I guess, my slight impatience, he glanced at his watch, and then remarked that we should make our way to the serpent house – where, he said, 'I have arranged an exhibition which I believe you will find engaging' – and led the way to a long, low building, the entrance to which was guarded by two gentlemen who on seeing Lord Cricklewood nodded and permitted us to enter.

The interior of the place consisted of a single room sufficiently dimly lit to deprive me for the moment of the sense of sight. Harry guided me to a seat, and as my eyes became accustomed to the gloom I saw that we were alone in a relatively small compartment, and that before us was a low stage or platform upon which stood a couch, behind which a velvet curtain hung. There was, however, no sign of any serpent – which somewhat relieved me, for I am no friend to these creatures, and would have been especially unwilling to encounter one in such a place and particularly in so dim a light.

However, that light now became somewhat less dim, for a young gentleman stepped through the curtain bearing a lamp, which he set down at the side of the stage. He was dark of skin, had long black hair, and was dressed in that manner in which illustrations portray the Indian – that is, merely with a white cloth wound about the loins. He now sat at the side of the stage, and producing a small flute or pipe began softly to play upon it. After a few moments, the curtain once more stirred, and there came upon the stage a young woman, her skin much the colour of the flautist's, clad in a length of silk which lay across her shoulders and around her body – called, I believe, in her native country, a sari.

She began slowly to move – I cannot properly describe her motions as a dance – to the sound of the flute, while I began to look somewhat nervously about me: this was after all a serpent house: so where was the serpent? Not, I trusted, loose about the place!

My anxiety was not uncommon, for Cricklewood had told me during our ride that some little time ago a large boa constrictor (which could swallow a donkey whole) had been supposed to have escaped from the cage it shared with a fellow, and great had been the anxiety of the inhabitants around the Regent's Park lest the serpent should have found its way into the enclosures. For a week no elderly gentleman stirred abroad without arming himself with a sword-cane, and not a ladies' boarding school dared venture to take the air for fear of some of the young ladies falling victim to the fatal embraces of the vagrant constrictor; nor, until the continuous lethargy and increased volume of the remaining reptile had attracted particular attention was it suspected that he had devoured his bedfellow.

But I digress: the young woman for a while was content to move her body sinuously to the music – but then, loosening her sari at the neck, reached inside it, and to my astonishment and consternation lifted out the head of a snake! Carrying it to her face, she allowed the darting tongue which could clearly be seen to play about her nostrils and lips: then, with a movement too obscure to be observed, somehow released her clothing so that the length of silk about her body slowly unwound itself, falling first from her shoulders, then slipping to her hips and finally to the floor, leaving her a perfect representation of Eve after the Fall – for she was clad in nothing but . . . snake!

I cannot say what sort of serpent it was which was wound about her, but it must certainly have been five or six feet in length, for while its head was still next to her cheek, its body curved down between her breasts, fell across her belly and then passed between her thighs, appearing once more around the crook of a knee, its tail lying just above her ankle!

Repugnance in me was accompanied, I must confess, by a certain sensual agitation: the very pattern of the snake's body against the light brown smoothness of the skin was arousing to the senses, and indeed when the woman – or girl, as I might more properly call her – slowly lowered herself to lie upon the couch and altogether released the snake, its sinuous movements as it slithered over her body would have excited an eunuch.

Whether the snake had been taught or not, I cannot say; but its movements were almost those of a lover: as its body slithered down between the woman's breasts, its curves seemed to rub amorously against their richness, while upon its head passing between them its tongue could be seen to flick out and touch one of its mistress's nipples – at which I fancied I saw her catch her lower lip between her teeth, as though to restrain a cry either of fear or of pleasure (and I do believe, the latter). All the time, she kept her loins slightly raised, the thighs open, so that the whole length of the reptile could the more easily slide downward between them, its body necessarily thus caressing her secret part – and (I could scarcely believe that I witnessed such behaviour in a mute beast!) on its head reaching that intimate location, it seemed positively to nuzzle against it as though claiming entry!

I could not prevent a shudder passing through my body, at which Harry gave a low and throaty laugh.

'The exhibition is perhaps more interesting than you expected?' he asked. 'But come, Andy – now is the opportunity for you to show your manhood!' – and rising, he took my arm as though to encourage me to the stage.

Although I cannot deny that the scene had raised my spirits to an extent, I was by no means eager to approach the lady – or, rather, her companion; she was herself a beauty – slim and without those over-abundant curves common in eastern women even of an early age, which attract some men but which I find less than engaging. Her viper friend however was not one with whom I wished a closer acquaintance.

Nevertheless, how could I refuse? I was too young at that time to do what would now be easier – that is, to excuse myself from participation; I was still much under the influence of a greater sophistication than my own, and attempting, I hoped successfully, to disguise my reluctance, stepped up to the reclining lady, and when she reached up to take my hand, allowed her to carry it between her legs and lay it not upon her flesh but that of the serpent.

To my astonishment, who expected coldness and slime, I found his body to be warm and by no means unpleasant to the touch – no less warm than the skin of the lady's thigh, along which it lay, its head nuzzled into the nest of black hair which lay about her pussy.

'Allow me,' said Harry – and I saw that he held out his hands to take my coat!

Again, I did not know how to refuse, and slipping out of my jacket could only go on to remove also my shirt, my shoes and my trousers – revealing, alas, that my excitement was more the produce of anxiety than of amorous animation, for that part of me which should have been standing was fallen.

Harry however showed no sign either of scorn or of disappointment with me – partly because he was busily removing his own clothing (his penchant for accompanying me in amorous pleasure might, I supposed, be disappointed – for I could not believe that in the presence of a serpent

I would be able to rouse my senses to any practical extent).

The young woman however now persuaded me to lie at her side, which I did – keeping a careful eye upon her companion, who did not move – but who, in a moment, was moved! – for to my unspeakable horror, she lifted him from his position, and making a kind of hoop or small noose with his upper body, curled him around my groin. If anything could further have reduced the size of my riding-muscle, I cannot imagine what it might be: indeed, so shrunken was I in that department that an onlooker might have found it difficult to discover whether I was of the male or female gender! I could not resist a tremor – but the lady now placed a gentle hand over my eyes, and another upon my breast, persuading me to lie still – which I did partly out of fear lest a sudden movement might provoke the snake to an action fatal to me, and partly because, I admit, her gentle touch, together with the calming music of the flute, was remarkably comforting.

Now a surprising thing occurred: the snake began slowly to move – yet its movement did not horrify me, as I had supposed it must. I could not see its movements, but naturally in so sensitive an area as that where its body lay, I was entirely conscious of them: and must confess that they were remarkably inspiring. Indeed, almost immediately I felt a flow of blood into that instrument so greatly in need of it; and as though the snake recognised the recovery, upon the organ swelling, it began to move its body against it, the warm scales imparting a pleasing friction which still further inspirited the organ.

After a while, the lady removed her hand from my eyes: when glancing down I saw what would only an hour earlier have harrowed me with fear – the serpent lay between my legs, its head actually lying along the trunk of my cock, which now reclined, not fully extended but showing a considerable enlargement, upon my belly! Gently, almost as though it took pleasure from the movement, the creature began to vibrate its head with a swift trembling motion against the crown of my prick, the resulting sensation being quite astonishingly animating, so that within a few seconds that part of me was of the consistency of ivory. I did not hesitate to reach down and lift the creature away from its position – whereupon Harry stretched over from where he lay at our side, and took the viper, permitting me to move my body into a closer juxtaposition with its owner, whose soft, smooth warmth was no less interesting than the unique embrace of her minion.

It was not long before we were fully embraced, and my cock was in the warm clasp of a cunny most delightfully tepid and liquid, with which she was able to milk me of all sensation in a time too short to be entirely satisfactory – except to Cricklewood, who impatiently (even somewhat roughly) thrust me aside to take my place almost before the final paroxysm had delighted me, and began to swive with a vigour which I now envied – the physical consummation of my excitement having failed to drain me of interest in the remarkable circumstance in which I found myself.

The snake in the meantime took itself off to a corner, curled up and went to sleep.

I looked on with some interest at the convoluted figures at my side – for although what is called by the French *voyeurism* is not (as I believe I have already remarked) a major pleasure for me, the contrast between Harry's white skin and the darker pelt of his companion threw into relief the juxtaposition of their bodies, the paleness of his thighs almost seeming to shine in the lamplight as they lay between the darker ones of his friend, which she had drawn up against her breast in order the more readily to offer his riding-muscle an easy hospitality. My impatience with myself was considerable, for though a couple of minutes only had elapsed since I had occupied more or less Harry's place, I was already resentful that I was not still in it! I was therefore by no means displeased to feel a gentle hand upon my hip, which in a moment began to creep over my belly.

Though the approach was welcome enough (for in those days my recovery from a bout was almost instant), I was somewhat surprised, for I had no idea that the lady had a companion. Of course she had: it was simply that I had not counted upon the musician taking that part in the proceedings which he now offered, nor that she was in fact female – though now that I turned my head I saw that the eyes were sufficiently large and liquid to be those of a girl, and certainly the lips which fixed themselves to mine were tender enough to be those of the most enticing of young ladies.

I succumbed to her embrace with enthusiasm, passing my hands about a slim waist, and falling upon my back allowing the flautist to lie full length upon me.

But what was this? Surely against my belly I felt . . .? I reached down and passed my hand over the cheeks of the young lady's arse. They were warmly smooth beneath my palms – but on reaching between them I felt the unmistakable presence of a pair of bollocks!

If I was for a moment at a loss what to do, the sophisticated reader must forgive me. Those familiar with the first volume of my memoirs will recall that while upon tour with a small theatrical company, I found myself in circumstances which resulted not only in familiarities of a sensual nature with a young gentleman, but in my inadvertent participation in that action which an unenlightened Government continues to regard as worthy of the most severe punishment.[4] I cannot say that carnal connection with a person of my own sex will ever be my first choice; but neither can I assert without deceit that it is never under any circum-

---

[4] The events to which I allude may be found described in the fifteenth chapter of *Eros in the Country*.

stances unenjoyable, and at the moment of which I speak the sadly brief nature of my recent bout had allowed my spirits to revive more speedily and more voraciously than would otherwise have been possible, and through the immediate spectacle of Cricklewood, still rogering his companion with an enthusiasm which positively shook the stage, reached such a peak of lust that (condemn me who will!) I took no action other than placing my hands upon my companion's shoulders, thus suggesting a course which he immediately recognised.

It may of course have been the Indian's skill as a flautist which had taught his lips and tongue the dexterity which he now demonstrated; placing his hands beneath my arse, he lifted it sufficiently to enable him to compliment not only my prick, but my cods and the adjacent areas, to all of which he paid attentions notable as much for their accomplishment as for their promise – while I must confess to closing my eyes and persuading myself that it was his beautiful companion who was so complimenting me. Rousing me at one moment to the point of discharge, he then refrained for just that brief period of time which enabled a partial recovery before once more bending to his task – so that when the moment of consummation occurred, not only did I recognise it with a cry of pleasure, but with a discharge so violent that (the Indian anticipating the moment and removing his head just in time) a jet flew up and over my shoulder, and fell upon the small of Harry Cricklewood's back, a moment before he, with a final lunge, did his duty by his own pleasure.

The flautist and his friend now rose to their feet, and with a little bow fetched from a corner bowls of warm water with which we were able to lave our bodies before resuming our clothing; whereupon Harry (as I guess from a clinking sound) passed some money to the couple before we stepped blinking into the early winter sunlight of the Zoological Gardens.

'Well, dear boy,' said Harry as he walked me to the entrance, 'I trust that you do not consider the morning entirely wasted?'

I could think of no comment to make, and therefore merely nodded. I could certainly not protest that I had not been an eager and happy participant in the events which had just occurred.

'And now,' said Harry, 'we will lunch at my club' – and hailing his carriage, instructed it to drive 'to Whister's'.

I had had no previous experience of the gentlemen's clubs of London. Those who do not know the metropolis would be astonished at the number of these which are to be found in the West End – the most fashionable and expensive part of the town. Here the great men of the place (as they would count themselves) lounge in the drawing rooms, flatten their noses against the windows, write their letters on club paper, seal them with club wax, impressed with the club seal; dine, if they have the wherewithal, on the one-and-ninepenny joint of the day, sip a pint of port in solitary dignity, then, lighting their cigar, wend their way home.

But what is home to them? If you ask where they live – at the club; how they live – by the *carte* of the club; what are their opinions? – the opinions of the club; who are the best fellows in the world? – Tom, Dick and Roger, of the club; where is the best wine in London to be had? – at the club; who have the whitest cravats and the reddest plush breeches in town? – waiters at the club; where is the best letter-paper to be had for the pocketing? – at the club; the best society? – at the club.

Well, the club is no doubt a very good place – no, better, for members of the wine committee, the dinner committee, the library committee and the other committees. To the committee the club is indeed a home – to all others it is only a place where they are tolerated; the committee as masters, the members guests; the committee are the decemvirs, the rest the populace; and although there are in every club one or two brawling tribunes of the people, they never make anything by their grumbling agitation.

Harry Cricklewood was, and had been for some time, the chairman of the entertainment committee of Whister's, in St James's; and from the press of people who came to speak to him as we ate our chops and drank our claret, a popular one.

'As you may guess, my dear friend,' he said as we smoked a cigar after luncheon, 'I have a little entertainment here tonight at which I would be happy for you to be my guest. Perhaps I might suggest that you spend an easy afternoon, for as a guest you are invited to a full participation in our evening's activities, which I think I may promise you will require the full recovery of your amorous stamina!'

To be frank, my amorous stamina was indeed for the moment enervated; and I was happy to take Harry's advice, and spent the afternoon dozing in a large armchair in the club's window, only faintly aware of the life of London passing by outside.

At seven, my friend returned and invited me to accompany him – when in the dining room we partook of some mulligatawny soup (that interesting and highly spiced produce of the Indian continent), roast pheasant, and other delicacies, in the company of half a dozen other members of the club, some young, some approaching middle years; the conversation was pleasant but without a great deal of verve or animation, as though the diners were for some reason conserving their energies.

After dinner, the company rose and drank a toast to the Master of Ceremonies – none other than my friend, who then led the way from the room and up some stairs to a handsome chamber containing nothing but a vast accumulation of comfortable cushions spread about the floor upon thick carpets. I followed the other gentlemen through the room and into an antechamber, where to my surprise it became clear that we were all to remove our clothing. Was this to be some sort of masculine orgy? If so, I must really excuse myself – for though (as I have explained) not finding such activity always and in all places contemptible, I had had enough of it for one day, and further, looking about me I could see no gentleman whose approaches I would not find embarrassing rather than warming!

My countenance must have silently spoken my thoughts, for Harry, placing a hand upon my shoulder, assured me that I had nothing to fear: the entertainment he had provided would, he was sure, be entirely to my taste – 'Though I dare say,' he went on, 'that you will find it as unusual as I believe will the rest of the company.'

We now returned to the larger chamber – which, I should explain, was warm almost to enervation through an enormous fire which burned in a large grate. There, we disposed ourselves upon the cushions, and Harry stood to address us.

'Fellow members, and our honoured guest,' he began, 'I have for this occasion – which as some of you know is the anniversary of my appointment as chairman of the entertainments committee of this club – provided a diversion which I think you will find as enjoyable as it is unusual. It has been produced not without some trouble and expense, but I am confident that you will find it memorable. James, if you would pass the box?'

One of my companions produced from a corner a small box with an aperture into which we one at a time inserted a hand – myself first, as became a visitor – to take out a small ivory ball upon which a number was inscribed (mine bore the number five). Each of us having equipped ourselves with such a ball, Harry then took up a small silver bell and rang it – when the door opened, and into the room walked eight young women, each clad in what appeared to be a white sheet, wrapped about their bodies. These were in startling contrast to their skins, none of which was white, but which ranged from the coolest coffee colour to the most entire black – not merely the brown of the snake-charmer I had encountered in the morning, but the black of night – blacker than it was possible to imagine.

Walking with that peculiar grace which seems always to be the property of both men and women of the southern countries, the young women stood in a row before us, and at a signal from my friend . . .

But the space allotted to me for the moment fails: Sophie must be allowed to continue her tale, and my narration must pause until my next chapter.

Chapter Six

Sophie's Story

I cannot say that the prospect of a visit to the British Museum filled me with an overweening excitement, though as we rattled over the bad road into town my friend Margaret did her best to interest me in the object of our excursion. The Museum had originated, she informed me, in 1753, through the purchase by the Government of Sir Hans Sloane's collection and library, and its chief glory (in her opinion) was the Elgin Marbles, brought over from Greece by that interesting archaeologist some two or three years previously, and still a great source of wonder to all visitors.

'There are, however,' she said, 'some other interesting works of art which I believe you will find appealing, and it will be my pleasure to arrange that they shall be shown to you – they are not on view to the general public, for they are supposed to be too stimulating to be contemplated by the lower orders.'

This remark did interest me, and I passed the rest of the journey in a state of mild anticipation.

It is certainly the case that the British Museum stands first in point of interest among our national exhibitions, as well as in the judicious liberality displayed by the trustees in enabling some of its more interesting possessions to be displayed to the discerning visitor. The galleries open to the general public on the day we visited it were extremely full with visitors, and it was a truly exhilarating sight to follow the inquisitive groups from room to room, to pause with them before those wondrous marbles that once adorned the Parthenon and the Acropolis, to listen to the unlettered criticism and quaint observations of the visitors, or to attend them through those apartments that bring before them, as it were, the world at one view.

It was delightful to observe the effects of the contemplation of the objects of curiosity congregated in this wondrous ark, even on the ignorant spectator. We were amused with the play of feature in the face of a smock-frocked countryman called up by the alabaster sarcophagi and porphyritic idols of the old Egyptians; the rustic beauty who accompanied him dropped her lower jaw in unaffected wonder, and whispered her astonishment in his ear.

Then came a bold dragoon, having passed with an air of military stolidity through the marble galleries, only to be suddenly arrested in his march by a bust of Minerva, and pointing out to his sweetheart with great minuteness the superior beauty and convenience of his helmet, which he had taken off to illustrate the comparison, over the helmet of Minerva, wondering who the colonel could be who would serve out such a helmet as that, and what regiment he belonged to!

Then there was a connoisseur in black gaiters and green spectacles, pointing out with evident gusto the perfection of some dancing fauns to a group of young ladies who stood looking everywhere but at the object of attraction, as if they imagined the contemplation of undraped forms, save in the unobserved seclusion of their bedchamber, a horrid crime.

It was from the gallery containing these figures that Margaret led me through a small door (opened after she had passed her name to the attendant) and into a long room filled with objects which, she exclaimed, could never be displayed to the general public, for reasons I would clearly understand, on observing them.

There now stepped forward a young gentleman, dark and slim, plainly but neatly dressed, who was introduced to me as Mr Meredith Whalley, an employee of the museum, and keeper of *libidinotica*, who agreed to display the works on view in the gallery, while my friend excused herself on the grounds that she must pay a call elsewhere in the museum.

Mr Whalley led me first to a rough carving which (he explained) was made four thousand years ago of the ancient Egyptian god Min. From the roughness of the carving, its age was clearly apparent. Min, it appears, was the god of fertility – and demonstrated this by the gesture of his left hand, in which he firmly clutched a sturdy prick (with what satisfaction it was impossible to guess, since the statue was headless). Nearby stood a statue considerably more graphic, portraying a bearded gentleman apparently pouring something from a jar on to a similarly sturdy commodity (which indeed was risen to a somewhat more emphatic angle than Min's). This, Mr Whalley told me, was the god Priapus, who played Min's role among the Greeks; sometimes (he said) the divinity held a drapery full of fruits above his prick (which was always upright), in allusion to his function as god of fertility; in this case he was anointing that article with oil.

'You may be aware,' said Mr Whalley, 'that in ancient times there was much use of oil in erotic play, as it was believed that the slipperiness which it produced between skin and skin was especially lubricious.'

I must confess that I glanced at my companion, wondering whether his statement was directed at arousing a lascivious interest, or whether he was really unaware that such a use of oil was still made in these more civilised times; but his face was that merely of a scholar intent on the explication of historical fact.

'Here,' he said, 'is a somewhat similar statue, though

from the island of Cyprus – it is, as you see, a portrait of a satyr. These creatures were, as you may well be aware, attendants on the Greek god Dionysus – boisterous creatures chiefly of human form, but with some bestial aspect. Here, you see, he has a tail; there can be no religious excuse for him, however, for as you see he raises his hand as though to say: "Look at my remarkable organ!" '

I was in no doubt that my guide was right: the bearded creature with the tail bore with him a member of truly splendid size, supported on two spheres in remarkable proportion.

'It seems possible,' said Mr Whalley, 'that the sculptor's imagination was permitted full play, for I must confess that there seems a certain lack of proportion in his depiction of the satyr's parts.'

'He is certainly extremely well hung,' I commented; 'though, you know, if he hailed from the Mediterranean it may be that the artist was simply copying from nature, for some of the men of those parts . . .'

I paused here, not wishing to offend my attendant's susceptibilities; but he merely nodded gravely, and drew me on to a large bowl set upon a table.

'Here,' he said, 'is a particularly fine example of a Dionysian scene painted, as they so often were, upon amphora, Dionysus being the god of wine. It is a very frank depiction of an orgy held between young gentlemen (the Greeks, you know, being frequently lovers of their own sex): you see that here is a gentleman with his lips firmly about the prick of another gentleman, while a third penetrates him from the rear – again, a practice regarded by the ancients as entirely proper, though as you know at present frowned upon by our Government. It is a taste well recorded also in literature: Strato, the poet, wrote of his boy, Kyris,

Why lean that ravishing backside
Against a wall? – The stone

Can do nothing, so why tempt it?

and of another young friend,

The gymnasium bench gave Graphicus's bum a pinch.
Even a bench has its fancies – and I'm a man!

'You regret the fact that such days are past?' I enquired.

'Not at all, madam; my own emotions are entirely fixed upon the female sex – and indeed many of the Greeks were equally lovers of women, though frequently seem not to have been opposed to connection with either sex. But here, you see, is a sleeping satyr bestraddled by a winged female figure, his prick about to enter that part of the other sex at which most men would be happy to aim.'

And so we proceeded through the gallery – from large marble figures to small intaglio carvings, all having in common the depiction of sensual enjoyment. My companion remained, as it seemed, entirely composed, his face a politely indifferent mask; but as I bent to look more closely at a small seal upon which was a representation simply of a prick and attendant cods, he (I am almost sure, by accident) stepped somewhat too closely up behind me, and I could not miss the fact that while his face might be composed, in another part of his body there was certainly a disturbance of an interesting nature.

Immediately he was conscious of the closeness which had betrayed his awakened state, he drew away with an apology:

'I fear, ma'am, that while I have examined them a hundred times, a close observation of these artefacts always result in a certain warming of my nature – even my familiarity with them cannot deprive them of their vitality.'

'My dear sir,' I replied, 'please do not apologise: you are of course right – one can feel through the senses the vital pulse which raised the blood of the artist as he carved

or painted these scenes. And indeed the emotions felt by
the models who posed for him, for' – and I laid my hand
upon the large and shapely prick (seeming warm and soft
to the touch, though hewn from marble) of a satyr who
leered down at me in stone from a nearby plinth – 'for
surely no artist could have imagined so splendid and handsome a weapon as this! Certainly no woman could fail to
admire both the artist's skill and the emotion which drove
him to depict it with such realism.'

My guide nodded, and I could not but observe that
he now regarded me with somewhat more warmth than
previously. I continued to stand for a moment, my hand
resting tenderly beneath the cool white spheres which hung
below the riding-muscle of the satyr, my bosom (as I
believe) somewhat animated by the emotion of the
moment – which was quite genuine, for the figure was
indeed so real and lively that it was not impossible to
believe that at any moment he might with a leap begin
to ravish one!

After a long moment, 'I wonder, ma'am,' said Mr Whalley, 'whether I might offer you refreshment in a room
which I have furnished for my convenience, nearby?'

I was as a matter of course happy to accept the kind
invitation, and the gentleman ushered me from the gallery
– carefully locking the door behind him – along a corridor,
and opening another door, showed me into a room delightfully and tastefully fitted out, dark green hangings making
it seem somewhat gloomy, but the gloom perfectly relieved
by the cool winter sun's shining through a skylight above.

I remarked upon the admirable proportions of the chamber, which was (Mr Whalley explained) or had been a
studio used by artists for restoring paintings or sculpture
brought to the museum; but lately a larger room having
been set out for that purpose nearby, he as the head of his
department had been offered the room for his private use,
and had made of it a sitting room where he could receive
guests.

'I can offer you a dish of tea,' he said, 'of if you are to lunch shortly with Lady Cricklewood, perhaps I could offer you a glass of Madeira wine?'

'I would be very pleased to take one,' I said; 'but, Mr Whalley, perhaps first we could engage in the assuaging of the emotions roused by those interesting carvings and paintings you were so kind as to display to me? – for, if I may be so bold as to say so – I observe from certain signs that you were as warmed by them as I am myself.'

The reader may perhaps be shocked that a person so young as myself should express herself so boldly to a young man to whom she had not for more than half an hour been introduced; but upon the other hand it may be the case that the more observant peruser of this account has already remarked to himself (or herself) that in such matters I was even in those days no neophyte, nor was troubled by the reticence which prevents so many young women even of mature years from taking advantage of an opportunity for a pleasant amorous interlude.

Mr Whalley, if he was surprised, was gentleman enough not to show it.

'My dear Mrs Nelham,' he said, 'how charming to discover so young and beautiful a woman as yourself as ready to express herself in these matters as a man! And as quick to recognise that your captivating frame – the intriguing lines of bosom and lower limbs (if I may so express myself) so enchantingly revealed by the fashion of the moment – cannot but drive the admiring male to the point of derangement!'

I cannot say that Mr Whalley looked to me positively to be on the point of derangement; but the forcefulness of the expression in those piercing dark eyes beneath black beetle brows, the sensual fullness of his slightly parted lips, were a sufficiently strong hint (together with the almost threatening proportions of the bulge which lay over his lower belly, unmistakably shown through his tightly cut trousers) that he would be a virile and robust lover.

I lost no time in slipping from my clothes, and upon my laying my dress down upon a chair and turning, discovered Mr Whalley clad only in his shirt – the front of which was raised by a staff too prominent to permit of its being concealed. I confess to wondering for a while whether the gentleman was one of those who preferred to retain some clothing while performing the act of love – but the case was simply that gentleman's formal clothing is somewhat more complex as to the arrangements of buttons, braces et cetera, than ladies', and therefore necessarily takes longer to remove, for Mr Whalley now took hold of the hem of his shirt and with a swift movement removed it.

He was, I was delighted to observe, as well built as I had supposed from his superior posture and carriage, with a broad but unfleshy chest tapering to a narrow waist and hips, his lower limbs as shapely as could be wished by the most critical of ladies, and covered by a thick mat of black hair, which – sprouting also on his breast and belly and curling about the root of his manhood – gave almost the impression of a satyr; with the thick and curly black hair upon his head and those aforementioned beetle brows, he would not have been out of place in a sylvan Greek grove, peering through a thicket at a bathing nymph! There was an additional feature which struck me as remarkable: the left nipple of his breast was pierced by a small round gold ring, of no more than half an inch in diameter, which hung there like a ring in a lady's ear!

I was not, of course, so rude as immediately to comment upon it, rather stepping forward happily to permit an embrace – but was not prepared for Mr Whalley placing his hands beneath my arms and (being considerably taller than myself) lifting me until, slipping a thigh between my own, he enabled himself to press his staff against those gates between which it was so eager to pass that I could positively feel its heartbeat! I was not entirely devoid, myself, of a similar pressure of emotion, and placing my

94

arms about his neck supported myself while he set his palms beneath the cheeks of my arse, when on throwing my legs about him I felt without any pangs of distress or trepidation the invasion of a stave sufficiently bulky and powerful to afford convincing proof of his admiration,

Inspiring as was the pose which we had adopted, it is not one which permits of a great deal of animated motion, and carrying me to the side of the room, he carefully placed my bum upon a side-table, thus permitting himself to devote his hands to an exploration of my body, while the necessity to carry me no longer obtaining, he was able to move his lower body in that manner which is normally to be expected in the act of copulation.

I have already remarked that Mr Whalley's prick was not conspicuous by its modest proportions, and though I had only had a relatively brief glimpse of it, it seemed to me from the emotion I now felt that it must be somewhat remarkable in amplitude – and on looking down saw that indeed it was splendidly thick, so that upon leaving my person it drew the flesh of the interior of my cunny with it with a splendidly affectionate gesture, and upon returning to its desired abode pressed in with a remarkably pleasing insistence, filling me with a delicious gift of charming flesh.

I will not pretend that a passage of love in a sitting room often carries with it either the comfort or the convenience afforded by a well-furnished bedroom; on the other hand it is frequently inspiriting simply through being unusual – and if we were not able to lavish upon each other those caresses which other circumstances would have made possible, the situation was certainly not devoid of pleasure – which was none the less keen for being protracted through Mr Whalley's ability to press home his amorous advantage with what seemed unassailable vigour, my emotions being stirred to the utmost on no less than two occasions before (upon my being forced to cry out aloud in the access of pleasure brought on by my third paroxysm) he allowed himself to reach the summit of his own ascension, being so good (since we were only recently introduced) as to withdraw his weapon just before it fired off.

Dismounting, my paramour kindly assisted me to a chair, and falling to his knees mopped the proof of his passion from my breast with his pocket handkerchief.

I naturally thanked him for the generosity with which he had paid me his compliments, but was immediately silenced by his own protestations of gratitude: for (he said) although a number of ladies had been kind enough to alleviate that passion naturally aroused by a study of the artefacts which he had shown me, there were few who did so with such freedom and enthusiasm as myself – and moreover few who demonstrated with such completeness the fact that the female beauty of our own time was no whit less than that depicted by the ancients.

I, of course, demurred, instead complimenting him upon his staying power (which I think pleased him); and also now remarked upon that strange phenomenon, the ring through his tit – which, he said, he had had inserted by a young Albanian soldier some years previously: 'I was in those days more impressionable,' he said, 'and believed him when he said that it would make me more interesting to the ladies!'

I was able with honesty to remark that at least it made him no less interesting; but had the operation not been a painful one? To which he remarked (with some blushes) that it was not particularly so, and that in any event he had been at the time distracted by the attentions paid to another quarter of his body by the young Albanian's lover, a youth particularly skilled in the art of . . . of . . . – at which words failed him; but I was able to assure him that I followed his meaning.

'It is not the case,' he went on, 'that I was even as a young man particularly susceptible to such pleasantries, but, you know, when in Rome, or rather Albania . . .'

I assured him that I knew what he meant, and reminded him that even such a discriminating person as Lord Byron had been susceptible to similar advances, having (as I believe) been persuaded by Veli Pasha, the son of the ruler of all the Peloponnesus, to succumb to his blandishments.

Mr Whalley nodded, but said nothing else until we were both dressed, when he seemed about to make a further remark, but suppressed the thought; whereupon naturally I wished to hear in full what he had to say.

'If you have an hour,' he said, 'it will be easier for me to demonstrate what I had in mind than simply to explain it' – and upon my agreeing to which, we left his room and proceeded through various corridors and passages to a door which led into a sort of small balcony or conservatory, from which there was a view into an artist's studio.

'This,' said my companion, 'is a part of our perpetuation department, where we repair those statues or paintings which are damaged. In this case, as you see, Mr Fortescue, a fine young sculptor, is engaged in replacing those intimate parts of a piece of statuary which was disfigured in ancient times by one of the less lascivious Popes in whose collection at that time the piece resided.'

Slightly below us was indeed the figure of a young gentleman, chisel in hand, at work upon a large piece of marble depicting a young lady in the embrace of a satyr. The young lady was held aloft by the human-animal, and poised above the place where one might expect to see that extended article of flesh with which he would hope to penetrate her. Alas, that essential object had been removed; and it was it which the sculptor was about to counterfeit in a large piece of marble which had been connected or welded in place.

In order to assist him at his work, a lady and gentleman had been engaged to pose in the attitude of the figures of the sculptor: the satyr was a young man who from his

97

appearance may have been a costermonger or market worker – a probability demonstrated by the muscular nature of his thighs and arms, and by the fact that he had no difficulty in suspending the female in the position required by the sculptor. Happily, he was of a quite remarkably hirsute appearance – considerably more so even than Mr Whalley. Dark hair grew so thickly upon his back and buttocks that it would have been difficult to believe he was not animal had it not been for the cheerful and perky expression upon his face.

Alas, however, between his thighs there was no sign of activity; and as this was the part of his anatomy the representation of which was vital to the repair of the sculpture, this presented a difficulty. The problem lay, I had no doubt, in the undesirable appearance of the female who he was holding aloft, for she was sufficiently thin to be described as scrawny – of female breasts there was little evidence, while her face was pinched and small and her haunches bony and without luxury – she had not, in fact, a figure likely to raise any young gentleman to a demonstration of virility, and I could not but remark upon this to Mr Whalley.

'You have made my point before I could put it into words,' he said.

But surely there could be no difficulty in procuring the services of a young lady personable enough to fulfil the requirements of Eros? I said – a number of handsome women were available upon payment of even a moderate fee.

'Ah, but you are not aware of the stringency with which we are afflicted by a Government always unwilling to make monies available for the support of artistic endeavour, and in particular for the upkeep of this place,' said Mr Whalley; 'moreover, those gentlemen charged with the payment of that ever-diminishing sum set aside for the Museum always search for excuses to withdraw their patronage – and I suppose that the rendering of an account for the hire of such a young woman as would readily make herself available for such a purpose would not be greeted with equanimity.'

What could I do but volunteer my services? Though I was not raised in a home where the arts were given a great deal of attention, it was always my pleasure to pay tribute, where I could, to the skills of painters or carvers; and this was a case in which such a contribution could be made without pecuniary expense, while at the same time making use of those gifts with which I had been graced by a beneficent and kindly Creator.

Escorting me to the floor of the studio with considerable enthusiasm, Mr Whalley introduced me to Mr Tom Fortescue, a young man and Member of the Royal Academy of considerable talent as a sculptor, who – I later found – was no less accomplished at rendering statues of his own designing than in repairing the carvings of the ancients.

On Mr Whalley's explaining my offer to replace the female model, Mr Fortescue could not disguise his pleasure – although, as a gentleman, he thanked with perfect courtesy the young girl who the costermonger replaced upon the ground; who, receiving the two pence which was her salary, was extremely pleased at the extra sixpence which, out of charity, I pressed into her palm – then accompanying her behind a screen where she replaced her clothing and assisted me to divest myself (for the second time) of mine.

When I emerged, the young costermonger (if indeed that was his occupation: I was never to learn it) was allowing himself to rest by reclining on the rug which stood upon the floor of the studio, and again I was struck by his resemblance to the satyr he impersonated – for now that I saw him alone and in isolation, I could see that the hairiness of his body was indeed remarkable – a positive pelt covering the front of his body no less than the rear, his chest bearing a mat or forest which extended down over his belly and thighs, between which that bush which normally marks out the territory of masculine virility was undetectable, since it was at every point a part of that forest which enveloped the rest of his body! While he made a pretence of not examining me, I could see from his sideways glances that he was by no means dismayed at my appearance.

Mr Fortescue need not pretend to be unaware of my appearance, for after all it was vital to him; and that his frank examination of my person led to a happy conclusion was signalled by his smiles, and by an attentive kissing of my hand – whereafter he called to Joe to resume the post. Sitting upon a stool (which in the carving was depicted as a rocky eminence) the costermonger placed one foot out and slightly to the side, then taking me by the waist lifted me bodily in the air, while the sculptor taking one of my hands placed it about the young man's neck, my fingers just running into the hair at the back, while he set the fingers of my other hand upon the satyr's breast, where within the hair I could feel the protuberance of a tit rising beneath the pressure of my finger and thumb. Catching young Joe's eye, and seeing a bright twinkle in it, I could not resist closing my finger and thumb upon his titty, when it swelled yet further – and in a moment I felt my lower lips nuzzled by a Something which (since both Joe's hands were at my waist) could only be the risen mark of his virility!

Mr Fortescue – of whom I had a full view – was delighted by the sight of that object whose presence I was positively aware; and first approaching and with eye and hand measuring the dimensions of that part which he wished to reproduce in marble, took up his chisel and set to work with a will.

It was unsurprising that having to preserve our pose for some time, and under the necessity to hold me in mid-air, Joe – whose physical strength could not be in question –

was not able for an indefinite period to maintain his standing prick; but happily upon its beginning to shrink (which
I could feel, from it falling away somewhat from my own
parts) a little tickling from my finger and thumb upon his
tit resulted in a recovery; and when this precaution failed,
after a while, by whispering I persuaded him (without
difficulty) that the moment he began to feel his carnality
weaken he should lower me slightly in order that by con-
tracting the muscles of my quim – a trick which every
young lady should master – I could tickle or even partly
enclose his prick, thus enabling him through a combination
of sensation, imagination and promise to retain that
appearance of his nether body which was of most practical
service to the sculptor.

Over half an hour must have passed before Mr Fortescue
laid down his chisel and informed us that he had made
such progress that he would be able to finish the sculpture
without any further assistance from us. Setting me down
with a nice mixture of relief and reluctance, Joe led me
(with permission) to the carving, where he was delighted
to see the massive and handsome proportions of the satyr's
prick; indeed, he questioned whether it could be a portrait?
– at which I softly whispered to him that from the observation I had made, it was no less!

The fact was that the past minutes had been remarkably
pleasant; and that, as was normal with me, propinquity to
a handsome male (especially one whose physique was so
remarkably decorated) had raised my spirits to such a
degree that they demanded, rather than merely requested,
satisfaction. I believe that Mr Whalley was aware of this,
for he suggested to Mr Fortescue that they should retire
in order to allow myself and my fellow model to resume
our clothing. The sculptor, though somewhat reluctant to
be drawn away from the admiration of his work, concurred,
and they left the room – whereupon I without hesitation
laid my hand between Joe's thighs, in order (as I explained)

to rouse his passion to the extent when I could make a proper comparison between the original and its representation.

He was clearly unconvinced that that was my true reason (and was, after all, correct in his suspicion); for taking me in his arms, he tumbled me immediately upon the mat, and kneeling over me took in hand an instrument which, now that I had an unhindered view of it, was indeed a splendid example of its species – its fine head bald where the hood had been withdrawn (no doubt by the manipulation of those fingers which held it aloft) and shining slightly, its stem handsome in its proportions, looking like a splendid, tall white column whose base was hidden in a black thicket.

I could not but take it in my own hands, and sitting up, pay it the tribute of a kiss – but Joe was in no mood for such niceties (he had after all been considerably the subject of teasing manipulation during the past hour!), and unprevented by me forced me upon my back, and placing himself between my thighs in a moment had plunged to the hilt, and was assailing me with a cheerful forcefulness, his lips fixed to my breast, and his haunches (covered in their cloak of hair) bounding with an ebullience which spoke of a happy recognition of the joys of the act.

By its very nature, our pleasure could not be indefinitely prolonged: for though Joe was as cultivated a lover as one of his class could be expected to be, and as well educated in pleasing a lady as could reasonably be demanded, the titillation which had been afforded him had raised his spirits to a height from which a fall must be the inevitable and relatively speedy result.

Happily, my participation was the result of a desire to reward him for his admiration and to some extent out of a curiosity to experience just such an encounter as a nymph might have had with a satyr in ancient times. Mr Whalley had after all already taken the edge off my sensual appetite. Thus although I must counterfeit rather than truly experience a pleasure as keen as Joe's, I believe that he was happy that he had satisfied me; and on our recovering our breath, rose and donned his clothes with a contented mien, and took his leave of me with a merry smile, on his way out collecting his sixpence from Mr Fortescue – who then thanked me with a politeness which seemed to suggest that he had no suspicion that the pose which he had required of myself and the costermonger had led to a natural consummation, though from his glances Mr Whalley suspected otherwise – who now escorted me to the front hall of the Museum, where Margaret awaited me, enquiring solicitously whether my visit had been as interesting as she had hoped – a query which I could only answer in the affirmative.

Chapter Seven

The Adventures of Andy

The sight which now delighted my eyes was one which any young man with pretensions to vigour would have found equally pleasant. To remind those of my readers whose attention has been distracted from my own narrative by that of my friend Mrs Nelham, I found myself in a private room of a gentleman's club in the West End of London, with seven agreeable companions, after an excellent dinner and some good wine; this delight now being capped by the appearance of eight young ladies whose faces varied in hue between the light brown and the jet black – and who now showed that the impression was not the result of any colourant which had been applied to their skins, but, stretching out their arms and lifting away the white sheets which covered their bodies, revealed those bodies in complete nakedness!

It will not surprise the reader when I say that I found it difficult to know where to focus my eyes – and on my glancing at the gentlemen around me, found the same to be true of them: indeed, the eyes of one or two of them (the younger and therefore more impressionable) stood out like hat pegs as they attempted to take in the whole picture before them in its completeness and variety.

The ladies were remarkably similar in build – that is,

of that happy degree between the positively fat and the emphatically thin; much of a height, their breasts were equally handsome, jutting forward and seeming to pout, the nipples pointing slightly upward and away from their chests; their bellies were slightly rounded but taut with all the firmness of youth, while between eight pairs of strong and finely tapering thighs, uniformly black bushes only slightly disguised those parts to which a gentleman's attention must always, in certain circumstances, be forcefully directed.

Harry, my host, had done well; indeed, I could not imagine how he had been able to collect together such remarkable specimens of womanhood, who must surely come from a number of different countries – for I was unable to believe that the ebony miss at the right-hand end of the line, whose skin was only relieved from utter jet by the handsome tone of purple which shaded the inside of her thighs, could belong to the same race as the young damsel at the other end, whose skin was more nearly the shade of one of our English maidens given to lying unclothed in the sun!

We were now required to examine the numbers on the ivory balls which we had chosen – while the young ladies, revolving, revealed that each one bore upon one delightful haunch a similar number, printed upon their skins in some white substance. My number corresponded with that upon the left buttock of the darkest of the beauties. I was not displeased – not only because it had never been my pleasure to be familiar with someone of her race, but because she seemed to me to have the most beautiful body – or at least, it appealed particularly to my senses, though from their attitude I believe that each of my companions was similarly pleased with the young women allotted to him.

Bella – for that was her name – led me from the room, and without troubling to cover herself, proceeded down a corridor and to another, smaller chamber in which a bed was to be found. The sight which I enjoyed as I followed her was not one which in any way persuaded me to regret my choice: her tapering waist was set upon hips which swayed delightfully as she walked, imparting a similarly delicious motion to twin buttocks somewhat highly set, which could almost have been compared to those of a boy had they not had the distinctive pear shape of the female posterior; indeed, so entrancingly tempting were they that I must exercise all my powers of restraint in order to endure the sight without attempting to confirm the elasticity of the skin by placing my hand upon a surface!

The cell into which we now stepped was comfortably furnished as to a large bed; but the fact that apart from a screen in one corner and a large mirror conveniently placed, it contained nothing else, persuaded me that the pleasures which presumably awaited me there would be nothing new to the carved cherubs which overlooked the bed's head, and that those couplings which I confidently expected would shortly be reflected in the mirror would not be surprising to the genie of that piece of furniture!

The young lady now turned to me, and without ceremony – but with the most provocative motions – began to assist me from my clothing. By the time she knelt to remove my trousers, she found some difficulty in that operation, from the prominence of my riding-muscle, which a combination of her beauty, my expectations, and the motions of her hands about my half-naked body had rendered so swollen as to force her to take it in one hand to persuade it from beneath the waistband of my nether garment.

No man in such a circumstance can perhaps completely believe an expression of pleasure from such a partner as she to be entirely honest; yet her declaration of surprise at its size seemed to break so innocently and spontaneously from her lips as to seem sincere – and indeed without even pausing to assist me to step from my trousers, she ran her fingers tenderly along its length, and even went so far as to place a kiss upon its empurpled head – then looking up with a shy appeal, as though I might be angry at the familiarity!

By now, no reader will be amazed to hear that I was in a high state of spirits, nor that I hastily wrapped the young woman in my arms, impatient to lay my naked flesh against hers; her body, once in my arms, proved as delicious as sight had suggested – there was none of that over-ripe softness which cloys, but rather the absolute relish of a frame as firm and vigorous as could be wished by any man who preferred an active partner to one who might prefer simply to lie back and allow herself to be loved.

There was but a short pause – during which I allowed my lips the pleasure of tasting her own (whereat she sucked upon my tongue as though upon a tasty sweetmeat, then running her own tongue gently about my lips, sighing with pleasure and exhaling a sweet breath) – before I bore her to the bed, and laying her upon it in no brief period instructed my lips to move from her lips to her cheeks and chin, her neck, her breasts (but here for some time they paused to graze upon such enchanting uplands), down over her little round belly until, gently parting her thighs (which moved apart without reluctance), I was able to feel the wiry prickles of hair upon my cheek, and at last those other, fuller lips of hers part beneath the pressure of my own.

I have had, as has any gentleman who has permitted himself a certain latitude in the lists of love, the happy experience of exploring the love nests of a great number of charming females; but if I remember one puss as being perhaps the most perfectly formed, it must be that of the young lady who I am presently describing. Certainly, the skin about her most intimate parts was as black as that of her cheeks or breasts – though there it was shaded to a dark, purply red; but that apart, the actual form was classic in its proportion and construction. In repose, the lips lay together snugly but not tightly, so that there was no impression that the castle keep was so designed as to repulse all comers; and at the top, just jutting from between them, appeared a little swelling turret of flesh which, as I closely observed it, was seen to be an almost perfect simulacrum of my own cock – complete with a tiny head embraced by a band of skin.

Upon my touching this with the tip of my tongue, a shiver of pleasure shook the young lady; while on my positively taking it between my lips and sucking upon it, she cried out so loudly that I feared for the horses in St James's Street! However, swiftly recovering herself, she thrust my head aside – though without more violence than was concomitant with the act – explaining in decent English, though with a heavy accent strange to me, that it was her duty to pleasure me, rather than the other way about. Naturally, on my part I assured her that it could not but be the duty of a gentleman to ensure that his partner enjoyed the act as much as he himself; but she insisted that I should lie back and permit her to display those skills for which my host had employed her – and seeing that she was likely to be upset by any more protestation on my part, I decided for the moment to give way.

Upon my doing so, she threw a long leg across my body and lowered herself until that remarkable black bush fell upon the underside of my prick, now pressed firmly against my belly by the extent of my excitement. I have already remarked that the locks which lay about the portals of her pleasure cave were bristles rather than tresses – and as she began to move her lower body to and fro in a gentle rocking motion, these rasped against my prick, imparting a sensation almost painful through the roughness of the hairs – the unusual quality of the feeling together with the sight of such a black fleece placed against the white of my British flesh being remarkably inspiriting, so that a shudder rapidly ran through my body and goose pimples rose upon my flesh – at the sight of which she smiled charmingly, and lowering her head flicked at my neck and breast with her tongue, tickling the small points of my nipples, which had grown hard as little pebbles with the pleasure she was already giving me.

Perceiving my delight, she now moved her hips down, and laying her body along the length of my own, permitted me to experience with all my flesh the softness of her own, which though muscular rather than flaccid was never in the least masculine in quality – for though her breasts (to mention but one feature) were firm, and even when she bent over me had retained their charming shape rather than depending from her body like the dugs of some female animal, they were also soft; even the nipples, full and rigid though they were, were softer than my own (a phenomenon I have noticed in women, even in the utmost throes of pleasure).

But now her lips had moved from my breast to my belly, and at last (though accomplished in a brief period, the movement seemed prolonged!) reached my prick, over the length of which they moved with little soft kisses, until (perhaps pitying me, for my entire body was now rigid no less with expectation than desire) she opened them and welcomed the instrument within them.

For those who have never set eyes upon a member of the African race, I should here explain that both in the men and the women their lips are fuller than those of the white races, giving them an advantage in oral love-making which is envied no less by those who enjoy rousing their partners by these means than by those who relish receiving such caresses. This young lady was naturally adept at the task to which she now applied herself, and her lips, being richly soft and slippery (through a ready flow of saliva which soon applied itself to my skin), passed over the column which now lay between them with a gentle yet firm pressure, embracing almost its whole length (for though my prick is no less long than average in a young man, she proved able to swallow it almost to the hilt), then drawing back until with the most delicate motion they withdrew over its head, remaining in contact until at the very last moment they reluctantly relinquished the last morsel, a little thread of liquid only connecting my organ with her tongue, with which she gave the most tender flick at its very end, before once more allowing its tip to make its way into the warm and tender grotto so eager (it seemed) to receive it.

It will not surprise my male readers to hear that after a few minutes of such work, which was accompanied by charming movements of her hands upon my torso, I had reached a point at which my spirits were in imminent danger of gushing forth in such a manner as to put an end to the proceedings. I therefore made as though to lift my friend into such a position as to permit her to embrace me from above in a manner which would at least (as I hoped) allow me to relieve her own feelings somewhat – but she declined to take the hint, and now taking my stalk at its root quickened her motions, those thick and loving lips seemed to impart the most delicate *frisson* to every area of an instrument which, while not unfamiliar with such a motion, had perhaps never been complimented by such devoted and sympathetic proficiency.

To cut my narrative short, it proved impossible for me to resist; and in a moment I felt that tightening of the lower belly, that irretrievable pressure in the groin, and finally that irresistible and forceful explosion of emotion which was ended only by the expulsion of the liquor of life. Some ladies have a dislike to receiving this in their mouths, which is why I am invariably prepared to do them the courtesy of spending in another manner; my companion, however, far from flinching seemed positively flattered, and continued to suck upon my prick as upon a teat, not removing her lips until the paroxysm which accompanies the moment of joy had fully ceased, and even then, reclining with her cheek upon my upper thigh, retained the shrinking member until it was a mere squab, after which she finally relinquished it, raising her head only to give me the sweetest smile, and to thank me for the pleasure I had given her.

I was, needless to say, almost ashamed to receive such a compliment; for to be sure I had played no part in the affair other than simply to allow her to pleasure me – but though I protested, and gathering her in my arms drew her head to my breast, I was for the time quite incapable of repaying my debt! I therefore allowed myself the luxury of simply reclining in that state most satisfactory to a man – with a beautiful woman in his arms, both of them being in a state of nature, and – speaking at any rate for myself – bearing what Mr Blake has called 'the lineaments of gratified desire'.

What was my sorrow, however, to feel upon my cheek, as I pressed it against the young woman's, a wetness which spoke of sorrow; and indeed could now feel by the heaving of her breast that she was sobbing, though as restrainedly as was possible – hoping no doubt to disguise the fact from me. No one will doubt that I immediately took upon me the responsibility for discovering the cause of her melancholy; and after some time drew from her the following story:

She had grown up, it seems, in that part of Africa known as Senegal, a country of some 75,000 square miles, upon which the French (that nation so irreconcilably avaricious where territorial possessions are concerned) have ambitions. Her origin had been in the town of Dakar, which has been in the possession of the French since 1677. It seems that this town is the centre of the slave trade – a circumstance which resulted in Bella being seized, some two years ago – at the age of only fourteen, as I would guess (she herself having no idea of the date of her birth). The piratical slave-traders who seized her were, I am sorry to relate, British; and she found herself upon a ship bound she knew not where, and thrust with many other women into a hold which also contained a number of men, also seized along the coast of Africa – but from the Portuguese colony of Gambia.

I should remind my readers that even in the years of which I write, it had been for some time entirely illegal to hunt down men and women and to carry them into slavery. For full fifty years it had been the law that as soon as a slave set his foot on the soil of the British islands, he became free, while it was in 1807 that Lord Grenville's bill for the abolition of the slave trade was passed by the Lords and then by the Commons. But while this bill effectually ended the large-scale trading of slaves in England, the business still went on by the back door – it being extremely difficult to prove the fact, for most of the black men and women brought here were too terrified or ignorant, or both, to protest or to support the protests of others, for fear of their lives – and a justified fear, for the bodies of slaves who had escaped or attempted to protest against their miserable state were often found in the Thames or, their throats slit, in one of the less salubrious districts of the capital.

But to return to Bella's narrative, the men with whom she now found herself imprisoned had themselves already been incarcerated in the hold for some weeks, and despite being somewhat starved of food, their carnal appetites being considerable viewed the women now thrown to them as so much fodder for those appetites, and fell upon them with an enthusiasm which they had previously had to slake among themselves (the younger men among them having been used for the purpose without mercy). Bella was fortunate in that she had fallen – quite literally – into the arms of a young man of about her own years and indeed of her own village, who was less rapacious as to his sensual passions than some others; and taking her in his arms had not attempted to force himself on her, but rather had (by dint of rolling into a corner) protected her from the ravages his compatriots were now wreaking upon the other women.

However, nature taking its course, these two young people, during a long voyage not notable for the provision of any entertainment for the enforced passengers, fell to that amusement which is either the concomitant of love or its provocation – that is, to the mutual examination of each other's bodies, and eventually to putting to their natural use those parts of their anatomy designed to give pleasure. Both (Bella confided) found solace in this activity, believing it to be natural, enjoyable, comforting – and a rouser of sentimental as well as passionate emotions; so that by the time they reached England, she and her friend had formed a bond of love which resulted in his protecting her from the passions of the other men on board, and in her regarding herself as his possession (for the women of Africa seem to be entirely free from any suggestion that their sex is equal, let alone the superior, of the male – a proposition often to be found, now, amid the educated females of this kingdom).

It was clear however from the manner in which she spoke of her friend that he was more than a man simply seizing the opportunity to slake his lust upon a pretty companion; he was a lover more educated (no doubt by a natural predilection) than might have been expected: his was not simply a habit of slaking his lust, for (she said) he always took care that she should get as much pleasure from the act as he, never leaving her unsatisfied; and his attitude towards her was as much that of a friend as of a lover.

Alas, on the ship's arrival in England – at a Westcountry

port, as I guess from the girl's description – the human cargo was unceremoniously unloaded on the docks in the dead of night, and immediately became split – some being herded in one direction, some in another; Bella and her particular friend remained for the time together, thrown into the back of a wagon where they lay for hours in extreme discomfort as it rattled over the road to London; but before entering the capital, the cart stopped and he was taken from the arms of his mistress, disappeared into the dim dawn light, and had not been seen again in all the six months during which the girl had lived (as I now learned) in a house with her seven companions, under the care of Lord Cricklewood.

It was, needless to say, a shock to me to discover that the gentleman who had befriended me was a slave-runner – for that is what he was, and he must be condemned for it, though the physical condition of the young ladies he had presented to us was excellent, and Bella made no complaint as to her treatment (except not being allowed out of the house unaccompanied by the woman who lived with the girls, and had been placed in charge of them).

She told me this story with some tears and much melancholy, but she was a merry child at heart, and the very narration seemed to free her spirits for the time, and seeing that my sympathies were such that her tale had lowered my own temper, she immediately fixed her lips to mine, begging me not to be despondent, for she was sure she would one day meet her man again, and would know how to greet him – at which she took my shrunken cock in her hand, and with a dexterity as much the result of natural feeling as of proficiency, soon worked it to a stand.

But I was determined now to return the compliment she had paid me, for the meanest female deserves no less; and pressing her back upon the bed gave way to her blandishments only to the extent that I assented to her suggestion that we should lie top to toe, in order that as I paid the tribute of Eros to her most intimate part, she could apply once more that dextrous tongue and those soft lips to that part of me happiest to receive the homage.

My previous disbursement of the consequence of passion was still sufficiently recent to dull somewhat the edge of my passion, and despite her endeavours (which were as delightful as formerly) I was able to keep my countenance, and to my pleasure felt her entire body shake not once but several times as the result of my attentions to the centre of female sensuality, that little bud which resembles the male organ no less in sensitivity than in appearance; indeed, she was rendered so incapable by her own pleasure that all she could do was gasp, even relinquishing my cock, and merely grabbing at my buttocks to bury her face between my thighs in happy embarrassment at the state almost of swooning to which I was able to reduce her.

I was determined however to conclude the matter properly, and reversing our positions, gently laid myself between her thighs, which happily embraced me; and there began those motions most common between a man and a woman, my prick now in so excited a state as to resemble a bar of iron or some equally adamant material; and thus continuing to provide in a more feverish manner that friction which my tongue had but recently left off. In a few moments, Bella's mouth opened in a soundless cry, and her back arched, positively lifting my body with it; upon which signal I relinquished my hold upon restraint, and we spent together, each (I am sure) with as much enjoyment as two persons of the opposite sex may be capable of.

Once more, we were now at leisure; and after a brief period of rest, resumed our discussion – or rather, I re-opened it, enquiring whether, should I give some attention to discovering the whereabouts of her missing lover, she would be agreeable to my attempting to obtain their release from bondage; whereat she consented – with the single reservation that it might be difficult for them to obtain employment in this country as free agents; but I insisted that this should be no problem, and that I should see to it – whereupon she was happy to consent to my interesting myself in her case.

I now raised myself as though to leave; but Bella informed me that there was no need – for the room in which we lay would not be disturbed until the following morning, and that it was the custom for a gentleman, unless he resisted, to remain; and she would as a matter of course be glad to remain also, in case (as she put it) I should desire further comfort.

I could not resist a feeling of compassion for so young a girl – for she could not be much more than sixteen or seventeen years of age – to be in the situation where she must not only give way to the desire of any gentleman foisted upon her, but must also remain in his bed until he agreed to her leaving it; but happily she seemed genuinely not to object to me, and I therefore turned her about so that her charming posteriors were pressed against my belly, put my arms about her and together we fell into a calm slumber.

We were awakened some hours later not by the light – for the mornings were dark – but by the entrance of a servant (a saturnine gentleman who from his lack of emotion or curiosity was clearly used to the tableau he saw before him) bearing a tray of chocolate; and were sitting up taking a cup when, unannounced, Harry Cricklewood threw open the door and hoped that I had passed an agreeable night.

'Young Bella is a vigorous quim, as you will I trust have found,' he said, with a coarseness unnecessary (in my view) in the presence even of a slave; though Bella had I suppose heard such talk too often to be affected by it.

I merely expressed my satisfaction – for if I was to look into Cricklewood's business I must not give any sign of disapprobation, or even suggest that I was aware how Bella had got into the position she found herself in. Sitting upon the bedside, the gentleman allowed one hand to fall upon Bella's shoulder, and placing the other upon her breast, planted a kiss upon her lips (to which she acquiesced with perfect grace; I was, I believe, more affected by it than she); then throwing back the bedclothes, hurried her from the bed – pausing only to ask whether I had 'finished with her', then allowing her only the time to throw her dress over her shoulders and vanish without so much as a backward glance.

'My dear Harry,' I said, 'I must express my thanks for a delightful night's work.'

'Well,' he said, 'you know what the poet says: "One charming night gives more delight Than a thousand happy days!" '

I smiled.

'I was not aware,' I remarked, 'that gentlemen's clubs laid up such splendid harems for the use of their members!'

'Ah,' said he, 'Whister's is somewhat unusual in that.'

He offered no further explanation, so after a moment I enquired how the young ladies had been obtained – and feared at that instant that I had gone too far; but after a moment's hesitation Harry asked whether I would like to know more about how the arrangement had been arrived at – for, he had said, it would form an admirable adjunct to a young person's education, though (he was good enough to add) he had no doubt that there was little which he or anyone could teach me by way of the ingenious means of setting up a similar establishment. Needless to say, I concurred, and he invited me to meet him at the club this same evening at eight o'clock, when I would learn more. In the mean time, I was free to make use of the premises, for he had seen to it that I was accepted as an honorary member for as lengthy a period as I might wish.

Chapter Eight

Sophie's Story

The day after my interesting excursion to the Museum, I had an unfortunate accident. Stepping somewhat too energetically forth from the front door of Cricklewood House, I failed to realise that ice had made the steps slippery, fell upon that part of my anatomy to which a cushion is kinder than a marble step, and on rising could not refrain from a cry of pain.

Devon, the footman, who had opened the front door for me with his habitual politeness, immediately came forward and taking my arm assisted me into the hall, where first I attempted to sit, but finding the exercise too painful, stood wondering what to do – for it seemed impossible that I should make any such exertion even as the simple stroll in the park which had been my intention.

Seeing my discomfort, Devon offered me his arm and suggested that my room was the only place in which I could attain any degree of comfort, and when I proved unable without some agony to mount the stairs, was good enough to catch me up in his arms (his frame was slender but he was possessed of very considerable strength) and shortly laid me upon my bed. Even this operation gave me some pain, the bones at the base of my spine seeming to be positively cracked.

Seeing (no doubt as much from my expression as from the care with which I moved) that I was in a state of extensive mortification, Devon with some hesitation suggested that he might be of assistance, and when I enquired how, replied that he had in his native village in Africa learned to administer what he described as 'plat-plat', which was of considerable assistance to the alleviation of pain. On my enquiring what this was, he hesitated to describe it more fully than to say that it somewhat resembled the massage which the Frenchies practise (more, in my belief, for pleasure than for the alleviation of any medical condition). I was doubtful whether such a thing could be of use, and if so, whether someone in Devon's situation could really have learned to administer it; but my discomfort was such that any suggestion must be followed, and on his admitting that this could only be done upon my removing my clothing, did not demur – except inasmuch as, movement being painful, I had to rely upon his assistance to draw my dress from me, leaving me bare as a needle.

I half expected the sight of my person to arouse those emotions in the young footman to which I knew he was susceptible – and the tender state of my fundament made me fearful of the discomfort which any amorous approach would inevitably involve; but (I must admit, a little to my chagrin) he remained completely cool, and his hands, when he assisted me to turn upon my face, were as dispassionate as those of any medical man.

He now asked to be excused, for there was something he had to fetch; and with my permission left the room, returning some minutes later with a large flask which proved to contain an oil or unguent of the most attractive yellowy-green colour, which he told me was the product of the administration of weight to the fruit of the olive, and which had been brought by Lady Cricklewood from Italy (no doubt at some expense; but her hospitality had been so generous that I did not protest at the footman's

intention to use it to succour me). This liquid, I subsequently learned, was more generally used for cooking,
or for the dressing of salads, but certainly was efficacious
in the task to which Devon now addressed it.

He first enquired whether I would permit him to remove
his uniform, for the liquid (he said) was inclined to stain
clothing to such an extend as to require its replacement.
Of course, I gave such permission; and even the pain from
which I suffered, and which at every movement shot
through my lower back, did not entirely arrest my renewed
admiration of his body as, for the second time, I saw it
emerge from its carapace. However, the prospect of someone in such anguish as myself being capable of amorous
play was positively laughable. My pain was such indeed
that I winced in anticipation as, kneeling upon my bed at
my side, he threw a leg over me, and knelt across my
buttocks. However, he was careful not to jar my recumbent
body, and the only contact I felt with it was the weight of
that remarkably massive cock of his, which now rested
lengthwise along the crack of my arse.

Now, pouring some oil into the palms of his hands,
Devon placed them at the base of my neck and began to
knead it with fingers firm almost to painfulness; then
to move them out along the tips of my shoulders. What, I
asked myself, had this to do with the pain in my lower
back? Yet I had to confess that it was quite extraordinarily
comforting. He continued a kneading, then a stroking
motion, now covering my shoulder blades and the top of
my spine. Then, it seemed to me that I felt some third
party giving little blows to my lower spine: it could not
have been Devon, for I could feel both his hands upon my
shoulders – yet surely no one else could have entered the
room without my knowledge?

Then I realised that those supple smacks, administered
with a soft, fleshy instrument, were being applied by that
appendage of the footman which, formerly lying slack

upon my buttocks, had now solidified and strengthened, elevated itself, and become sufficiently firm to be used as he was using it. I have from time to time come across gentlemen whose cocks have seemed to have an independent life of their own – or, rather, have been capable of autonomous movement: almost as much so as an arm or a leg! But I must confess that this tool of Devon's was most remarkable, for without moving his lower body (I could still feel his thighs pressed against my sides) he was able to beat with it upon my waist, spine and buttocks – and sufficiently strongly to cause pain!

But I lie: for while I began by wincing in anticipation of agony, so tender was that part of me upon which the fleshy weapon was beating, in fact I felt no discomfort – in some strange way, rather, a warmth was spreading from waist to knees, and each blow seemed to dissipate rather than promote the pain.

I now felt the footman remove one of his hands from my shoulders (though the other remained, still caressing them, and now moving to the nape of my neck, which he squeezed and manipulated); the other, as I guessed, he applied to his cock, adding manual strength to its own natural springy energy and thus increasing the vigour of the blows which rained upon that part of me which had previously been most tender.

After a few moments more, the regular throbbing pulsation ceased, and rather to my disappointment the footman lifted himself from his position astride me – only, however to place his palms upon my body, this time liberally oiling its lower parts and kneading the cheeks of my arse, from which to my amazement almost every vestige of pain had now vanished. I could now not fail to see as he stood bending over me that for whatever reason – I mean either because such a change had been necessary in order to perform the act of mercy he had just concluded, or because he was no longer devoid of pleasure in my company – his magnificent phallus now stood upright against his belly, engorged by a flow of that hot blood which seems to run naturally in the veins of the southern races.

Standing at my side, Devon continued the comforting motions of his hands for some time; and finally, having placed yet more oil upon my skin, which was now positively slippery with it, once more mounted the bed and laid the whole length of his body over mine, so that I felt the tight springs of his hair against my cheeks, and an instrument as hard as it was large once more lying between those other cheeks which were now glowing, warm and – as it seemed – devoid of pain. I attempted to part my thighs, for I felt as eager to reward him for his kindness to me as (I felt sure) he would be eager to receive a reward; however, he made no attempt upon my person, but instead began a writhing motion, sliding his body upon my own, his breast against my back, his legs upon my own, and his middle parts upon my backside, where, though the size and state of his weapon somewhat impeded smooth movement, the oil which now made both our bodies slippery and emollient made such a movement astonishingly inspiriting.

At last, again to my disappointment, he raised himself from the bed, and standing back enquired whether I thought I might be able to stand.

Somewhat gingerly, I attempted to rise: and to my astonishment found that only the very slightest discomfort attended the motion.

'My dear Devon!' I said. 'I am as delighted as I am amazed!' – and was about to go to my purse to find some tangible expression of my gratitude; when an expression at once somewhat rueful and more than a little imploring direction my attention again to his weapon, which was still at the present – that is, standing in vertical splendour, revealing beneath two pendant balls drawn up into his groin by the tightness of the skin stretched to an extremity in order to clothe so great an engine, and the whole now gleaming with oil which emphasised the muscularity of the main object, not only the huge vein which ran the length of its underside being accentuated, but the rings of muscle which decorated its barrel also being thrown into relief; the whole indeed seeming so urgent in its expression of desire that no guineas could, I believed, compensate their owner for being left in so urgent a state.

Stepping forward and placing my hand upon the pole, I softly enquired whether the footman would not prove to me that I was now entirely free from pain, by allowing me some more energetic exercise than merely walking about? However clumsily I may have expressed the invitation, he understood me immediately, and replied that should it not be inconvenient to me, he would indeed be glad of some relief – and taking me by the shoulders, gently turned me about, and encouraged me to lean forward, supporting myself by placing my hands upon the bed. Realising that his purpose was to try whether my recovery was complete or no by exercising just that part of me which had been most in pain, I now parted my thighs, offering him a target which he immediately pierced – his instrument and indeed my quim having been so oiled that despite the unusual size of the former I once more had no difficulty in admitting it without undue discomfort.

He began immediately what was at first a relatively slow motion, and only upon my assuring him that I felt no pain (indeed, pleasure was rather the emotion which immediately conveyed itself to that portion of my anatomy now most concerned) accelerated the motion. From my bending position, I could look between my own legs, where once more that inspiriting contrast between the white skin of my thighs and the dark skin of his private parts, a sheen almost of purple gleaming upon the dark column which pierced me, gave me an aesthetic pleasure which added in remarkable degree to the physical exhilaration conveyed by his vigorous swiving.

The shriek of pleasure which I could not but give as his motions brought me to a climax came too soon for him, for though, in gentlemanly fashion, he immediately paused, I could feel by the continued rigidity of his instrument that he himself had not reached an apogee; I therefore advised him to continue – but, realising that the position in which we had been connected had been one conducive to particularly keen pleasure in the female, he drew back, placed me upon my back, and once more mounting, was so inspired (as he confessed) by the sight of my bosom – raising himself to look upon it with that peculiarly limber motion of his fellow Africans, whose waists seem capable of almost unlimited bending and fluency – that upon my giving him permission to kiss it, which he did with lips as sensitive and loving as they were fleshy and prominent, within a very short time, and with a convulsive shudder, he again withdrew: and just in time, for immediately a positive fountain of frothy liquid was thrown upon my body from belly to neck; whereupon, though still gasping, with a politeness by no means invariably to be found in more conventional lovers (and perhaps born of his servantly status) he seized the sheet and carefully wiped my body before preparing to withdraw.

I was now not only grateful to him for having so completely cured my pain, but had a kind of loving curiosity about him: his friendliness, consideration and kindness were married to so unusual a talent in bedroom accomplishment that I could not but ask myself what was his history – whence, for instance, his strange name, which I had previously known only as that of an English county? I felt impelled to discover the truth, and having drawn from him the admission that during the next hour or so he would normally be at leisure, expressed a desire that he should remain with me. However, at that moment

I was too exhausted for talk; and he also showed a certain degree of fatigue; so placing my head upon a chest so beautifully moulded as to have been designed and executed by a master craftsman, and laying my left arm along his body (the hand, I must admit, upon his now relaxed but no less grand engine, the limber fullness of which made it so comforting a bauble) I fell into a doze in which, by his regular breathing, I believe he accompanied me.

We did not, I think, sleep for more than fifteen or twenty minutes, but awoke considerably refreshed – except that I was extremely thirsty. Upon my expressing the fact, Devon advised me to ring for a dish of tea. When this was brought, he made no attempt to conceal himself, nor did the maid who brought the tray show any surprise at his presence – or at that state of undress which he made no attempt to disguise. This, I may remark, was no doubt all part of the manner in which the aristocracy of England conducted itself in that period about which I write, when it would have been considered vulgar in the extreme for any servant to take notice of the behaviour of his or her superiors. No doubt that behaviour was well discussed in the servants' hall, but even the most extreme conduct on the part of a master or mistress (or any of their guests) must be ignored by their domestic servants.

In this case the tray of tea was simply placed upon the table at the side of the bed, the girl not seeming so much as to glance at the two persons lying in a state of nature upon it – the sheet, I may say, presenting sufficient evidence that they had recently been indulging in an activity which rendered them so ready for the refreshment of the liquid that (as Mr Pope put it) cheers but not inebriates.

We took our tea still in that state of undress which (when a room is as pleasantly warm as mine was, the cheerful fire still burning in the grate) is more comfortable than any clothing; and as we did so, I asked whether I might enquire into the form of those adventures which had brought my companion to London. His answers to my questions I now set out in the form of a narrative in the first person; it may be that my words are not precisely those of the footman, but they are not too distant, for he was a naturally educated and well-spoken young man. The sense of his story I convey as precisely as my memory carries it – and I have subsequently read the account to Devon, who has been so kind as to say that could he write, the tale is told just as he might have told it.

'I was born,' he told me, 'in the town of Dakar, in the French colony of that part of Africa known as Senegal. Although parts of that town have through the influence of the French become relatively civilised, the suburbs (as we would call them) remain in a rude and uneducated condition, consisting of a number of villages as little accustomed to what might be called "civilisation" as those far out in the plains.

'The family among whom I grew up lived in a hut constructed of reeds and cow dung – and none the worse for that, I may say, for that material is such as to keep the extremes of heat out in summer, and protect us from the cold during what we call winter; though truth to tell there is little difference between the seasons in my native country.

'My father, when at home, dressed in the traditional manner of our people; but during the day put on a shirt and trousers, and went off to the house of the French consul, where he was a gardener – being rewarded with an income considerably larger than that of our neighbours, though by the standards of this country too trifling to be of consequence. I was schooled by the local mission school, and being quick to learn could by the age of fifteen command a vocabulary in French, and could even write – though not with great fluency.

'My father, eager to show off my accomplishments, took

me along with him to the consul's house, where I helped him in the garden – chiefly in keeping it watered, for the heat was such that an inordinate amount of water was needed if anything was to be kept growing. A pump had therefore been set up over the well, which must be kept almost constantly in motion to supply the hose which it was my duty to wield – the pumping itself being too arduous a task for a youngster whose muscles were not yet fully developed, so my father performed that task (though I was well formed enough, my diet being considerably better than that of others of my age, for my father was able to bring home scraps of food from the consul's kitchen and a good diet together with my naturally vigorous and lively movements kept me lean and fit).

'M. Douclerc, as the consul was called, was a charming man in early middle age, who took a liking to me and eventually agreed to take me into service as a general servant, to be employed not only in the garden but on general duties about the house.

'One day there was considerable stir, for M. Douclerc's daughter had travelled from France and was to stay with him for some months, consequent upon some illness which prevented his wife from joining him – and upon his desire, I believe, to broaden Mlle Douclerc's horizons. Every hand was therefore employed in cleaning and painting the house and making the place ready to receive a European lady – which would be the first I had seen at close quarters, for there were few enough in Dakar, the climate not being considered sufficiently salubrious for their health.

'It will not surprise you that I found the lady an extra-ordinary vision of beauty. I suppose that she was of no more than average attraction – but my lack of acquaintance with white-skinned women gave her a sheen of beauty which I found completely magical. She must at that time have been of no more than sixteen or seventeen years of age (she was the eldest of the consul's daughters); and her very fair hair made almost as much impression on me as the whiteness of her skin, while what I could discern of the shape of her body was sufficiently different from the profile of our own women as to be particularly attractive. I was in fact struck dumb by the apparition, and was so unnaturally quiet at home that evening that my mother believed that I was sickening for some illness.

'I went off to work the next morning eager to set eyes once more on that paragon; but she made no appearance – being I suppose closeted in her bedroom, resting after the exhausting effects of the long voyage, to which was now added the fatigue of extreme heat. The latter was of course no inconvenience to me, and I set about my task of watering the stretch of grass which lay behind the house, while my father, around the corner, was employed at the pump. I suppose I must admit that I chose that particular part of the garden because I knew it to be next to the room which Mlle Douclerc occupied – I had myself whitewashed its walls in preparation for the reception of the guest.

'I had been occupied for about ten minutes when I saw some movement of the curtains of that room. It will already be clear to you, Mrs Nelham, that I wished to make as close an acquaintance with this lady as was possible between a servant and his master's daughter – the gulf between us being greater than can be imagined in this country, for to the fact that I was merely the youngest and least important servant of the house was added the phenomenon of my colour, which set an even more considerable barrier between us. Or so I thought. The truth was otherwise: for what I did not consider was that the blackness of my skin made me as fascinating to Mlle Douclerc as the whiteness of hers was enticing to me! Moreover, it did not occur to me that she might find my person attractive, for I had no notion in detail of that magnetism which draws the male to the female.

'That is not of course to say that I was not a fully developed male animal in every sense other than that of the emotions: perhaps because of the climate, we come of age early in our continent, and I can have been only ten or eleven when I first became conscious of the capacity for pleasure which was seated between my thighs. My family being a large one and our hut small, it was impossible to enjoy that privacy which is common in this country, and at night I was curled up closely with my brother and sister (the former older, the latter somewhat younger) in a state of nature which made it impossible that they should not become conscious of the development of my body.

'My brother had already for some time enjoyed those sensations which were the result of kneading and stroking his own organ, and indeed had taken me in hand, in the expectation of being able to introduce me to similar delights; and when this happened took some pleasure in experimenting with various means by which they could be produced when more than one person could participate, it soon becoming clear to him that the insertion of our cocks into some aperture or other was one particularly pleasing method; he at first experimented with hollowed fruits of various kinds, and then smearing some of this fruit upon his instrument persuaded me to taste it. The pleasurable sensation achieved by the application of my tongue and lips to his tool was so great that I found myself pressed into such service several times a night – and insisting on a change of roles, found the feeling thus aroused was indeed so pleasing that I was no longer surprised by his enthusiasm.

'The next and no doubt inevitable experiment was in his wishing to introduce his tool into the only other orifice in my body considerable enough to accept it. I trust that I do not offend you by this statement' (I assured him that he did not, for as a keen student of human nature I found his narrative fascinating) 'but knowing no better, and finding the sensation delightful when greasing his finger with oil he introduced it into my fundament, I felt pleasure rather than pain when he replaced it with that other feature of his person which happily was by the measure of our country not particularly large.

'My brother assured me that the enjoyment afforded by the action was quite as considerable as that which could be conveyed by the lips, and once more, on our changing roles, I found it to be so. Our sister, meanwhile, looked on with no more than slight interest, being too young for the true delights of sensuality to have arisen; and while consideration for the feelings of women is not (I regret to say) great in our country, we had a natural affection for her which over-ruled any interest we might have had in making her the object of our experiments – other than in our examining her person to discover in what respects it differed from our own.

'The additional orifice with which she was equipped seemed too minute to be used for the purpose for which we would have wished to use it; but on our transferring our attentions to our girl cousins and the other girls of the village, we discovered with some pleasure that they (being of our own age) not only possessed apertures sufficiently capacious to receive our ready cocks, but were by no means reluctant to permit us to make what experiments we wished, for their enjoyment in such trials seemed to our surprise to be quite equal to our own.

'By the time I was fifteen, then, I had had as much experience with members of the opposite sex as with my own – and more, I would guess, than most European boys of my age.

'But to return to the main thrust of my narrative, I had never so much as seen a white-skinned woman; nor did it occur to me, as I have remarked, that she might be as interested in the colour of my skin as I was in hers. I therefore took extreme care not to be seen to be looking in

131

Mlle Douclerc's direction when the curtains of her window stirred on the morning after her arrival. She however felt under no such restraint, and throwing back those curtains stared with frank curiosity in my direction. I was clad, as was my custom, in a pair of somewhat large trousers which had once belonged to my father, and which were caught about my waist with a piece of rope. Being extremely capacious, these covered the whole of my lower person; but my chest and back were quite bare, and Mlle Douclerc I suppose found the sight of such a quantity of jet-black skin of sufficient interest to provoke a closer examination. She therefore stepped from the house and while appearing to stroll idly in the gardens, took care to find herself eventually within a few feet of where I was watering a stretch of grass already burned brown by the scorching sun.

'Once again, I thought it proper to ignore her, and simply continued my watering. What provoked her to the jest she then played on me I cannot say – it would be improper I suppose to suggest that she foresaw the consequences – but she stretched out her hand to me, took the hose (which of course I immediately surrendered to her), and turning it on me, soaked me from head to foot.

'I need not say that this did not distress me, and the peals of laughter to which the young lady gave vent encouraged me also to laugh, whereat she was the more delighted, and once more turned the hose on me. In a few moments I had quite forgotten the respect due from a native boy to a visiting white lady, and we was skirmishing with much the same good humour as that in which I played with my sister – and seizing the hose, had turned it on her. In a moment, I realised the enormity of my action – but happily, the young lady, while I think she had not anticipated such an action, was not unduly distressed by it: indeed, the heat was such that she positively relished the coolness of the water – while my own pleasure was greater in the sight of the curves of her body emphasised by the wetness of the material of her dress, which now adhered closely to her thighs and sides, and even her bosom.

'However, young as I was, I realised that such a situation must not be encouraged, and putting the hose down made the young woman understand by my gestures that our hilarity must cease. She pouted a little, but then becoming conscious of the wetness of her clothes, withdrew. I once more began my watering, but curiosity overcame me, and seeing the curtains of Mlle Douclerc's room close, could not resist the opportunity to spy upon her, and making my way to the window, stood upon an upturned bucket and applied my eye to the glass, the curtains being just sufficiently ajar to enable me to see in.

'What I saw was as fascinating as I had hoped, for Mlle Douclerc was, at that very moment, peeling her dress from her body, which was completely unclothed. Her back was to me, but that was a cause of no distress, for she seemed to me to be much more beautiful than any female I had previously seen. This was not surprising, for my experience had been confined to the girls of the village, and those who would permit my attentions, who were so close to my own age that their bodies were underdeveloped and immature: here was a young lady whose person had filled out, whose hips were broad, whose waist was narrow, and whose bottom was as rich and full as any fruit, positively inviting a bite!

'She now, happily, turned, offering me as clear a view of her front as I had had of her back: her breasts were firmer than those of the village girls, which by the time they were seventeen or eighteen had begun to be heavy, drooping and unattractive; these were slightly upturned, and with nipples of a charming pink – her creamy flesh was luscious, and the bush of yellow hair between her legs so entrancing that I felt almost faint with the desire to bury my lips in it.

'I suppose, recollecting the scene, that there is no doubt that she must have seen me – or at least my shadow – at the window, for she now indulged in a series of movements which can only have been devised to show her body off; she seemed to examine every part of it with care, in case it had in some way been damaged – lifting each breast in the palm of a hand and stroking it with her fingers, passing her palms over her sides and belly, placing a foot upon the bed and opening one thigh, thus exposing her most secret parts more fully to my delighted eyes – which could now clearly see that the yellow curls were merely a garnish to full, pink lips immeasurably more attractive (as it seemed to me) than the coarser, dark red lips of the similar parts of the girls I had been permitted to fondle.

'But now, so quickly that I had no time in which to retreat, she darted to the window and threw back the curtains. I was aghast. Without doubt, she would denounce me to her father, and I was sure that my punishment would involve more than mere dismissal. I looked pitifully at her, and stepped down from my perch – only to see that she was smiling and beckoning. Nervous of the consequences, I shook my head – but she only beckoned more insistently, upon which you will not be surprised to hear that I made my way around the corner of the house, and careful not to be seen by any of the other servants – or by my father, who continued pumping water through my rejected hose-pipe – slipped into the room which Mlle Douclerc occupied, and (obeying her first gesture) slipped the bolt of the door home.

'She was still entirely unclothed, and now reclining upon the bed – an item of furniture which I had greatly admired as being considerably more comfortable than the mat upon which I normally slept. I stood inside the door, hesitating; what could so handsome a young lady want of me? (Yes, I was so naive as to ask myself the question.) But she was again beckoning to me. I approached the bed, conscious that my wet trousers, adhering to my body, showed all too clearly the state to which her beauty had reduced – or rather enlarged – me. She sat up – and reaching out, in a moment seized the piece of string which held my trousers about my waist, and jerking upon it, undid the knot. Being so capacious, the garment would have fallen to the ground, had not my excitement resulted in the obstruction which prevented such a revelation.

'Observing this, Mlle Douclerc once more reached out, and . . .'

But my allotted space has been fully absorbed by my friend's story and I must not any longer intrude upon the flow of Andy's narrative; let me therefore pause, allowing Devon to continue his account in my next chapter.

Chapter Nine

The Adventures of Andy

I must confess to having been tempted to remain at Whister's all day: it would have been a positive pleasure to present my compliments to any one of those smooth-skinned ebony young ladies of whom I had been vouchsafed a glimpse on the previous night; but even at a young age I had already learned in the course of such temptations that an excess of amorous delights, while charming, can lead to a satiety which may prevent one from fully enjoying yet more delightful pleasures should they present themselves, and so I took myself out into the chilly air of St James's and walked about, doing a little shopping, and calling upon my man of business at Messrs Coutts' excellent banking establishment in order to ensure that my affairs were in order (which was certainly the case).

Just before dinner time Harry presented himself, and after we had dined we settled ourselves with a bottle of port, and he offered to deliver that narrative he had promised, and which I now report in (as far as I can recall them) his own words.

'I never knew until my seventeenth birthday,' he began, 'how it came to be that my father had become one of the richest men in England, for as far as I ever knew he was the son merely of a country squire from the neighbourhood of Compton Pauncefoot, in the Westcountry of England. Yet from my earliest years of comprehension he had ever been the possessor of both town and country establishments, and in command of an income which allowed him the complete freedom known only by those to whom money is of no account.

'He had certainly not acquired his wealth through marriage, for his wife had been a young woman of his own village, the daughter of the local parson, and upon dying giving birth to me, had left him no other legacy than my poor self.

'Upon my leaving my college at Oxford and celebrating sixteen years upon this earth – that is, on the morning of my seventeenth birthday – he took me aside, and put to me the very question: how I supposed him to have made his fortune.

'On my confessing that I had no idea, he then went on to enquire what, in life, gave me the most pleasure?

'An answer immediately sprang to my lips which many a young man would have hesitated to give to his father: but we had always been on the terms of the utmost frankness, and moreover he had seen to it that my education had been much more complete than that vouchsafed many young men of my age. So I did not hesitate to give voice to my first thought, and replied that commerce with a pretty young woman was at present what gave me the greatest satisfaction. (I should here say that from the time at which I was ready to show an interest in such things, it had been my father's care to ensure that all the charms of female companionship had been available to me, taking me to my first brothel at the age of fifteen, and ensuring that at Oxford the best young women of the game were mine by my having a sufficiently deep purse to afford them.)

'As I had expected, my father gave no show of surprise at my reply – and indeed, clapping me upon the shoulder congratulated me upon my taste, for, he said, at my age that had been his chiefest pleasure; and moreover continued so.

'I, in turn, showed no surprise at this remark; for I had been used from infancy to seeing my father in the company of a variety of young women – he had never married again, but placing me under the care of a comfortable and motherly old biddy, had determined (as he put it, in the parlance of a racing man) "to play the field". Indeed, one or two of the fillies in and out of his stable had given me my first lessons in trotting, not only with his connivance but I believe at his suggestion. However, though I could tell you some warming stories of my sentimental education, that is not the purpose of our present conversation.

'My father, as I have said, rather approved my choice of the delights of love as primary in my list of pleasures, and gave the impression that he shared that preference (though he seemed to me to be old, as he spoke, he can have been no more than thirty and seven or eight, and but for a sickness of which I was then not cognisant, appeared still in the prime of life).

' "You will forgive me for reminding you," Father went on, "that your circumstances, through myself being in a comfortable way of business, are such that those diversions which most please you have ever been freely available, and I guess your experience of them to be as considerable as that of any young man of your age. May I, without wishing to embarrass you, enquire what single amorous experience, over the past six months, has made your blood race fastest?"

'Only that frankness which was common between us enabled me to answer candidly; while I was upon the most familiar terms with a great number of young women, I had, six weeks previously, had the pleasure of an engagement with a charming member of the Italian race, whose body – darker in hue and somewhat fuller in limbs than those of our English girls – together with raven hair and sparkling black eyes, had entirely captivated me, so that I had returned to her upon a more regular basis than was usual with me – and indeed was still more than a little besotted with her.

'On hearing this, my father smiled.

' "And was it not the case," he said, "that it was the freshness, the strangeness of her aspect, the fact that she was not as our English girls are, which proved as moving as any tricks of her profession in capturing your heart?"

'I could not but admit it.

' "It is a phenomenon that I have myself observed," said my father, "and which led me, some fifteen years ago, to a conclusion which resulted in a business enterprise which has established me in my present happy state of finance."

'He then advised me that he had arranged a birthday entertainment for me, and invited me to accompany him to Whister's – a club of which I had heard, and knew my father to be a director of, but where I had never been a member. To cut the preliminaries of my story short, here, in this very building, I found a harem of young ladies gathered from all over Europe – long-limbed English girls, certainly, but also the plump-breasted young women of France, the thick-waisted dames of Italy, even the sinuous girls of the East. My father had made it his business to gather willing youthful females from as far afield as was then practicable – and finding that the wealthy young men of London (and indeed those whose years were concomitant with their wealth) were happy to pay a large fee to be in their company, also found his pockets swelling with the profits of the enterprise.

'At first I imagined that my father merely wished to give me the freedom of this establishment as a birthday treat – which, setting my eyes on a handsome young lady from Sicily, I thoroughly enjoyed; but I found that he wished me also thoroughly to understand the nature of his business; more – he intended that I should participate in it, and as swiftly as possible learn to conduct it; for what I did not know was that his physician had warned him that a weakness of his heart was likely to put an end to his life at any moment: which indeed was the case within only a few months of my being introduced to an undertaking which I then found it my duty to carry on.

'While there was a small committee of members who advised upon the conduct of Whister's, it was recognised that as my father's son I had the right to inherit his major function in it; and since my instincts were as I believe a reasonable counterfeit of his own, I had no difficulty in continuing to carry it on, making, from time to time, journeys into Europe, and even so far as Constantinople, to discover new young women of talent and amiability – for one of the features of Whister's has always been the charm of the females to be found there.

'The business continued upon an even keel, and given that care which my father had taught me to exercise, was entirely trouble free. There is, Andy, a sufficient profit always to be made from supplying first-rate goods to those with sufficient funds to pay for them.

'However, six months ago I began to arrive at the conclusion that the business was beginning to become somewhat stagnant: if there was no positive measurable falling-off, there was no enlargement – and so I took myself off on one of my regular visits to the continent, to see whether some fresh blood could not be found with which to liven up the establishment.

'I went directly to Venice – famous, you know, for centuries as a centre of the trade, perhaps because its situation as a port makes it a ready clearing house for goods from every part of the civilised world. There, at a house well known to me from former visits, the madame of which had often been of assistance to me in my commerce, I saw before me, amid a group of young women each of whom would have been an ornament to Whister's, one who was obviously a native of an African country. Those young black women who were at that time engaged in the profession in London, I had found to be somewhat less than appealing; they had for the most part been brought to England as domestic servants, and had entered whoredom upon concluding for some reason or another their domestic employment; they were for that cause no longer young, and their household duties had to some extent coarsened them. Even so, they usually found engagement in one or another of the *maisons de passe*, merely because the colour of their skin made them sufficiently unusual to engage the attention of gentlemen who would not otherwise have looked twice at them.

'The young lady I saw before me, however, was another matter: she was clearly of no more than seventeen or eighteen years, her breasts were carried high without any trace of that sagging too common with the natives of hot countries; her waist was narrow, her belly only slightly swelling, her thighs full without being over-fleshy, and between them a jet-black nest of tight curls set off to perfection a pair of nether lips purple rather than black. Madame had no difficulty in persuading me to taste those delights which were set before me; nor was I disappointed, the girl's bed manners being as enthusiastic as they were generous, and her enjoyment of the act (even were it counterfeited) being an agreeable relish. Though I believed myself by custom impervious to most novelties, I must confess to an afternoon of singular hedonism.

' "I have," said Madame, "three other such young women, all of whom have been received with enthusiasm here. Since I suppose that such persons would be a similar sensation in London, I have taken the liberty of summoning my friend Leon, who is my provider and will be happy to supply you . . ."

'Leon was able to show me two young girls immediately,

freshly arrived from Africa; and when we had agreed a price, I brought them back to England, where they were greeted with an enthusiasm so marked that the membership of Whister's trebled within two months, and I had to make it a rule that the two young Africans must serve only three men each on any one day, for fear that their lively spirits should be enervated. (I may say that they protested violently against my rule, being astonished by their success and delighted by the income they were receiving – which by their standards was unbelievably excessive!)

'A more stupid man than myself would have understood that the enlargement of the livery at Whister's by the addition of a few more swarthy mounts was obligatory; and being reluctant to hand over to such intermediaries as Leon the large sums they required, I decided myself to set out for Senegal – the country from which the two so popular young ladies originated. I therefore commissioned a ship and a small crew, set sail for Dakar, and there made my way to that small village (almost now a part of the town) whence my two young friends had been brought. There, I had some initial difficulty in conveying to the chief man of the place the reason for my visit. I showed him two little paintings which I had had made of the young ladies, displaying them in all the comfort of their private apartments at Whister's; and recognising them he became unusually excited, and sent for their parents, who being naturally delighted to see their daughters so well and comfortable, were amazed at the degree of their prosperity. Asked to explain how they had come to such affluence, I found that the few words of English commanded in the village were insufficient, and must resort to mime – the movement of my right forefinger through an aperture formed by the thumb and forefinger of the left hand producing much laughter, but then much confusion – for at first they supposed that I had myself married the two young women in question, and was in search of other wives; then that I was merely in need of a woman for my immediate satisfaction. However, after much gesticulation, I believe I made myself understood – and also made it understood that where those two had been successful, others could follow. As I had supposed, the result was the immediate application of every girl between the ages of twelve and thirty, to accompany me to a land so flowing in milk, honey, silk and satin!

'It took me no long time to make a choice of ten of the applicants, the elders of the village allowing me to make use of one of their huts, and the appearance of the candidates dressed in the manner of our mother Eve (for clothing is not a major consideration in that sweltering country) making my task the easier at least in a first selection. It was of course necessary for me to try their talents, which they understood well, but through I suppose some native form of diffidence they agreed to my doing so only in the presence of them all. Their shyness contrasted with an extreme brazenness – a contrast in itself remarkably stimulating; as indeed was the fact that in the matter of converse between the sexes the mere hint of any preference on my part for one resulted in them entering with all their hearts into the competition.

'This resulted in a scene participation in which would no doubt have commanded a considerable fee had it taken place at Whister's; even for myself, who had so often to undertake it for the purposes of trial that intercourse often seemed insipid and even on occasion tedious, being the single male in a circle of ten maidens, each chosen as being handsome members of their race, each eager to please (through a desire to emulate their successful sisters), was by no means without its agreeable side.

'I must confess that soon I was in such a swoon of pleasure that even had one or two of the girls been less active and interesting in their participation than the others, I would probably not have noticed. I believe that I was the first white man they had seen unclothed, which no doubt added some interest to the proceedings for them – and indeed even while one or two of them were engaged with me in the primary act, the others rather than retiring to a distance crowded about, touching and even licking such portions of my body as were available, as though eager to see whether the chalky colour of my skin had not in some way been artificially applied. Their fingers too were about every part of me, the pinkness of my ears engaging their curiosity as much as the redness of my cock (soon made the ruddier by use, recovery, and re-use). The hair upon my chest interested them as much as that upon the cheeks of my arse and beneath my arms (for their men are notably without such adornment); the fineness of the hair of my head was fascinating to them – indeed at one point I found that a young lady cradled my head between her legs, nuzzling her most intimate parts against it, and relishing (as it seemed) the softness of it. Even the hair which decorated the base of my cock seemed to them to be remarkably silky, compared I suppose to the wiriness of that of their own men.

'They competed eagerly to show me how quick they were to engage in any action which appeared to please me; upon one fixing her lips about my tool, the others would not rest until they had tasted it – and one finding that her inserting her finger into my arsehole resulted in my showing some appreciation, they all turned me about and, spreading the cheeks of my bottom, examined that aperture with the greatest interest, spitting upon their fingers and rubbing it with the most insinuating and supple movements, and even playing about it with the tips of their tongues.

'Alas, even practised as I was, I found it impossible to engage them all in the final courtesy: in a long night I fucked, I believe, only four of them – the others insisting (for it seemed to me a kind of honour) that I should apply my fingers to their parts until they were satisfied, two even taking my feet and (first having sucked each toe) using them for the same purpose.

'If I was unable to be entirely sure that each was as efficacious as the others in the task to which I would be putting them, neither could I possibly reject any; and in short made a gift of some gold to the head man of the village, and ensured that the young ladies would be ready to sail within two days. The celebrations which followed my decision lasted almost until the moment of their departure.

'In the mean-time, it seemed necessary to me to call upon the British consul, a Mr Trebetherick, in order to regularise my visit (though I did not have it in mind to explain its full nature to him). He lived in the centre of Dakar, in a bungalow which was one of a number occupied by those foreigners who represented their governments in that city. He received me kindly, and insisted that I should spend the two remaining nights of my visit with him – the local hostelry being, he said, no place for me. I was delighted to accept, the prospect of a quiet rest being one which was remarkably attractive after so *mouvementé* a night.

'We dined quietly, the consul's wife joining us – a pleasant woman in I suppose her mid-thirties; she and her husband seemed on very good terms, and when she withdrew and we sat over our port wine, I congratulated him upon having so amiable a consort. At this, he bowed slightly, but became thoughtful, and after a while confidential: confiding that while their life together was companionable enough, it lacked that spice added to a union by a close and engrossing physical experience of love. An unfortunate accident which had occurred to him just before his leaving England three years previously had deprived him of the ability to perform the function normally to be expected of a husband or lover.

'Marie – for that was his wife's name – had, he said,

been constant in her affection, but after some time, and particularly in the heat of a tropical climate, had confessed to him that she found it difficult to bear with life as a virgin, once having enjoyed the pleasures of love.

' "The situation, as you can imagine, is a trying one," said Mr Trebetherick; and indeed, I could see it . . . Loving his wife, it must be difficult to see her deprived of the expression of that love (quite apart from any strain upon himself, which he assured me was minimal, for the virtual removal of that instrument dominant in the expression of affection had left his own spirits lowered to the point at which he did not miss it).

' "She has from time to time benefited from the few visits we receive from colleagues," Mr Trebetherick told me; "but otherwise sadly lacks the company of a gentleman – for to form an alliance with a black man would be contrary to the policy of our Government expressed to its agents abroad." '

'I sat, silent; should I offer to console the lady? But I had not, to be plain, found her particularly attractive – though as I have said, pleasant enough; moreover, I was still exhausted from my efforts of the previous night. I therefore said nothing, rather I believe to my host's disappointment. Instead, after a short while, I made an excuse – or rather stated a fact: that I was tired, and wished, if he did not object, to take to my bed.

'Somewhat glumly, he assented; and we parted, myself to a charming but plain room at the back of the house, with a large and comfortable bed over which hung a canopy of thin material to ward off mosquitoes; into that bed I climbed with little hesitation and not troubling to pull the single sheet over my body (for the night was hot) almost instantly fell into a deep sleep.

'You may, Sir Andrew, already have foreseen what followed; and indeed it was with an inward sigh that I awoke, later in the night, to find myself lying in a pool of light from a moon which seemed several times the size it generally appears in England, aware that outside the mosquito net stood a figure – that of a woman; I was in little doubt that it was that of Mrs Marie Trebetherick. I determined not to move or in any way show that I was awake – I really could not countenance the idea of entertaining her in the manner she undoubtedly expected, after so active a night only twenty-four hours previously. Even the indebtedness one naturally feels to a kindly host must have its bounds. So I remained still, my eyes only half open – to see the woman lift the net and look down at my unclothed body for some moments with an intent gaze before unloosing her single garment and allowing it to fall to the floor.

'She now stood in the same pool of light which illuminated the bed, and the view I had of her person was one made almost cruel by the cold, white beams. However, considering her years, she was a woman of very considerable beauty; I suppose that the paucity of the kind of food to which Europeans are under more homely circumstances accustomed had prevented her from becoming over-heavy, but for whatever reason her waist remained narrow and her belly flat, almost as though she were still a girl; her breasts, though full, stood high and resolute, the dark aureoles clearly marked in the moonlight. My eyes now naturally fell to that part which is of most interest to a man (despite my sensual exhaustion, I wryly observed, I was quite unable to resist that masculine instinct which usually governed me!). There, between thighs which were large but firm, I saw a sex unshrouded by any form of protection, for – perhaps because of the heat – she had by shaving or plucking removed the usual mantle, leaving her lower lips quite naked; these protruded slightly, and by the top of that delightful incision I could see a nub of flesh which seemed (perhaps because of the clarity with which it could be observed) considerably larger than might have been expected even in a woman of fairly substantial build – and so clear was the light, I could even discern its head, slightly rosier than the surrounding flesh, an almost perfect simulacrum in little of the head of a gentleman's cock, and no doubt as susceptible to feeling. Normally, the sight would have aroused me to instant action; however, lassitude still made me remain passive.

'As I looked, the lady carried her right hand to her lips, and having moistened the fingers, placed them in the vicinity I have just described, and began with a gentle and smooth motion to caress that part I had particularly marked. I was alarmed to find that the sight resulted in a stirring in the corresponding part of my own body, for my prick began to awaken, thicken and lengthen, though happily by altogether closing those eyes which had only in any event been half open, and thus obscuring the inspiriting view which had prompted this awakening, I was able to prevent my weapon completely cocking itself for action, which would have been the clearest indication to my visitor that I was in fact awake!

'As it happened, I suppose that she believed that some dream had prompted the slight alteration in the size and shape of my organ; but whatever the cause, she clearly felt that she should take advantage of it, for I heard her move, and a moment later felt a warmth additional to that of the night about my nether part, and once more peeping, found that Mrs Trebetherick had fallen to her knees at the side of the bed and approaching her head to my middle parts was examining the evidence so closely that her breath fell upon it – causing it, once more contrary to my intentions, to stir slightly.

'The fact again prompted her to action, and approaching with the utmost caution, she lifted my prick gently between forefinger and thumb, and placed it between her lips. She did not begin immediately to suck upon it, but merely allowed it to lie upon her tongue like a piece of fruit the flavour of which she intended to savour to the utmost, before, so delicately that she might have been caressing the petals of a flower, moving her full, warm and liquid lips over its head.

'I suppose that you will not be astounded when I tell you that this had the result that my prick within a very short period had enlarged to the fullest extent possible, and that despite the adventures which had prompted me to suppose that nothing could arouse me further, my veins once more began to run with the liquid fire of desire. Nor will you suppose that the lady, feeling now between her lips an instrument sufficiently inflexible and substantial to perform its duty, did not wish to employ it for just that purpose.

'She was clearly under the impression that I slept; and I felt that to exhibit my wakefulness might embarrass us both – while in any case I was curious (unfeeling though this may seem) to see what course she would follow; I therefore remained inanimate while she, removing her lips from my better part, first raised herself upon the bed, then with the utmost daintiness placed one leg upon each side of my waist and for a moment knelt above me; when, first delicately anointing my prick with saliva carried thither in the palm of a hand, she drew aside her lower lips and lowering herself placed its head just between them before ever so slowly sinking so that its length gradually vanished within her.

'The expression on her face at this moment was instructive, for while I have had the opportunity of observing many ladies at the moment of joining our persons together, I had perhaps never seen such an expression of pure pleasure as now passed over Mrs Trebetherick's countenance – it was the look which one sees on the face of a woman enjoying an almost sacred experience, less carnal than spiritual, less joyous than ecstatic. I believe it to be, my dear Sir Andrew, the first occasion upon which I felt that the act of love, which we so frequently perform so thoughtlessly that we might as well be those animals whose actions we seem too often to mimic, must be inspired by some instinct higher than we may know. It is an emotion which I continued to hold, and is one reason why I believe that I perform a worthwhile task by enabling gentlemen to satisfy that urge some consider merely bestial.

'You may expect that the lady now began to ride me in the manner customary when the posture she had adopted is employed. But no: indeed she began to rise and fall in the manner of a woman riding a horse at trot – but with such slow and careful motions as were indescribably provocative, so that my self-control must be great in order to prevent myself losing all sense of decorum and revealing my wakefulness by thrusting upward with my hips to meet her downward movement. Her motions were far from unrestrained; yet, from the continued intent expression of her visage, no less delightful to herself. Her eyes never for a moment left the point at which our bodies were joined – and indeed the sight was an engaging one. Our observations of the motions of love are too often fleeting and inattentive; her manoeuvre was now so leisurely that every detail could be seen. She would rise until my prick was almost entirely exposed, drawing the foreskin up over the shining head, her lips caressing it gently until they seemed on the point of forsaking altogether their tender duty. Then, reversing her movement, she would begin to sink, and those same lips, naked as the staff they caressed, pushed down before them the folds of skin, so that they slowly encompassed that most sensitive area of the staff, its pink hue emphasised (as I suppose) by the frantic activity of the previous night, so that it was a darker tint than usual, and contrasted charmingly with the lighter pink of the flesh that enveloped it.

'Reluctantly (as it seemed) swallowing that titbit, the lips now descended the column below, only slightly detained by friction – both my staff and the lips themselves being now almost excessively lubricated – until they buried themselves in the bush at its base, its wires – as I believe – delightfully tickling the flesh as those two parts of our bodies met.

'Her movements were so slow, and the state of those parts which I have described were so greasy, that I felt almost no sensation: yet what sensation there was was of such a delicious nature as I had never previously experienced – almost devoid of salaciousness, while at the same time being more lascivious than I can well describe!

'One of the consequences of this was that (especially, I suppose, since I had been milked dry of all my more obvious carnality by the experiences of the previous night) I was able to contain my emotions without difficulty, almost able to regard the experience as a display devoid of sensation – while at the same time my prick showed no sign of wilting, and indeed seemed to become yet more adamant as the lady continued her motions.

'She, I believe, had more difficulty than I, for I now saw that a sweat had broken out upon her brow, and her dark eyes shone, while her teeth had closed upon her lower lip with such firmness that even a drop of blood (as I thought) stood out where she had punctured the skin. Now, she brought a hand down and placing a finger upon that nub of flesh which I had already observed in her, began gently to rub it while at the same time taking her other hand around and with its fingers gently stroking my cods. The former motion had the effect of bringing her almost immediately to her zenith, for I clearly felt her lips tighten about my prick, while her thighs also for a moment clasped my sides, and her mouth opened in a silent cry of pleasure. The sight of this, the apprehension of her pleasure, and the light touch of her fingers about me, brought my own pleasure to a reluctant height; and I felt my own parts contract and spill – though in the nature of things I cannot believe that a great explosion of liquid accompanied it, in view of the considerable downpouring which had not long since taken place!

'For a moment, the lady remained still, and then in a motion prompted I suppose by a mixture of gratitude and tenderness, she leaned down and placed a light kiss upon my forehead, before lifting herself from me and from the bed, bending to pick up her nightgown, releasing the net which fell once more over the bed and vanishing as quickly and silently as she had come.

'Next morning I slept late, and the household was kind enough not to waken me – so that it was almost half past nine o'clock before I stirred; then, walking to the window, I threw it open to feel what cool air I could upon my body, and looked out upon the small and shaded back garden, which itself abutted that of the French consul. As I looked I heard a commotion from that direction – cries in the French language and the voice of a gentleman, then a crashing as someone threw themself over the fence which divided the gardens and through the bushes, until suddenly a few feet away from me appeared a naked savage – or at any rate, a young black man whose staring eyes gave the impression of either fear or anger. Seeing an open window before him, even though a white man was standing by it, this young man threw himself through it, and in a moment was beneath my bed!

'Almost immediately, there was more rustling and commotion, and a white man, accompanied by a black servant, broke through on to the grass, and seeing me, the European broke into a stream of French only parts of which I could understand (through having spent a few months in his country). Seeing my confusion, he made himself understood in a combination of his own language and a badly broken English, enquiring whether I had see a fleeing black boy.

'I cannot be sure why I equivocated, except that I always am disposed to take the part of the pursued rather than the pursuer; moreover, I gathered that the boy was charged with attacking the gentleman's daughter – and while this might of course have been true, I could not but recall that I had heard no screams or protests, which seemed to indicate that the young lady concerned might have been only too happy to have been attacked. Moreover, the father was equipped with a dangerous-looking machete, which he seemed to have the intention to use.

'I therefore indicated as best I could that I had indeed seen a young man, who had run through the garden, round the house, and as I supposed out at the front gate. The French consul (for it was he) looked doubtful at this, but with his servant disappeared in the direction I had indicated; while after a few moments, I suggested to the runaway that he might find it safe to emerge from his hiding place, which he did with many protestations of thanks and of his innocence.

'He was nevertheless extremely frightened; for, he said, the man who had accompanied the consul was his father, who for the sake of his own employment was likely to give him up should he return home. Moreover, to attack a white woman was an offence punishable by death.

'To cut a long story short, I offered him a better way of escape – by accompanying me to England, where I could find him a post as a servant. He accepted this with alacrity, was without difficulty (helped by Mr Trebetherick, who had no love for his neighbour) smuggled on board my ship, and indeed brought to this country. I did not, I may say, set eyes on the consul's wife before leaving, though I have the kindest memories of her – as I hope she has of me.'

And what had happened to the young man? I asked.

'He proved so amiable that I decided to retain him in my own employ,' said Harry, 'and on our arrival in England, since he had a native name which it was impossible to pronounce, I christened him Devon – for we landed at Plymouth. The one slight difficulty I had with him was that he had formed an alliance, during the voyage, with the young girl who entertained you last night – young Bella – and was reluctant to part from her. She, however, proved so adept at her work (as you have had the opportunity to discover) that I cannot possibly spare her to a domestic life, and I therefore had to part them upon our arrival in London, Devon having been taken into my own house – where you will have seen him as footman.

'I should have said that just before my voyage I had married the young lady marked out before his death by my father and her own parents as a proper wife for me; and found her to be a person I could love, her agreeable qualities including that determination which I shared – that marriage should prevent neither of us from slaking elsewhere those appetites which were so keen that the attentions we paid to each other – by no means negligent nor unconsiderable – could not altogether satisfy them. Indeed, a few days after Devon had been introduced into our household she admitted to me that she had had him, and that his accomplishment in the art of love was (while lacking in refinement) so tenacious and forthright that she believed he would be a most helpful addition to the household, especially should I be for any time absent or too exhausted by those amorous activities which occurred during the course of my duties at this club to perform my husbandly duty.

'Bella, parted from her friend, for a while repined; but her vivacity and enjoyment of the game is sufficiently keen to make her, as you have discovered, one of the chief stays of this club. It is no doubt sad, but the emotions of the black races have not the depth of those we feel, and I cannot believe that the parting has provoked real distress.'

Here, Harry ceased his story. I took leave silently to doubt that the young couple of whom he spoke felt any less distress at being parted than Harry or I might feel – indeed my recollection of Bella's distress was clear – and

I determined to do what I could to reunite them; but would have to go to the task with care, for Harry had after all been my kind host, to whom I owed some duty not to cause particular difficulty.

Chapter Ten
Sophie's Story

Readers will remember that I was forced to close my last chapter just as my friend Devon had reached an important point in his narrative: I allow him to take up the story at the moment when we paused:

'Observing my state,' he went on, 'Mlle Douclerc reached out, and with a familiarity which suggested that she was not unacquainted with the physiognomy of young gentlemen in such a condition of excitement as that in which I found myself, pulled away at the waistband of my father's trousers, and releasing them from the obstruction which had formerly prevented their descent to my ankles, enabled them immediately to resume their downward motion, and in a moment revealed my entire person – and the particular feature of it which had previously impeded their fall: that is, a young cock which (although I did not at the time know it, for it was not remarkable as such characteristics go among my native people) was sufficiently massive to provoke an admiring stare from the young lady – and indeed, while I was still so frozen with embarrassment at my person being so exposed to a young white woman, provoked more than a stare: that is, it incited her to reach out her hand and tease and play with it as a child might tease a kitten or a puppy.'

Here, he paused, as though to make sure that I was not offended by the details of his story; my answer to his unspoken question being to take in the palm of my hand that very feature which had been so admired by Mlle Douclerc, and to assure Devon that I had been as impressed by its dimensions, on first setting eyes on it, as she had been, then begging him to continue his narrative.

'Well,' he resumed, 'in a moment I was convinced that her interest in me was such that in the first place she was not about to cry rape, or in any other way betray our being together, and that in the second place I was about to be honoured by being allowed the pleasure of satisfying not only her curiosity but her carnal aspirations. I was not so brave as to make any motion towards her, but stood perfectly still – which was no trial, for her next move was to kneel before me and, supporting my tool in her left hand and with the right gently pulling at its shaft so that the skin was peeled back, reveal its head (which again seemed to impress by its size), attempting to encompass it with her lips.

'She fell into some difficulty, for her mouth was petite and pretty, and even stretching it open as though she were about to scream she could not do more than, as it were, place a rim of pink flesh about its crown.

'How the situation would have developed, I cannot say – for at that moment the door opened, and there appeared M. Douclerc. If we were surprised by his sudden manifestation, our astonishment can have been as nothing to the shock felt by a father suddenly faced with the picture of a daughter, of an age which might suggest that she knew nothing of the other sex, kneeling before a young fellow whose colour naturally made him inferior and whose upright cock she was attempting to swallow.'

The father's reaction was what might easily be foretold: vanishing for a moment, he reappeared bearing a large and sharp machete which usually stood against the wall in the hallway (against the possible appearance of thieves), and showed every intention of separating Devon from the organ so admired by his daughter.

'She screamed; he lunged; I fled. The open window was just behind me. Leaping upon the bed, I flew through the window like a bird, and before the more cumbersome M. Douclerc could make his way around to the door, and then circle the building, shouting to my father to accompany him, I had broken through the fence into the neighbouring garden, and seeing another open window, without consulting the figure which stood in it had entered the house of the British consul and was beneath one of his beds!

'Thence I heard the gentleman whose room it was kindly misdirect the sweating Frenchman, and in a while emerged to meet the Viscount Cricklewood, who after some discussion invited me to accompany him to England. The prospect did not displease me; indeed, it seemed likely that I could make my fortune there. I was somewhat surprised however to find myself accompanied on the boat by no fewer than ten girls who I recognised as being from my own village, one of whom being that very one who had been so kind as to allow me to prove myself for the first time capable of that act which makes one a man.

'I had to sleep with a number of other men in a noisome and filthy hold, but during the day we were given the freedom of the decks, and I was able to keep company with Bella (as she now calls herself); her pleasure in the game was as keen as my own, and despite the fact that every activity must take place in public, we made the beast with two backs – as you call it in Europe – with great enthusiasm, there being little else to occupy us while the voyage continued. The only problem was that the other girls at first also required me to pay them those compliments I paid Bella, my other male companions being (they said) rougher and less adept at the game. It cannot be imagined that this endeared me to the other men; but happily I have some skill with my fists and was well able to defend myself – against them, if not against Bella: for on one occasion finding me engaged with one of her friends she hit me sufficiently hard upon the arse with a piece of wood to dissuade me from further skirmishes of that nature. The other girls henceforth had to content themselves with who they could get, or with each other – though my new employer or owner occupied his own spare time by teaching them the niceties which would be expected by the European gentlemen who might take them to bed – for he made no bones about the fact that they would expect a more inventive and individual approach than was usual with us.

'Bella was of course also required to engage in such lessons, to which I taught myself not to object – for not only must I endure what could not be cured, but she delighted in trying upon me those tricks which he taught her, which indeed were extremely entertaining, introducing me to those bed manners which made me, even before I set foot in this country, an adept.

'Alas, things were not to fall out as I expected: for landing at Plymouth, in the county of Devonshire, and being rechristened in commemoration of the event (or rather for the first time christened, without benefit of clergy), I travelled to London with my female friends only to be separated from them the moment we arrived in the city: for I was made to leave the carriage at Cricklewood House, while they were taken on, I know not whither.'

'And have you not enquired after them, and in particular after your friend?' I asked.

'Upon one occasion, yes,' said Devon; 'but my lord made it perfectly clear to me that Bella's whereabouts were no matter for me, and that I should forget her. Moreover, I was by that time occupied with my lady, who the moment she saw me informed me that I was to become a valued addition to her staff. She herself surveyed me, on that first evening, for my uniform; and in the course of those intimate measurements required for the perfect fitting of my breeches, certain familiarities took place, and upon her setting eyes on . . .' He paused, and I nodded to show that I understood.

'You will comprehend, Mrs Nelham, that in no protracted time I was firmly established as head footman, somewhat to the disgust of the other, white servants (with whom however I soon established a friendship), and was made firmly to understand that I was to be at the call and convenience not only of her ladyship but of any of her friends who should show an enthusiasm to taste "dark meat" (which was her ladyship's not particularly elegant description of that part of my body for which, from the first days, she showed a considerable predilection).

'And that, I think, completes my tale; you are now in possession of as complete an account of my life as can be given, up to this moment.'

The young man sighed and lay back upon the pillows, when, to show my sympathy, I pressed a kiss upon those full and expressive lips. I had been moved by his story, and not only by it: although the bout we had earlier enjoyed had been a most inspiriting one, I had been warmed by the close propinquity of our lying naked together upon a bed; and indeed had, perhaps impertinently, allowed my hand to continue to caress, in I trust an inoffensive way, that fascinating prick of his, which so comfortably lay between my fingers and filled my palm with a palpable and warm presence. I was now conscious that I began to wish that it might be more interestingly placed; but on my smiling at the young man and pressing my lips upon his shoulder, he looked at me with what seemed an apology, and asked whether he might be excused from that action to which I seemed to invite him: for, he said, it would undoubtedly be the case that he must shortly wait upon his ladyship, when she would expect of him something of which he would prove incapable should he once more . . .

I looked, I suppose, my regret – for he now raised himself upon one elbow, and suggested that if I would not find the action offensive, perhaps he might . . . and with no further words lowered his head, and having placed a kiss upon each breast, ran his lips down to my belly, and, by a gentle pressure of his hands inviting me to spread my thighs apart, planted a similar kiss upon my most tender part, and proceeded to variations upon that theme which any woman would I believe find delightful.

The act is of course now common with us, and though the puritans despise it, has always charmed womankind: indeed, this seems to have been the case from the earliest recorded times, and in every part of the world – a traveller recently assured me that the T'ang Dynasty Empress Wu Hu was so devoted to it that she insisted that all government officials and visiting dignitaries should pay homage to her Imperial Highness in the manner which Devon now complimented me: indeed, there is an ancient scroll depicting the Empress, her robe held open by two dignitaries, while a third kneels before her, and . . .

I need go no further; except perhaps to say that Devon proved himself to have exceptional skill in the task he had set himself: when I later questioned him upon the matter, he confessed that he had acquired that skill entirely by practice, and expressed his surprise that not all lovers were as skilful, for (he said) it was simply a matter of observation: noting which actions most delighted your companion, and teaching oneself how best to perform them. I believe however that he had not only a natural talent, but natural physical qualifications: his lips seemed particularly soft yet at the same time to possess muscles of their own which allowed them to suck most appealingly upon my flesh, while his tongue was perhaps longer than is the average (could it be that this was linked with the old wives' tale which relates the length of tongue to the length of prick?). At all events, he seemed able to insert it almost to the depth of the average cock, with the additional characteristic of course that it could be moved about in a manner which the latter instrument is incapable of.

My enjoyment was intense – but I was unable properly to return it. Indeed, Devon at one point turned his body and threw a leg across my shoulders, the better (by placing his palms beneath my bottom) to approach his subject; this set his splendid apparatus immediately above my head, and I was sad to note that that admirable instrument which I had hoped might be put to its proper use now hung lax and limp – though still of a quite uncommon length and breadth – above me. But on my raising my head in order to take it between my lips, Devon gently lifted himself so far as to make the action impossible. It was clear that he feared too close an engagement, which would make it impossible for him to pay to Lady Cricklewood the compliment he believed she would demand of him.

I therefore lay still – or as still as my enjoyment of his attentions permitted me to be – and gave myself over to pleasure, allowing him to bring me to the crux within a sufficiently short period to grant him time to replace his footman's uniform and prepare himself to leave me; which, in time, he did – taking with him my thanks, for although I had not (I confess it) enjoyed the experience as much as if he had found it possible to lie with me fully, I was grateful to him for his kindness and consideration.

Before he went, I promised him that I would attempt to discover from Lord Cricklewood the whereabouts of his friend Bella, and see if I could not contrive some means of bringing them together; though privately I had few hopes of it, for apart from any other consideration I could not imagine that Lady C. would be pleased to have living under her roof a young woman to whom her footman would wish to pay, perhaps with too much enthusiasm, those attentions she regarded as peculiarly her own property.

I had privately concluded that it was time I thanked my lord and my lady for their hospitality and took myself to rooms in town; while their hospitality had been most kind, I have never been particularly fond of living in the houses of others, and began to long now for that complete freedom of movement which comes with being entirely one's own mistress.

I therefore, having dressed, walked along the corridor and knocking at her ladyship's door entered to find her still abed (as I had supposed), while at the bedside Devon stood in his shirt, just having removed his footman's buskins.

'My dear Sophie,' said Margaret, 'I hear you have had a fall. I am delighted to see that it has not incommoded you to the point at which you cannot get about.'

I assured her that it had not – but without telling her of her servant's attentions to me; I had the feeling that she was a lady plagued by jealousy – and that while she might offer me her servant's attentions, she would not be best pleased to hear that they had been offered (or accepted) without her knowledge: it was a feeling reinforced by the sudden look of anxiety which clouded Devon's face, but which lifted at the moment when he realised that our connection was to be kept private.

'This is the time at which I take some relaxation with our friend . . .'

'My dear Margaret,' I said, 'please let me not interrupt you!' (at which she gestured to Devon, who whipped off his shirt and during the remainder of our brief conversation occupied himself in drawing back the bedclothes, unbuttoning my lady's nightshirt, and rendering her as bare-skinned as himself).

I broke to my lady the news that I had decided, with great thanks for her hospitality, that I should now quit the house. She expressed regret, but I believe was by now too eagerly anticipating the immediate pleasure ahead to give me much attention – for she had already begun caressing Devon's cock, which she regarded with an admiration which could, I thought, scarcely have been keener had she never seen it before. I must confess that I envied what lay ahead of her, for though Devon's actions had been kind and to a degree satisfying, it was a taste of a second course which I had had, rather than a meal.

However, having thanked Margaret Cricklewood again for her hospitality, and sent my compliments to my lord, I took my leave, a last glance attempting to assure Devon that I had not forgotten my promise to him.

The weather outside was cold almost to an extreme; carefully negotiating the steps, I took myself into the carriage which I had ordered (the last time I would take advantage of Lady Cricklewood's assurance that I should use her house as my own) and rode into town. Despite my warmest cloak, I was sufficiently cold by the time I reached Piccadilly to instruct the driver to stop at Meanwell's coffee shop on the corner of Albemarle Street, and hurried into the warmth meaning to commission a cup of chocolate before walking around the corner to the Haymarket and Andy's rooms, to which I had a key, and where I hoped for the time to take refuge (for his bed, though small, could bear us both for a night or two).

The coffee shop was not busy, and a boy took me directly to a box or cubicle, as they call it – the shop being divided into little square rooms, each of about five feet by five, and surrounded by partitions about five feet high, thus giving some privacy to those who wished for it. As I sat, my eye caught those of the lad, and immediately a spark seemed to fly between us. This is a curious business, which I have noted before: there are some men with whom one instantly establishes a harmony of some sort – with whom one at once knows that a connection will be not only possible, but welcome. How this can be is a mystery to me: but that it is something to do with the glance, with the exchange of eyes, there is little doubt – poets have commented on it through the ages, apart from which one has oneself remarked upon it. I believe, myself, that perhaps the very physical appearance of a woman's or man's eyes speaks, as it may be through the central part being enlarged through admiration, and therefore signalling an interest.

At all events, the regard of the white-aproned lad was clear to me the moment my eye met his; and I suppose that my own must have signalled that I would not be averse to toying, partly through my still being randy (to use the common term), and partly because he was a pretty lad – of about my own age, lean and quick, with a pert and round little bottom (as I saw when he turned for a moment away) and small, firm hands (one of which now nudged as though by accident, against my thigh as he pretended to brush some non-existent crumbs from the seat, and encouraged me to take my place).

My not shrinking from this delicate approach encouraged him, and when he brought the chocolate I had ordered, in placing it before me with his left hand, he placed the other frankly upon my shoulder, and (on my again making no objection) while enquiring whether he could serve me with anything else, slid that hand beneath the neck of my gown until it lay upon my breast, where the coolness of his fingers provoked my nipple to a stand – this again being no doubt regarded by him as an indication that I was not averse to his solicitation – though this may also have been clear from my placing my arm so that it lay against his thigh, and then nuzzled gently at that bulge which lay within it.

The boy now, realising that he had all to hope for and nothing to fear, quickly disposed his hands beneath his apron, where he busied himself for a moment, and then taking my hand placed it where his own had been – upon which I discovered him to be unbuckled, for what met my palm was a naked prick which, while no doubt it might seem insignificant when placed beside that black bludgeon which it had lately been my pleasure to caress, was sufficiently sturdy to give pleasure – my attempts to ensure that it was so by grasping it between my fingers led the lad's eyes to roll, and his voice somewhat to shake (for all this time he was continuing to favour me with his animadversions upon the weather – no doubt for the purpose of disabusing any nearby customers of any idea that what was in progress between us was in fact in course of development).

He was now in such a state that some risks must be taken if the business was to go forward, and standing at the entrance of the little box, or room, he drew up his apron, revealing to my view what my sense of touch had already discovered – that is, a cock in a healthy state of elevation, the skin about its head drawn back, and a little opaque tear already standing in its eye.

His look of appeal was irresistible, and he lifted his instrument in his hand in a positive invitation to me to press a kiss upon it – but though it was within my reach, I hesitated to assent – really, there are some actions which are too dangerously performed in a public place, even a relatively deserted one. However, noting that a dish of butter had been left upon the table, I dipped my hand into it and applied it to his prick, the flesh now shining delightfully in the light of the candles which (the day already being dark) stood nearby. It was now possible for me to move my fingers, indeed my palm, upon that weapon to such exquisitely slippery effect that for a moment the boy found it impossible to continue his conversation, and merely panted loudly: a state of affairs which might have been suspicious had we been more closely observed than we were.

I was now too far gone in amusement not to proceed

further, which I did by handling his cods with my left hand, which seemed further to increase his relish; the knuckles of his hands whitened as he continued to grasp his apron, though from his eyes – which were on my imperfectly concealed bosom – he wished they were elsewhere.

It would have been easy for me to continue my motions until the inevitable inundation; but that would have been to deprive him of the opportunity to pay me any compliment other than that of his eyes – so I unhanded him (to his dismay), but then rising bent across the table and threw up my skirts, revealing the promised land, and that furrow ready to be ploughed.

'And, madam,' he said while edging himself into position behind me, 'I am assured that as far as Shepherd's Bush there are at the side of the road carriages which through the obstruction of ice cannot go further.'

In no time at all I felt his cock nuzzle against my pussy, and immediately slipping into that place where it was ambitious to be.

'Do you tell me,' he enquired in an even shakier voice than previously, and beginning that plunging motion which gave me no less than him immediate pleasure, 'that you have been unwise enough to travel from Knights Bridge without any assistance other than that of a coachman?'

This question demanded no reply; and a reply would have been difficult to deliver, for I was myself by this time somewhat breathless. My impression of the boy had been correct: he was vigorous and lively, his prick no less muscular than I had supposed, and as he made use of it I merely gave myself over to pleasure.

But what was this? – my standing had brought my head over the top of the box – and what was my surprise to see, not three feet from my eyes, the visage of Mrs Plumtre, a neighbour of mine during my brief married life!

'Why, Mrs Nelham!' she remarked. 'It must be two years since I last set eyes on you. How do you do, indeed? But

I fear you are unwell, for you are flushed and breathless: a winter cold, no doubt.'

My voice was somewhat uncertain as I replied, for the servant lad's enthusiasm had increased by what it fed on, and his prick was now so energetically at work that his belly was battering my arse so as to make my whole body shudder.

'Why,' said the amiable Mrs Plumtre, 'why, dear, you positively shake with a fever! You should be at home and in your bed.'

I protested that I found it too boring to remain at home all day, and that my cold – which had indeed been a bad one – was being cured by the variety of experience to be found in town.

'Indeed,' remarked Mrs Plumtre; 'it is not my experience, for I find much more to interest me at home than I do here – except of course at the milliners' and jewellers'.'

I should explain that Mrs Plumtre was plump, plain and fifty, and known for her lethargy. While she short-sightedly peered at me (for I was fortunate in that her eyes were not as clear as once they had been) I managed to continue a desolutory conversation – allowing her the best of it – while Jack the Lad swived until with a positive shout he reached his apogee, at the same time accompanying his action by pinching my bosom with his hands, which had been thrust into it no less to afford him a grip upon me than to afford me entertainment.

I now felt him withdraw, and excusing myself for a moment, turned to see him wiping his prick with his apron, while I pulled down my skirts. He then insisted upon fetching me another cup of chocolate (the first having gone cold while we were toying), and I must take myself into the neighbouring compartment in order to converse more sedately and at greater leisure with Mrs Plumtre – which was tedious, but necessary in the way of neighbourliness.

'What an amiable young man,' she remarked, after Jack

(I know not whether this was indeed his name, but use it for convenience) had brought me yet another cup, and solicitously hovered about us.

On my bidding my friend goodbye, he showed me to the door, assuring me that I would always find him waiting, ready and able should I wish for some relief from the cold or any other distressing circumstance. This somewhat amused me, for I felt it to be unlikely that I would trouble him again. Yet he was indeed an amiable lad, as Mrs Plumtre had remarked; and after all it had been to a degree at my invitation that he had proceeded as far as he had. Moreover, the pleasure he had afforded me had been no less than that I had given him – and so we parted on agreeable terms, and I walked to the Haymarket, where, looking up at his window, I saw Andy regarding me with surprise as I approached.

Chapter Eleven

The Adventures of Andy

Making my excuses to Harry, I now returned to my little rooms in the Haymarket – for should I become involved in some plot to reunite Bella with her lover, as I fully intended to do, it would be improper for me to do so while living under the roof of a gentleman to whose pecuniary advantage it was to keep her in his employ.

My rooms had been well kept during my temporary absence, and I must confess that it was pleasant to come back to them – for however much one enjoys spending time in luxurious surroundings somewhat superior to those which one's own purse can command, it is always pleasing to be able to attain solitude when one desires it, and not continually to have to keep in mind the wishes or convenience of one's host or hostess.

What was my surprise, as I took breakfast on the morning after my return, sitting in the window which looked out over the busy street, to see none other than Sophie making her way towards my door through the crowds of morning shoppers. When we had greeted each other and I had poured her a dish of tea, she began immediately upon a narrative with which the reader will already be familiar – that of the footman Devon, to whom she had clearly taken such a fancy that had I been a jealous husband I would have entertained the suspicion that their acquaintance might be more intimate than she immediately revealed. Knowing Sophie, I was quite certain that she was upon warmer terms with the gentleman than those of mere acquaintance – as indeed was the case, as she admitted, even entertaining me with some details relevant to their friendship.

Nor had she concluded the story before I realised that indeed it was the case that the young lady with whom Devon had formed so close a friendship on the boat which had brought them to England was none other than Bella; and that the lover whose loss she so sadly mourned was the footman!

I lost no time in acquainting Sophie with the facts – and we could not but smile at the realisation that the two lovers were already in a sense reunited through the accident that while the young man had been pleasuring my friend, I had been delightedly making the intimate acquaintance of his mistress! We agreed that they must be well suited – and agreed too that they must be brought together and released from the necessity to live apart, even should they continue in the Cricklewoods' employment.

But how was this to be achieved? It seemed that we must act without the knowledge of the two young persons' employers, for it was no more likely that Margaret Cricklewood would be happy to give up so vigorous and useful a servant – beneficial to her household not only through his personal services to her but by entertaining her female friends – than that Harry Cricklewood would wish to release from his club a young woman infinitely the most popular among the harem he had established there.

It was agreed that the first and easiest task would be to persuade Bella to leave Whister's, where she would be less likely to be under continual observation than her friend would at Cricklewood House. To that end then, after we had whiled away the morning in negligent conversation, I took myself to the club after lunch. Happily, the head butler, who would instantly have recognised me as a friend of Harry Cricklewood, was not in attendance, his place in regulating the appointments of the young women being taken by another, who consulting his book regretted to inform me that Bella was already engaged, and would be so for perhaps a further forty minutes. Would I care to take a drink – or could he persuade me to accept the hospitality of one of her friends?

'All the young women,' he said, 'are expert in the game; though of course it is understood that gentlemen must have their particular favourites. However, I can especially recommend young Jessie . . .'

He must have rung an electric bell concealed beneath his desk, for there now appeared a cheerful, small and lively negress, who upon my accepting her invitation to accompany her, led me to her rooms. She was charming enough – to tell the truth, I could scarcely bear to disappoint her when she offered her services; indeed, in other circumstances I might have . . . But it was more important to me to talk to Bella, and should I exhaust my powers with her friend, what excuse could I have to meet with her?

Jessie pouted prettily when I made my apologies, asking whether we could not merely enjoy a drink while I waited? I had (she said) 'a nice smile' (something which touched me, for it seemed to indicate that normal affectionate conversation might be the exception, rather than the rule, in her circumstance). She seemed however not altogether dissatisfied with her lot, and confessed to enjoying the commerce which earned her her living – suggesting that the women of her race were naturally more hot-blooded than their European cousins, and therefore able with greater ease to accommodate themselves to the life she led. When I enquired whether she believed this to be equally true of the men of Africa, she paused before replying reluctantly in the affirmative (as though afraid of insulting me!); and when I questioned the truth of her statement, said that in my position a young man of her race would not have found it difficult to entertain her while retaining enough of his manhood also to divert her friend, half an hour later.

I then asked whether she did not find it troublesome to spend much of her time in commerce with elderly gentlemen, when she most certainly must prefer the brisker company of young chaps (like myself, I meant, though I did not say so). Why (she replied) she rather preferred the elderly: they were more amusing than young men, they took their time when the former were all dash and flash, and they had experience, which was a *sine qua non*.

I could scarcely credit this, but in one way was happy to hear it, for one day I should be past thirty and grateful for the attention of anyone younger than myself.[5]

Despite my equivocation, she evidently found it difficult to believe that I was not prepared to take those liberties with her for which most gentlemen hotly competed.

'But perhaps,' she said, half mockingly, 'English gentlemen need a little persuasion?' and pointed in enigmatic manner to what appeared to be a large wardrobe set at the side of the room. When I showed no sign of understanding what she meant, she lifted an eyebrow, and rising persuaded me to approach it, opening the door and ushering me into what was almost a small room, occupied entirely by an armchair and a footstool. Inviting me to sit in the chair, she herself took the stool at my feet, and closing the door behind us, so that we were in complete darkness, appeared then to draw a blind, revealing a small

---

[5] Now that I am over sixty, I am happy to confirm that what Jessie said has proved the case, for I find no shortage of young ladies happy to accommodate my years, and complimentary upon my powers.

window giving into the neighbouring room (where doubt-
less the glass presented the appearance of a harmless
mirror). I had of course heard of such devices before, but
this was the first time I had seen one in use – though later
I was to make use of similar apparatus for my own purposes, in the house of pleasure I established, and which I
have fully described elsewhere.[6]

The scene now presented to me was one which at first
somewhat disturbed and agitated me, for I was not then
in command of so much information about the unusual
predilections of some gentlemen as I have later collected
– indeed at the present time it would be difficult, I believe,
to produce any evidence of curious amorous connections
between man, woman or animal which would shock me!
However, at that time I must confess to being surprised to
see – as the first object that presented itself to me – the
naked body of a gentleman stretched upon a table, his
arms and legs secured to its four corners by straps.

It did not immediately appear to me that this was anything but a scene of violence in which no sensible man
could have become involved of his own choice – though
unless those who had restrained him had left the room,
the man before me must lie there by consent, for the only
other occupant of the room was a woman, who through
her sex would scarcely be able to command the strength
to subdue him (he was a well-built, young and vigorous
fellow). I had heard that some elderly gentlemen on
occasion required unusual forms of stimulation, in the bedroom, to rouse their spirits, but I did not suppose that
vigorous young chaps such as myself (and the victim before
me appeared to be of not many more years than I) could
do so, and it certainly did not suggest itself to me that

---

[6] *Eros in Town*, still available from the publishers of the present
volume.

anyone should simply *enjoy* being placed in such circumstances.

The lady in the picture, I now saw, was none other than my friend Bella, who, fully clothed, appeared to be securing the last of the straps which restrained her companion – while he showed no signs of struggling either to prevent that, or to release his limbs. Having done so, she turned from the table, and removing her shirt to reveal those fine breasts which I had already admired and caressed, bent to pick up from the floor what to my dismay I saw to be a whip – and standing at the side of the table, raised it in the air and brought its several cords down upon the body of her companion.

The latter had clearly anticipated the action, and seemed to find it not entirely pleasurable, for between his thighs rose no proud conqueror, but lay merely a little squab fellow, disinterested to the point of positive shyness. As the whip struck home, leaving five or six red weals across his chest, I saw his lips open, and though I could not hear his cry, could not believe that it could be one of pleasure. Bella now repeated the blow, not once but several times, the whip upon each occasion laying its stripes upon a different stretch of his body – now upon the belly, now upon the hip, the thigh, the arm, the shoulder – and (I could not but flinch as I saw it) even seeming to assault that chief characteristic of man, though it was so shrunken that one could scarcely call it that.

But what was this? As the cords of the whip played over the young fellow's belly and thighs, his manhood began to stir, and within a few strokes had risen to a state of pride which would have shamed no cavalier. He now raised his hips from the table, and as far as was in his power separated his thighs, so that the ends of the whip, laid over a thigh, curled about his very cods.

He had ceased to cry out, and a sort of wild grin had spread over his face; he seemed by his expression to be

making a plea, and in a moment Bella laid down the whip
– but only in order to step out of her skirts, revealing
herself most completely to him (and, as she bent to pick
up the whip again, presenting to myself a view of her
backside which was extremely tantalising).

Now she again wielded her weapon, most carefully (as
it seemed to me) laying on, in order that no part of his
body should be spared; and the more she laid on, the more
excited her prey became, his cock seeming to grow with
each blow – though indeed I believe that all that truly
occurred was that it jerked, thus appearing to swell; for I
could not believe that any instrument could continue to
expand at such a rate without bursting! To add to the
interest, Bella now carried that hand unoccupied by the
switch to her lower lips, and caressed herself with what
appeared to be relish, presenting to her victim a picture
from which he could not avert his fascinated eyes.

So interested was I by the spectacle, that I scarcely
observed that my companion had not been inactive during
the performance I have described; sitting in the most convenient position to do so, she had (virtually, I assure the
reader, without my noticing it) undone the buttons of my
breeches, and drawing them down – I must without thought
have raised myself in my seat sufficiently to enable this –
had taken in hand my own prick, which, the spectacle
before me being so interesting, had already risen to its
not inconsiderable apogee, and had even wept those tears
usually the prelude to congress, so that Jessie's fingers and
palm slid over its surface with an indescribably libidinous
sensation.

It is interesting, is it not, that even those of us who do
not search out such scenes as that which I have
described, not needing the stimulus, never fail to be excited
by them? It is, I suppose, but a further step to that which
is found in the consultation of lascivious pictures; but
whether the excitement comes merely from the contem-

plation of what is before one or from the imagination which substitutes ourselves for one of the persons in the representation or tableau, I cannot say.

However it may be, I now found myself in the confusing situation that my emotions were engaged both by the scene before me, and by a certain keen sensation in my lower parts which (glancing down) I found to be the result of my companion's lips, now fixed about my cock, and moving upon it with the most delicious softness and sweetness.

My confusion was not to last long, for now Bella was concentrating her whipping upon the middle parts of her patron's body; that some pain was involved I cannot but believe, for I now saw that while no blood had flowed from any of the stripes, they were red and livid across breast, belly and thighs; but, I trust with less violence, she was now laying the cords of the whip about the base of his prick itself, so that their ends curved around beneath it, tickling or perhaps even smarting at its base and the spheres which seemed to support the column – with the result that in a very few seconds his whole body bent like a bow, and a fountain of liquid gushed from its source to splash plentifully across his body, drops even reaching over his shoulder to fall to the floor. Then, after a certain twitching, his prick began to diminish as his paroxysms pantingly expired.

Bella, turning towards me to lay down the whip, would have seen – had it been possible for her to see through the glass – my own grimace of pleasure; for at the very moment at which she had provoked her companion to orgasm, my own friend had succeeded in milking me to my own.

I must confess to feeling somewhat ashamed as, rising to her feet, she insisted on washing my parts and assisting me to adjust my dress: it was scarcely a compliment to her to have rejected her advances and then to have permitted her to pleasure me while watching a scene which interested me only on the basest level. Yet had she not assisted me to such a scene? And in any event, she seemed not at all discomfited by the circumstances, showing neither irritation or disappointment – though indeed the latter would in any event have been assuaged by the present I gave her, which was perhaps somewhat larger than would otherwise have been the case. And we must never forget, in our commerce with even the most delightful wh*re, that she is engaged in business rather than pleasure, and in the end it is the size of the income which is more productive of satisfaction than the commerce itself.

It was now possible for me to meet with Bella (though Jessie enquired, with perhaps the merest twinkle in her eye, whether I still felt it necessary to do so!); and in a very brief time I was shown into her own room, where I found her clad only in the most revealing of dress, and presenting a picture which would have tempted any man who had not very recently been bereft of those virile juices which arouse desire.

Having smilingly assured her, after her initial embrace, that I had not come for amorous purposes, I lost no time in informing her that I and my friend were advised of the whereabouts of her former intimate companion – who she knew by some local name, but we referred to for our own convenience as 'Devon', which was the name by which we knew him – and intended to help her to a reunion with him. She was naturally delighted at this, and redoubled her embraces, which were so warm that I already began to feel the stirrings of an amorous recovery! However, I now asked whether she could leave Whister's without being observed. She replied that it was impossible, for since one girl had attempted to elope some months previously, the single door which led from the rear of the building was carefully watched.

For a few moments we were nonplussed: but then, very hesitantly, she said that she had thought of a possible way to escape – but that it would involve me in some inconvenience, and might indeed place me in an embarrassing situation. I replied that I did not in the least mind inconvenience, while embarrassment was an emotion I only rarely felt, and never minded.

She then explained that in each room there was kept a set of masks, to be used by gentlemen who wished for some reason to disguise themselves – perhaps from inquisitive friends, or even from jealous mistresses or wives. It might be possible that . . .

But, I said (without permitting her to finish), surely no female was on the premises but the – I hesitated, not liking to use the term 'wh*res' – the ladies themselves, and therefore anyone in female dress would be stopped?

She nodded – but before she could go on, I caught her meaning. If those fine breasts were excepted, and a certain broadness in the hips, we were much the same build; if she could be got into my breeches and jacket, her hands concealed by my gloves, and a mask hide her face . . .

Meanwhile I, of course, would be left without clothing. But we would cross that bridge when we came to it.

Though she tried to protest that I was too kind, both my sense of adventure and my sense of humour were now aroused, and in a moment we were disrobing – a ceremony which did not take long with Bella, whose single garment was off before I had removed my shoes and stockings.

There was remarkably little difficulty in what followed: tearing a strip of sheeting, I bound it about her upper body, compressing her breasts as completely as could be without causing acute discomfort. My shirt on, which was fully cut, there was no immediate suggestion of femininity. There was more trouble with the breeches, which had to be slit behind with my pocket knife before they would close over her hips – but the damage was covered by my coat tails. Her hair, naturally curly and cut short, was easily packed beneath my hat after a close-fitting velvet mask had been placed over her face – and there stood before me almost a counterfeit of myself. Before the mirror we could not forbear to laugh, for here was a youth perfectly clad in the latest fashion, while beside him stood another, naked and white as a plucked chicken!

I must confess that the necessity to handle Bella's limbs as I assisted her to dress had resulted, despite my very recent engagement, in an amorous interest, and Bella could not but observe it; placing her hand upon its most manifest sign, she promised that she would repay me for my kindness – after which, pausing only to enquire how I hoped myself to escape (which I could not answer, for I had not so far thought of a way), she wrapped my large cloak about her, walked boldly downstairs and, I trusted, safely from the building.

Now, I was left naked and alone. I could of course disguise myself in Bella's clothing, and at that time was sufficiently young and pretty to pass as a girl, provided that the examination were confined to my secondary features; but there would be little point, since any female attempting to leave the club would be immediately arrested.

I poured myself a glass of sherry wine, and sat before the fire for a while in thought. Outside, from leaden skies, a little sleet had begun to fall, sending passers-by scurrying for shelter beneath. Even had the door of the club not given on to a populous street, for me to dash down the stairs and from the building unclad, in such cold weather, would without doubt have results more damaging physically than to my reputation (for which I cared little) – although in the event of a fire, I reflected, inhabitants of the place must leave by what means they . . .

At that very moment, there was a disturbance in the grate, and a glowing coal fell out and rolled almost on to the carpet. Aha! I rose from my seat, and looked about the room. It was completely bare except for the bed, furnished

with clean linen against the next visiting cavalier's convenience; by its side lay the torn sheet from which I had
ripped a piece to bind Bella's breasts. I now took the rest
of it, tore it in half, and stuffing one portion up the chim-
ney of the small fireplace, in which the fire was sufficiently
low for me to do so without being burned, I took a small
part and soaked it in water from the basin by the bed.
Then, taking the dry portion, I placed it upon the fire –
which immediately began to give off a satisfactorily dense
cloud of brown smoke. Clapping the wet cloth over my
face, I now took a chair and with it beat out the window,
from which the smoke at once began to vent. Straightaway,
it was seen, and a cry of 'Fire!' was given. Taking a deep
breath, I threw down the wet cloth, and pausing only to
wrap a towel about my waist, burst out of the door. As I
went, doors began to open on either side, and ladies and
gentlemen in all degrees of clothing (and lack of it) were
looking forth and exclaiming in perturbation at the sight
of the smoke which issued after me from Bella's room.

On my descending the stairs, already I was passed by a
number of alert servants with pails of water, while downstairs there was such a bustle that I was scarcely noticed,
despite my eccentric garb – which was much that to be
expected of any male occupant of the rooms upon the first
floor. Leaving the club, I was fortunate enough almost to
be run down by a passing cab, into which I hurled myself
with only the curtest direction to the driver. Seeing the
smoke billowing from the broken window – though by
now accompanied by steam, which seemed to suggest that
things were under control – and aware (I believe) of the
purpose for which the club was most generally used by
gentlemen, he agreed to drive me the short distance to my
rooms whence, having rushed upstairs, I threw him down
a purse from my window.

In the shop below, a gentleman more voluminously clad
against the cold than myself – a handsome black fellow

whose somewhat feminine face was inviting libidinous looks from another male customer – appeared to be deeply interested in a volume recently published upon the flora and fauna of North America; on his being invited upstairs, he threw off my cloak and embraced me enthusiastically before setting to and rubbing my body with a coarse towel in order to restore its usual rosy warmth (for the brief journey to Haymarket had chilled me to the bone).

Even after several minutes of chafing, I was still shivering, and Bella now paused in her ministrations, and taking me by the hand drew me into the bedroom, where first lighting the fire which was laid in the grate, she removed my garments from her person, drew us both between the blankets and laid her warm body along mine.

I had heard that this was the treatment afforded to mariners chilled to the bone by being doused in the seas, when a young midshipman is generally chosen to revive his shipmate in just such a manner (the stratagem often leading, I am advised, to that informality which has confirmed the description of His Majesty's Navy as being devoted to rum, bum and hornpipe). That the embraces of a naked companion are an efficacious remedy cannot however be doubted by anyone who has tried the panacea, for in a very few moments my veins once more ran with spirited blood, and even my chief male appendage, which had been shrunken to the size of an infant's, began to revive and enlarge, paying its own tribute to Bella's ministrations.

Feeling this, as she must – for it now thrust itself between our bellies – she smiled, and passing her hands around my buttocks drew me the closer to her, inviting me to rest contentedly in her arms until the room had thoroughly warmed – for she fully intended (she said) to express her gratitude to me, but not under the restriction of heavy bedclothes, which she had found to be a particular hindrance to the activity she had in mind!

I could only agree, for sheets and blankets are as dampening to love as is darkness; perfect freedom is as important, in lovemaking, as is light – for who could wish to couple with their movements restricted by the weight of bedclothes, or under the cloak of darkness which prevents the eyes from enjoying the pleasure relished by the other senses?

I therefore lay still, now turned about so that Bella lay behind me, her breasts against my back and her wiry black bush tickling to engaging effect the sensitive spot just where the divide of the buttocks joins the small of the back. She occupied the time by allowing her fingers to play with perfect freedom over my chest, my tits, my belly and what lay below – not grasping my prick, but fondling it with the lightest touch, playing her fingernails along its length, wetting a forefinger and thumb at her lips and running them about its crown, until the memory of Jessie's caresses, which had until lately seemed to deny the possibility of a renewed connection, were quite forgotten.

A happy result of my rooms being small was that it was not long before the fire had heated the bedroom to a degree which made it possible for us to throw off the sheets and blankets, when, turning, I saw once more before me a body which delighted no less by its appearance than by the knowledge that it was a playground upon which I could roam at will. Even now, however, Bella refused to allow me to approach her, and on my attempting to throw a leg across her body, pressed me back upon the bed, and kneeling at my side stopped my lips with a kiss.

I must here pause to express the unusual nature of her kisses. Those of my readers who have never seen a native of Africa will by now through the drawings of M. Georges Dauphin or M. Le Page be familiar with their physiognomy, the most marked feature of which is a thickness of the lips remarkable when compared to those of European women. This results, when kisses are exchanged, in a sensation very different to that felt when similarly embracing a European: a sensation very like that felt when one bites into a juicy fruit, for both upper and lower lips are full, firm yet yielding, and sucking upon them is a sensation remarkably pleasant – though there is the disadvantage that it is more difficult for the ladies to suck upon one's own lips, the thickness of theirs preventing this. However, their tongues are sufficiently active to compensate for this failing (if so it be), and seem almost prehensile in the manner in which they can probe one's mouth – to say nothing of the way in which they can explore the inner recesses of the ear, or the more intimate parts of the body – while the lips are perhaps more conveniently formed to give pleasure in that area than those of the most accomplished English or French wh*re.

Bella's intention was now, it went without saying, to give me the most complete pleasure which could be furnished by a woman to a man. I have been fortunate in my life in being frequently in that situation – due perhaps to a natural desire to be helpful to those females who I find in any kind of distress; and on almost every occasion of experiencing their grateful embraces I feel, while the loving engagement is in progress, that I am experiencing the keenest delight possible. This cannot, of course, be the case; but I must confess that now, some years later, I still recall the caresses of the young lady of whom I write as being particularly charming. Her lips and fingers played upon every part of my body – and I mean *every* part: not just those to which any mistress must direct her touch, but those which few gentlemen would assert to be associated with sensual pleasure. She licked, for instance, at the crooks of my arms and legs, raising goose pimples of pleasure along my limbs; she sucked upon each toe, slightly biting with keen-edged teeth, not so hard as to break the skin, but sufficiently vigorously to give a momentary sensation almost of anticipatory pain; my armpits were caverns in which her tongue took refuge, and she drew upon the tender hairs there with her lips, the result being an enchanting sensation somewhere between tickling and stinging.

Neither did the more obvious parts of my body go short; my tits were especially chosen, those sharp teeth nipping at the raised buds, while at the same time her fingers were busy between my thighs with an attention as devoted as it was ingenious, as provoking of pleasure as it was teasing.

Finally, I could no longer remain inactive, and raising myself to my knees seized her in my arms and gave her a kiss which was meant to signify gratitude as well as lust. Now it was her turn to fall upon her back, when, inserting my knees beneath her thighs, I raised her middle parts until her lower lips, as fleshy as those which had been fixed to my breast, were drawn slightly open, and my cock could nuzzle at the entrance to heaven – whereupon with a smile she invited me to pass through the gates!

This was achieved by her placing her arms about my neck and pulling herself upright so that she sat a-cock-horse, my thighs her saddle and my prick the pommel. The disadvantage of this posture was that I could make no vigorous movements; the advantage that she could certainly do so – though at first she restricted her motion to a slow and deliberate rise and fall, a movement more caressing than vigorous, the black wires of her bush one moment knitting with my own, and then with (as it were) a farewell kiss withdrawing as her lower lips slid up the fleshy shaft, stroking its skin with an ineffable tenderness, and – as the crest was reached – drawing the skin after it over the rosy cap; there, a pause ensued, only the very tip of my instrument still embraced within the mouth of that delicious cavern, while she pressed more kisses upon my lips, and ran her fingers down my spine.

Then would begin an equally lingering descent, her lips pushing the skin back over the bulb and stretching it delightfully as they passed over the rim and almost seemed to suck my soul in with the length of my prick as it passed within the dark purple passage.

A dozen or so such passes reduced me to a single bulk of luscious sensation, each nerve seeming to swell with pleasure, currents of delight running out from my loins to every extremity. As my eyes closed almost in a swoon, Bella somewhat accelerated her motion, and then gradually increased it as though riding to a canter and finally a gallop – while I, reluctant to give myself up to a paroxysm which would end the passage, attempted to concentrate my mind on recalling the details of the road from Cambridge to London, passing through Baldock, Ware and Dunmow. However, it was a fruitless exercise; with a mischievous grin, Bella at one moment fixed her lips to mine, sucked my tongue between them and nipped it with her teeth, while with the long nails of her fingers she nipped at my tits.

The stimuli were too much, and deep within my belly I felt the knot of pleasure explode, and as Bella lifted herself from my prick there burst through it with an almost painful gush a flood of viscous liquid propelled with such force that it fell upon her breasts, agreeably lying in droplets upon the black skin there.

I say agreeably, for it was clear that she welcomed what some women might have regarded as an unpleasant demonstration of my pleasure – for in common with some other inhabitants of the continent from which she had travelled, she regarded the male ejaculation as a magical display, and the liquid expelled as a result of it to be a mystic potion especially productive of beauty in females: she therefore now, with the greatest care, began to spread it over her breasts, ensuring that no drop was wasted – and even thanked me for providing it in such quantity (this had indeed surprised me, for the amount of liquid expelled, as every male reader will know, somewhat diminishes should expressions of love follow each other too closely).

It will surprise no one that we both, after this charming interlude, fell into a sleep; after which, waking towards evening, I sent out for some food and we spent a pleasant time until nightfall, Bella continuing to show by her tenderness her gratitude not only for what I had already done for her, but what I hoped to do – and this gratitude was itself rewarded in no short time, for there came a knock at the door just after noon, and who should stand there but Devon!

Chapter Twelve

Sophie's Story

Andy having volunteered to rescue his young friend Bella from the company in which she found herself, I was left to release Devon from his bondage at the Cricklewoods' house.

Andy's volunteering to look after the young Negress was not, I inferred, entirely devoid of self-interest, for it was clear that he had found her a charming companion in those exercises to which he as much as I was devoted, and I am sure looked forward to her expressing her thanks in a manner which he would find most gratifying. The truth of the matter is that while, like most men, Andy had no hesitation in purchasing love when he felt so inclined, he preferred it to be offered freely and without any financial transaction complicating the occasion. It is true, of course, that he would in a sense be paying Bella by the act of rescuing her from Whister's, but no actual exchange of money would take place, though Bella might be expected to be inclined to be particularly generous through gratitude.

All this may make my friend sound a paltry fellow; but he was merely what is called a realist, and eschewed those false protestations of undying love by which many men persuade women into their bed, only to reject them the

189

following morning. With Andy, every woman knows where she is (which is usually in his bed); and I have yet to meet one who has expressed herself as any the worse for an amorous encounter with him.

But to continue with my narration, I went off to visit Lady Cricklewood without any particular plan in my mind: to be plain, I could think of none, and in any event I am somewhat given to ingenious improvisation rather than to careful planning. On arriving at the house in the middle of the morning, I simply rang the bell, and when it was answered by none other than Devon, enquired whether I could exchange a word with him in private. First taking my heavy cloak and outer coat and hanging them in the hall, he led me quietly into an anteroom, where I informed him that at this moment (as I trusted) Andy would be removing Bella from Whister's Club – though I did not explain the nature of the work she had been doing there, nor indeed the nature of the establishment; that would be a matter for her to tell, if she cared to, upon their reunion.

Needless to say, the young man was delighted to hear of that possibility, and embraced me with enthusiasm – then, to my amusement, apologising for any discourtesy in doing so (which in view of our former encounters was supererogatory!).

I now asked how easy it would be for him to leave the house for some place where we could conceal him from the Cricklewoods' attempts to discover him (for I was in no doubt that Lady Cricklewood, at all events, would wish to do so). He was doubtful: he was, he said, carefully watched (for upon one occasion, desperate to go into London in what would have been a vain hope of discovering his friend among the multitude there, he had been discovered attempting to leave and threatened with immediate dismissal – though on his showing every sign of acquiescing, the threat was instantly withdrawn, and an increased show of affection substituted).

Another obstacle was that each morning between the hours of ten and two (it was now half an hour of ten o'clock) he was likely at any time to be sent for by Lady Cricklewood, who always insisted on his attending and dressing her, for (she said) he not only had hands as tender as any maid's, but a means of providing that comfort no maid could dispense, to which upon occasion she felt particularly disposed in the mornings.

But could he guarantee, I asked, should I detain Lady C. for an hour or so, to find his way out of the house and into London, to an address with which I would furnish him?

He could (he said); but slowly, for he had no money for a cab, and would have to walk.

I of course pressed a guinea upon him, together with the address of Andy's rooms in the Haymarket; after which (and an expression of thanks as warm as anyone could have expected) we returned to the main portion of the house, and I was soon introduced into Margaret Cricklewood's bedroom – where I was sure I could engage her attention for some time with a hot tale or two which would interest a woman of her libidinous nature.

She was sitting up in bed in a négligé which revealed much of a bosom as attractive as that which any younger girl could have displayed; and I no longer wondered (as I had been tempted to do) how Devon could rise to provide, at any moment, the services for which he was valuable to her – for her age was such (she was over thirty) when most women's attractions may be expected to fail somewhat. Yet really one could have taken her for a girl of much my own age, except that her features were a little coarsened.

She invited me to sit on the bed, and dismissed Devon – for, she said, she was sure that Mrs Nelham would be glad to lend her any aid she required upon rising. I thought I saw the boy give the shadow of a wink in my direction as he left, but confined myself to expressing the hope that

I had not disturbed her ladyship, nor deprived her of any exercise which it was her custom to take in the mornings. A raising of an eyebrow signified that she knew what I meant; but she was quick to express satisfaction at my visit, and the wish to know more of my life than I had previously rehearsed to her.

This was my cue (to use a theatrical term) to tell her of my marriage, and my adventures in Cambridge among the undergraduates; one particular excursion fascinated her which took place in that interesting form of river transport the punt, and which had taken me into the country in the company of four young gentlemen each possessed of that virility which lends high spirits to boys of an age when they are (unrealistically) expected to confine themselves to the company of their own sex for the purposes of study. The occasion was not devoid of erotic interest, and by the heaving of her breast I could see that my tale particularly raised her spirits; yet (I was, remember, though more experienced than many maids of my age, not widely learned in the manners of women of society) I did not expect what followed, which was that she placed her hand upon my thigh, and with the other upon my shoulder drew me nearer to her, and enquired whether I would not care to remove my clothing, which must surely make me over-warm in this heated room – where indeed there burned a fire set in a fireplace of remarkable proportions for a bedchamber.

Knowing that it was my duty to keep the lady occupied, I could scarcely refuse, and to cut the story short, indeed divested myself of my clothing and at Margaret's invitation joined her in, or rather upon, the bed. On my placing my clothes upon a nearby chair, I found when I turned about that she had unbuttoned the négligé which so became her, and thrown it aside, thus displaying her entire person to me – which I inferred I was meant to admire.

This was not difficult, for as I say she was remarkably

well preserved, indicating that with care a woman's beauty may long outlast her teens – something which gave me some comfort, for then eighteen years of age, I had assured myself long since that I had but two or three years of beauty before me, after which I must prepare to sink into that state where no member of the other sex could possibly find me attractive. I now find, of course, that this is entirely a false idea – for being of an age which I do not care to divulge, I find myself still attractive to gentlemen, and not short of that spirit which persuades me often to accept their advances (in which context I should remark that I once asked the Dowager Lady Fiddle, a lady of considerable experience who has now reached the remarkable age of ninety and nine years, at what age the desire for connections with the other sex died – which she replied to by asking to what address she should send her answer, which she would do as soon as she had experienced that death of the senses, which had certainly not yet occurred).

Margaret Cricklewood was, then, a lesson to those who believe that at thirty and some odd years a woman is past her best: her breasts, while they could not be described as pert, showed no signs of that descent towards the waist which marks the decease of beauty: while full, they were still proud, the upper line somewhat depressed, the lower showing that beautiful, ample curve which must be admired (by gentlemen) above the lean and somewhat starved look of the bosoms of too many younger girls. Her nipples, too, had no depressed appearance, but stood arrogantly out from the dark circle in which they were set. Her waist was narrow, her hips broad without being over-generous, and – to my surprise, for I had not previously seen such a thing – every hair had been removed from her private person, which might have given her, in that part, the appearance of a very young child, were not the lips so prominently displayed, their colour a delightful pale rose, darkening about the aperture to almost a dusky brown.

'I am not, you see, quite yet decrepit!' said the lady: to my shame, I had been staring at her, unable to disguise my surprise. It was best in such a circumstance to be frank, and I told her that if my expression had been one of astonishment it had been at her beauty, which must be impressive whatever her years.

'But age must always give place to youth,' she remarked, placing a hand again upon my thigh; 'I shall never again possess a bosom as fresh and flowering as your own!' – and leaning forward, she placed a kiss upon one bubby, taking it between her lips and pressing it between them.

I hesitate to record what followed, for it is of an intimate nature; yet I shall do so – not as a warning to young women who find themselves seduced by older matrons (for that is quite the wrong term to apply to an exercise more one of pleasure than of pain), but because I had not previously had the opportunity to discover what passes in such circumstances; and my younger readers should, I believe, be informed on the matter, for occurrences of this nature are more frequent than they may imagine.

I found myself, the next moment, positively embraced by the lady, her bosom pressed to my own, one leg thrust between mine, and her hands clasping me to her, while her kisses were as ardent as those of any masculine lover whose caresses I had so far experienced. Closing my eyes, I gave myself up to an attempt to discover whether the embrace felt in any way different to that of a man: the lady's body was, of course, softer – not only as to her bosom, but through the flesh of her back and bum being pulpy and the covering of tissue thicker. Even her kisses were different, through the skin of her chin and upper lip being devoid of that stubble the pricking of which is always to be felt even should a lover have recently shaved his face: but as to the movements of her lips, the sucking of them upon my tongue, the playing of her tongue within my mouth – there was nothing there to distinguish between the sexes.

Pressing me back upon the pillows, she turned her attention again to my breasts, with many complimentary exclamations which, though they took the form of gasps and groans rather than of words, were none the less flattering: she seemed not to know which was the more important thing, to press kisses upon them, to caress them with fingers and palms, or merely to gaze upon them – and, in fine, she did all three, to an extent which would have persuaded me that she was madly in love with me had I not known that she was equally given to the love of men.

Now, while her kisses continued to be conferred upon my bosom, her left hand had strayed below, and, persuading me to open my thighs, had found its way to my cunny, which she was now fondling, stroking, toying, first upon its lips and then within them, inserting first one then two and even three fingers – a gesture I find most men eschew, presumably from the feeling that such an intimacy should be performed by that part of their body more obviously furnished for the purpose. I cannot say that the emotion provoked by her touch was identical to that of a gentleman's prick, much less to be preferred to it; but that it was unpleasant, I should lie to say; and indeed my passion was now sufficiently roused for me to return her kisses and caresses in an equal measure – the sensation of a woman's breast beneath my palms being a strange but by no means disagreeable one; while on my taking my hand to her lower body, which I found lubricated by the juices of desire, the impression was even odder – yet her cry of pleasure on my first approach was such that I could not doubt that she found it enjoyable, and that very fact persuaded me to continue the gesture.

She now for a moment broke away – for what purpose I could not predict; but it was to turn about so that she lay with her face approximate to my middle parts, when passing her arms about my waist, she buried her face between my thighs and began lapping with an urgent complimentary motion. Finding my lips now within reach of that strangely naked groin of her own, I could not but in common politeness pay it complementary attention; and found somewhat to my surprise that the exercise was by no means repugnant – her skin was sweet and clean, and the taste upon the palate of that liquidity which bathed the area was, far from being sour or disagreeable, somewhat sweet and cloying. It is also the case that I find giving pleasure to my partners a significant diversion, and the shudders that ran through Margaret's body as my tongue first stroked the cool outer lips, then found its way between them into the warm interior, when finally my lips fixed on that little knoll of flesh, the only prick woman possesses, increased until she began to buck and moan with exultation.

After a while, somewhat to my surprise, she broke away – just in fact as I, somewhat slower than her to react to the caresses of a person of my own sex, was beginning to move towards a pinnacle of pleasure – and suggested that I might be interested in something she could show me. I wondered at this, for she seemed already to have shown me every part of her person which could properly be examined; but she did not refer to her own body, but rising from the bed fetched from a table a beautifully carved ebony and lapis box, which when opened contained a row of remarkable objects.

These, I must immediately inform the reader, were those objects known as 'dildos', which he or she may be cognisant of, but of which I at that time had no notion. Seeing my puzzlement, Margaret took one from the box – a fine article made of ivory, which as soon as she had it in her hand appeared for what it was: an extremely accurate approximation of an erect cock, correct not only as to its general shape, but to the most minute detail – the wrinkles in the skin about the bulb, the crown itself and the tiny aperture at its centre; while the veins of the shaft, and that main one through which is expelled the liquor of life, were equally finely expressed by the master craftsman who had made it.

When I had congratulated her on its beauty, she explained that it had been carved 'from the life' – that is, her grandfather, the Hon. Peter Latchsphere, a well-known roué of his time, had posed for it to a celebrated Venetian carver; and it had been used in the family ever since.

Used? – I enquired: at which Lady Cricklewood understood that I knew nothing of the purpose of the implements which lay before me.

She now kindly explained that such objects had first been employed – as far as history could tell us – by the ancient Greek women whose husbands were away at war, or preferred (as was sometimes the case) their girlfriends to their spouses. To satisfy the self by the use of such aids was then regarded (she said) as entirely acceptable, and the use of what were called *olisbos* was common; the city of Milebos indeed based its entire economy on the production of these useful objects, manufacturing them either in wood or padded leather, and exporting them together with that olive oil with which they were commonly anointed before use.

'I have even seen performed in a private theatre in Athens,' said Margaret, 'an ancient dialogue between two young women, Metro and Coritto, which was entirely devoted to the subject. Of course, the *olisbos* were used not only by married women, in private, but by the *tribads*, or women who invariably preferred the company of their own sex to that of men: I have read in Plutarch, the ancient historian, that "at Sparta *tribad* love was held in such honour that even the most respectable women became infatuated with girls" – rather in the way that in Athens seasoned warriors and politicians were infatuated with boys.'

All this was fascinating to me, who then knew nothing of ancient life.

The *olisbos* – Margaret preferred that term to the coarser 'dildo' – were not always used without shame; in the Middle Ages, it appears that nuns who made use of them were particularly hardly treated. In Europe, there had always been a caution about artificial amorous aids, while elsewhere – particularly in China (she said) – there was almost complete freedom. Why, perhaps I would care to examine one of their products?

She lifted from the case a remarkable contraption: an *olisbo* covered in ribbed leather, with a sort of harness attached to it. Seeing my puzzlement, Margaret buckled this about her waist, and lubricating the 'jade stalk' (as the Chinese call it) invited me to insert it in her 'Cinnabar Cleft' – the Chinese name for the natural receptacle of such an object.

I was somewhat nervous of this, for it seemed an object larger than it would be in nature; however, Margaret held the lips of her private part aside, and inserting the machine I pressed it steadily home, meeting no particular resistance, and even hearing her breath expelled in a hiss of pleasure as the ribs of the stem pressed against the sides of the fissure.

When it had been pressed home, and only perhaps an inch of it remained in sight, she reached into the box, and produced a similar piece of equipment – but this time comprising only the stalk itself, which she then attached to her own by a simple mechanism: when I must be sufficiently honest to confess it looked very much as though it were a gentleman's prick, set at a very similar angle, and of much the same appearance, though of a generous size.

I could not but agree, driven no less by a sense of obligation than by curiosity, to place myself upon my back and admitted the lady between my thighs just as I might a male lover. First generously oiling the *olisbo*, she inserted the tip and, pressing down, ensured that the machine entered me with remarkable ease and indeed a very inspiriting sensation as the ribs passed my lower lips – whereupon she began just those movements which might be expected, the harness she wore ensuring that that end of the implement embedded within her body remained there, giving a steadiness and intractability to the other portion, which moved within my body just as a prick does when one swives.

I was surprised that she appeared to be getting as much pleasure from the exercise as (I must confess) did I – for surely there can have been no friction involved, her portion of the apparatus remaining more or less stationary; the contrivance which ensured her pleasure (as she showed me afterwards) consisted of a little bump or protuberance embedded in the leather of her *olisbo* just at that point where it came into contact with what doctors term the clitoris, but which we may know as 'the man in the boat'.

I will now cut the scene short by saying that I need have had no fear that I could not engage Lady Cricklewood for a sufficient period for Devon to escape from the house – for of course one point much in favour of artificial cocks is that they neither tire nor fail, and since the novelty of the situation continued to interest me almost as keenly as the various *olisbos* gave me pleasure, my lady was happy to remain with me for several hours, until each of the half-dozen pieces of equipment in her magic box had been proved. I believe that her pleasure in watching me try them, and occasionally showing me how their use could be varied, was as great as that which she experienced when joining me. As for myself, my interest was keen and my expectations sometimes amazed: for instance, although I was perfectly aware of the pleasure which a lover could give by inserting a finger into that orifice adjacent to the one more usually employed for congress, and even by kissing it, it had never occurred to me that a woman might enjoy the insertion of an object rather larger than a digit. I had never believed that pleasure was experienced by the recipient of those attentions lavished upon each other by gentlemen engaged with members of their own sex: the active partner must experience, after all, much the same emotion when engaged in the act of sodomy as when swiving with a mistress; but I had always supposed that the passive partner must at best be bored and at worse positively pained by the deed.

I was proved wrong, however – at least if my experience could be credited; for in the course of the morning, when I had been reduced almost to tears by the keenness of my emotions, I suddenly realised that as I lay atop her, still pierced by the *olisbos* which was attached to her own, another – certainly somewhat slimmer than the others – was being slowly inserted in that second orifice, and more-over not inflicting pain, but offering positive pleasure, the slight stretching of the muscles about that place being astonishingly pleasant.

Lady Cricklewood could not but laugh at my surprise.

'You will learn, my dear,' she said – not unkindly – 'that it is unwise to reject any action offered to you by way of physical pleasure until you have tried it. Indeed, it is a lesson I would offer my children – if I had them – that one should try everything in this life except perhaps incest and bell-ringing.'

This curious remark would have made me laugh, except that she accompanied it with a final push of the *olisbos*, at the same time complementing it by upthrusting the other; the joint sensation reduced me to a mass of emotion which had much the effect of a display of fireworks; and I must plead to the lady to allow me to rest, which, with a laugh, she did.

Although it was clear that my companion had enjoyed the extremity of love not once but (from her grimaces and exclamations) several times, she was still not exhausted, for as I lay at her side in the happy exhaustion which follows amorous intercourse, she could not resist allowing her hands to wander about my person and even, from time to time, to bestow a kiss upon those parts which only a lover normally visits with such caresses. I am not, as my particular readers will know, averse to lubricious play – and it is true that the female, brought to the point of ecstasy, is immediately able to continue toying, while the man must have a pause before he is able, at least actively, to proceed; but I must confess to finding Margaret's continued petting more an irritation than a pleasure – though I did not show this, for I must detain her as long as possible.

But with the best will in the world I must make my excuses when she produced from her box an *olisbo* the size of which would I believe have frightened a much more experienced woman than myself; and upon her offering to introduce it into my person, protested that it would be too large, and would certainly damage those parts upon which I set too high a value to offer them such violence; whereupon she laughed, and pausing only to pass a palmful of oil over its surface, slid it into her own cunny without apparent resistance or discomfort, then taking my hand and placing it upon the hilt, encouraged me to move it to and fro while at the same time continuing to pay both manual and oral tributes to my beauty.

After a time, and some shuddering and shivering, even she had had sufficient play; and rising, pulled upon a bell, and was surprised when instead of Devon a maid entered. Her enquiries were met by the information that the footman was nowhere to be found, at which she looked first puzzled and then irate; a search of the house was ordered, and made, and still (as I knew would be the case) the whereabouts of the errant servant were not discovered.

I am glad to say that she in no way connected me with his disappearance; nor did I offer comment either on his absence or her choler at it – though this was considerably higher than might have been expected in a normal household. Having taken advantage of the offer to immerse myself in a bath of hot water, thus warmed I dressed myself in my thickest clothing, and taking leave of my lady – too much aroused by the unwonted disturbance in her household to pay her departing guest more than cursory attention – was soon in one of her carriages, and on my way back into town.

Chapter Thirteen

The Adventures of Andy

The joy with which our two ebony-skinned friends were reunited can be imagined, and my pen is certainly not sufficiently talented to convey in anything like its full intensity the pleasure with which they greeted each other upon my opening my door to the knock of young Devon, who had escaped from the Cricklewoods' establishment under the circumstances narrated by Sophie in the preceding chapter.

I was happy that Bella and I had risen from bed some time previously, for while the gratitude of the two young persons would surely have over-ridden any painful feelings which might have been aroused by our being discovered in such intimate circumstances – and while indeed both parties seemed particularly devoid of the emotion of jealousy, which wastes so much of the spirit and so distorts our emotions – it was still much more agreeable that they should meet as they did, and be able (as they were) to retire instantly to the bedroom, whence issued sounds indicative of pleasurable reunion.

After only a brief hour – so keen was their gratitude to me that they cut short the time which surely they had rather spent in each other's company than in mine – Bella, considerably less completely dressed than previously, presented herself to me in the sitting room with the request that I should join them, for they wished to express their thanks to me once more.

There was (I said) no need, for the delight they had shown at their reunion had in itself been sufficient reward; but she insisted, and led me into the bedroom, where Devon immediately jumped up from the bed and wrung my hand anew. He was also in that state of undress into which the pair had rendered themselves, no doubt, in order properly to communicate their joy to each other, and I must confess to being astonished at the size of that part of him which I supposed had been exercised during the past half-hour: though I assumed that exhaustion must surely have diminished its dimensions somewhat, it seemed to me of massive size: I am not expert upon the subject, but of those gentlemen's pricks I have seen it was immeasurably the most monumental, and even in its slackened state (for it swung between his thighs in a manner which expressed repose) it must have measured at least nine or ten inches in length, while it seemed almost of the thickness of my (or certainly Bella's) wrist – I could not even resist a glance at her nether parts in order to assure myself by the absence of blood that he had not done her a damage.

But now, I felt Bella's hands on me, divesting me of that shirt which I had thrown on – and then of my trousers. I was somewhat disquieted at this or if not positively disquieted at least a little perplexed, for it could surely not be the case that Devon would celebrate his reunion with his beloved girl by wishing to see me engaged with her by way of coition?

Upon my being rendered in that state in which they already were – that is, pared to the buff – each of them took a hand, and leading me to the bed disposed me upon it, one on each side of me – Bella lying beside me while Devon knelt by the bedside (the cot being too small to take us, all three, and yet allow space for amorous manoeuvre).

The pair now began to caress me with such wanton yet tender care that although during the previous night I had (as I thought) been completely drained of emotion by the lascivious and delightful attentions of Bella, in no time my cock was as taut as a bow (if, I must confess, somewhat sore through the uses to which it had been put during some very active hours).

Bella now occupied herself by kissing me upon the lips with all that sensitivity I had already experienced from her – but at the same time I could not but be cognisant that Devon was paying me such compliments as, in general, are not exchanged between gentlemen (except of course those whose habit it is to engage in such play as is outside the law). His hands were playing about my nether regions – with, I must confess, an ingenuity and tenderness equal to Bella's own. While I was of course aware that the caresses were those of one of my own sex, I must confess that I found the sensation itself indistinguishable from that provoked by female hands; and since my eyes – as she redirected her kisses to my chest, her tongue flicking delightfully at my nipples – were upon Bella's face, I had no visible reminder that the hands which were manipulating my prick and cods to such diverting effect were other than female.

Were I not aware of the circumstances, could I (I thought, while enjoying those sensations provoked by Devon's activity) possibly distinguish between his caresses and those of a female? – and for answer, must accept that I could not. It may be that in some circumstances (where, for instance, a man's hands may be particularly rough or callused) it would be possible to do so; and I suppose that should there be any circumstances in which his face came into contact with any sensitive part of the body, his beard must give away the game. But in this case, I must admit, it was certainly impossible to swear that had I been blindfold, I could tell . . .

But now, Bella moved her body so that my head fell

between her thighs as she sat upon the bed, my cheek upon one of them, and my neck resting upon that snug little nest of tight black curls which hid the entrance to that nirvana I had recently enjoyed. It was a ravishingly comfortable position – and at the same moment was accompanied by a distinct alteration in the sensation about my nether regions, where in the place of the unmistakable stroking of fingers there was a softer and more liquid feeling – which upon my lifting my head and glancing in that direction, proved to be the result of my staff having been placed between Devon's lips. These, as full as Bella's, were somewhat less luscious, but deployed (I must confess) with even more originality, and with motions resulting in an even higher degree of pleasure. Devon, being a man, was aware of what most pleasures a man; and played upon the instrument with all the dexterity of a professional, so that even had I been one of those men to whom the very idea of connection with another man was horrid to the point of nausea, I could not but have appreciated the delectable emotions which he aroused.

After a while, it became clear to me that if I could not persuade my friend to give over, the result of his ministrations would be an immediate culmination; but both my friends at that very point must have reached the same conclusion, for Devon lifted his head, and approaching his lips to Bella's ear, whispered something into it. She looked somewhat doubtful, and raised an eyebrow; but he gave a decisive nod, and lowering her head she informed me that her friend wished to offer what was in his country the chief gesture of friendship and gratitude, only in adult years exceptionally proposed to another man.

I could not understand her; but Devon had now risen, turned, and presented to me an arse which I must confess was a charming sight – as succulent as that of any woman, yet through its configuration (resembling two apples placed together rather than the fuller and richer profile of a peach) unmistakably masculine.

What was being offered was now clear to me. Could I refuse? Would it be proper to reject the keenest and most honourable gesture that Devon could make in recognition of my assistance to him and his friend? Clearly, it would not – though it was with some nervousness that I now saw him lie upon his back on the bed and, pulling his knees upwards so that his thighs lay open upon his breast, present to me in that pose that aperture at which it would otherwise never remotely have occurred to me to set my ambition.

I believe that Bella saw my anxiety, for she smiled as though in encouragement, and persuaded me to place myself in proximity to her lover, just as though I were lying with a woman, and, taking my prick in her hands, placed its tip at what seemed too tiny an opening. However, on my pushing slightly forward, there was a yielding and a softness which seemed to suggest that I could do no hurt either to myself or to my young companion by going further; and indeed without any hindrance my prick was accepted – I almost would say ingested – with as much loving acceptance as it had ever found upon entering the quim of the most delightful mistress, while Devon's face showed by the most provocative smile that my action was not merely tolerated but welcomed.

I suppose that he would have accepted with equal equanimity the most enthusiastic swiving which might have followed; but my spirits had been so heightened by what had gone before and by the singular situation in which I found myself – the odd sensation of his own enormous cock now compressed between our bellies, his hands clasping my buttocks as though to encourage me to action, together with Bella's smiling approbation as once more she bent her head to press her lips to mine – that all my emotion gathered itself into a great knot, and was released in a discharge so violent that it shook every atom of my being.

As though in sympathy, at that very moment I felt Devon's prick shiver and pulsate, and in a moment give forth the evidence of his own pleasure.

When we have indulged our passions in a manner which seems in a calmer moment to be regrettable, the moments immediately after a release are those in which repulsion is sometimes felt. But in this case, I felt no such nausea. Raising myself from Devon's body, I turned myself and lay upon the bed – whereat both he and Bella kissed my cheeks, the latter reaching for a sheet and wiping both our bodies before reclining, like us, in a tangle so tightly knit that even the confines of a small couch enabled us to sleep for some considerable time.

On our awakening, it was my turn to express my gratitude for so remarkable a turn of events – whereat many protestations were heard against any such demonstration; all that had occurred was that my friends had shown their appreciation of my assistance in the best manner they could, and they declared themselves even yet in my debt.

Having washed and dressed ourselves, we sat over tea, and I began to wonder what more I could do for them; for I could not presently afford to employ both upon a permanent basis, and though the time might arrive when it would be convenient to do so, I did not in any event at present wish to fetter myself in such a manner; I preferred to be a free spirit, capable of easy movement and uncluttered either by domestic servants or by luggage. Yet how could they earn their living? Devon had, it is true, experience of domestic service – but through his association with the Cricklewoods was too well known in London among those who might otherwise have employed him.

All I could do – and I did it – was to make it clear that for the moment they were to rely upon me for sustenance, and to that end presented Devon with a guinea, and the advice that he should take a room for them in a quarter of the town where it would be easy to keep out of Crickle-wood's way should he instigate a search – advising that rabbit warren, So Ho, where a network of narrow lanes would make escape as easy as possible should they be spotted.

On finding such an address, he was to let me have a note of it, and I would advise them of my plans for them (when I had any, I added to myself, *sotto voce*!).

They had not long left the rooms, hand in hand like happy children, when the door again opened, this time to reveal Sophie, who lost no time in assuring herself that Devon had safely reached me; I gave as distinct an account as possible of the reunion of the lovers – after which she was so eager to favour me with an account of her morning's activities that I had no opportunity to describe how they had shown their gratitude to me – though at that time I might in any event have hesitated to do so. I heard Sophie's narrative with as much interest as amusement: it struck me that had the circumstances been reversed, I should have borne with less equanimity the attempts of Harry Cricklewood to make love to me – but then remembered recent events, and concluded that in the right circumstances our sensual selves may be capable of actions which in cold blood might seem impossible.

'But what,' Sophie then asked, 'are we to do with our two black friends?' – a question which I could not answer, and which we debated for some little time without reaching any advantageous conclusion.

It was then that – in the course of a day becoming increasingly busy – another knock came upon the door. Sophie retired to the bedroom, for it was our immediate thought that the Cricklewoods might have come to call. On the contrary, however, the visitor was a welcome one: none other than Frank – my friend and Sophie's half-brother, Sir Franklin Franklyn, of Alcovary in the county of Hertforshire. To say that we were both delighted to see him is an under-statement, Sophie indeed throwing herself into his arms with a warmth that would have been regarded as suspicious had he been her full brother – but the distance set between them by the fact of their having different fathers had already persuaded them to allow such familiarity between them as would be unusual had the connection been closer.

What, we asked, was the cause of his visit to London? – for already Frank was showing that unfortunate taste for rural seclusion which was eventually to remove him, largely, from those scenes which most appealed to us.

We must know (he said) that in fourteen days' time he was to celebrate his twenty and first birthday. (A glance passed between us: sadly, we had entirely forgotten the fact.) He looked forward to our returning to Alcovary for the occasion, when the local gentry, and a number of his friends from college at the University of Cambridge, would attend a great party. The problem which exercised him was the entertainment of the latter.

'Sir Bunting Bilbury, Lady Clossett, Mrs Twitchen and the others,' he said, 'will be content with food and wine and dancing; my friends however will expect more – and I am in a difficulty to consider how to amuse them, for their tastes you know, are . . .'

'Are very similar to our own,' said Sophie, grinning. 'So you want us to find some merry girls for them to rollick with?'

Frank did not deny it; but, he said, could not there be some additional entertainment? He could not think what, but . . .

'Leave it to us, my love,' said Sophie. 'And now, let us dine' – for it was four in the afternoon, and we had had no food yet that day.

We went to Glaiscow's, in the Strand, and made short work of some beef and potatoes and a pie or two, when Frank said that he must find somewhere to lie; it was his

The Adventures of Andy

intention to remain in town only for a couple of days – he
had some discussions with his man of business in connection with additional monies due to him upon his majority.

Naturally, we could not permit him to stay at an hotel,
and pressed him to sojourn with us; my rooms were
small, and Sophie had not yet found herself a lodging –
but we could in some way accommodate him without too
much discomfort. He protested, of course; and it was true
that his funds were such that he could have afforded to
take the largest suite of rooms to be found in the city. But
in friendship we over-ruled him – and having collected his
single small bag of luggage from the inn at which the
Cambridge coach had concluded its journey, and taken it
to the Haymarket, we swept him off to the theatre for a
performance of Mr Wycherley's *The Country Wife*, which
we thought might amuse him, and at which indeed he
laughed immoderately.

Returning to our rooms, we easily solved the problem
of where to sleep by piling into the single bed which the
establishment afforded! – this, I had already proved capable of supporting three persons, though they had best be
on terms of intimacy, as the three of us were. We had
known each other for a sufficient number of years to be
so familiar with each other's persons that we could now
settle down in perfect comfort, and – the weather still
being briskly cold – greater warmth than would have been
the case had there been two, or one of us!

Sophie properly occupied the centre of the bed, with
Frank on her left and myself on her right. She and I, I
believe, fell asleep almost at once – we both had energetically exercised ourselves during the course of the day, and
ardent lovemaking is a great provoker of pleasant fatigue.
I awoke at I know not what hour, but perhaps at three or
four, and was conscious of some kind of movement. Looking about in the combination of flickering light from the
dying fire and of the full moon which was just beginning

211

to wane, I saw that Frank (who I suppose was not as fatigued as we) was wakeful, and since in the heat of the room we had thrown the bedclothes from us, was gazing at Sophie's unclad body, and quietly exercising his left hand by manipulating a cock clearly appreciative of the beauty of the sight.

Catching my eye, he looked for a moment abashed – but then remembered that we were as affectionate and open together as brothers, and that indeed our first experiments in sensual pleasure had involved just such an exercise as that he was presently engaged in, and grinned wryly. Knowing that Sophie would be sorry not to afford him some relief, I shook her shoulder, and instantly awakening (for we were young enough to find even a couple of hours' sleep sufficient to recover us from most exhaustions), she saw what was the matter, and as I had expected immediately reached up, grasped Frank's head, and pulling it down to her own gave him a welcoming kiss, at the same time (and meeting with no opposition) persuading him to lift his body into such a position between her thighs that a union was not only possible but immediately effected.

I now took myself from the bed, where there was little room for three except in complete quiet or complete union, and sat myself down by the fire, sufficiently warm despite my state of undress – and not for the first time within twenty and four hours found myself in the position of watching a gentleman achieve sensual satisfaction with a lady.

I must confess that although I knew both of the parties extremely well; and although this was not the first time I had seen them similarly occupied (for we had lived in close proximity for some time, and moreover during the summers at Alcovary had passed our time bathing in the lake, an occupation which almost invariably led, on our lying down to dry upon the warm grass in the sun, to such familiarities); although I had spent an extremely pleasant and active night in Bella's arms, and followed this by the extraordinary events I have described in this chapter which might have been expected to have milked me not only of desire but of physical energy; despite these facts, I say, I must confess that the spectacle of my friend's lean and shapely buttocks plunging with enthusiasm between the thighs of my other friend – together with their low exclamations of satisfaction – moved me so that my own prick was soon in a state similar to that in which Frank's was now proving its efficaciousness as a weapon of love.

Attempting to distract my thoughts from the situation (though I was entirely unable to avert my eyes from so provocative a sight) it occurred to me once more to wonder why men (especially, though also many ladies) found such sights entertaining. The taste ran through all classes – even the princes of the church had organised similar spectacles: was it not one of the Borgia Popes who had arranged at the wedding of his sister a display in which the most attractive and shapely whores of Rome had cavorted in the courtyard of his palace, the Pope throwing down gold pieces for them to scramble for, in order that he and his guests might enjoy the lascivious postures in which the exercise placed them?

At this point however, Sophie, distracted for the moment from her friend's attentions by his request that they adopt, before the final *coup*, a different posture, set eyes upon me and observed my state – or rather that of my prick – and called to me to join them upon the bed. I did not hesitate to do so: for one thing I never recoiled from any opportunity to express my affection for both Frank and Sophie; for another, the alternative was the employment of Mrs Palm and her five fingers – pleasant enough should there be no alternative, but ever a somewhat drab activity when compared to an invitation from a pretty woman.

As I approached the bed, Sophie whispered something to Frank, at which he seemed somewhat surprised – however, upon her advice laid himself down upon the bed, his bum right upon its edge; whereupon in a moment Sophie had placed her knees on each side of his hips, and impaled herself upon his weapon – and observing my slightly abashed look, whispered to me that as she had recently learned, I would do her no harm by taking an alternative route to heaven.

I had not – remember, I was still a mere youth – heard of such a thing where women were concerned, though very recently I had proved myself capable of enjoying such an activity, even not considering myself to be one of those bum-batterers whose regular activity this is.

However, since I was invited, since Sophie seemed eager to accommodate me, and since Devon's arsehole had accepted my cock without any signs of discomfort, I spat upon my palm and liberally bedewing my prick, approached and – upon Sophie slightly raising herself from Frank's body in order to present me with a better mark – presented myself at the gate. The ease with which this opened, together with what seemed a sign of appreciation and positive enjoyment from Sophie, persuaded me to press home, and though I hesitated to make any vigorous movement, I found the sensation offered by the posture to be no less devoid of pleasure than it had been some ten hours previously – though in some ways more curious, not least because I could clearly feel the movements of Frank's cock, which seemed separated from my own only by a thin barrier or membrane.

Sophie showed no discomfort at all, and indeed remarked in a somewhat trembling voice how pleased she was to comfort her two closest friends at the same time, and asked whether we did not feel that it established an even closer bond between us?

I believe that we *did* feel that; and it was certainly in literal terms the truth, for my cods and Frank's jostled in the most familiar group of four ever to have danced together, while the distinctive sensation of our being aware of each other's pricks, and aware too that we felt much the same emotion, heightened our feelings to a point at which they could no longer be contained. Catching Frank's eye, I saw it widen and then squeeze shut just as my own performed a similar movement. Provoked beyond measure, we reached at the same moment the acme of pleasure; and Sophie too seemed to accompany us on what was first a leap and then a decline as the three of us, now perforce breaking the strange connection our bodies had with each other, fell exhausted to the bed – or rather, Sophie and Frank fell to the bed; I fell off it, happily upon my back, thus avoiding the infliction of an additional shock to an organ once more reeling, now indeed positively sore, from yet another adventure.

We now fell into a yet deeper sleep than before, from which we awoke (I am ashamed to tell you) only at eleven o'clock on the following morning, so that it was twelve before we breakfasted, and then found time to tell Frank the story of Devon and Bella, and the situation in which they found themselves. He was a little surprised, I believe, at the closeness of the association we had formed with these two young persons – he, himself, though randy as the next man, always took care never to form any close bonds with one of his servants, and clearly thought it somewhat strange that we should find the couple so delightful – but then, he had not had the opportunity of meeting them; and (so close was our association) in the end must accept our assertion that when he *did* meet them, he would be as anxious to help them as we were.

As the reader will have guessed, Sophie and I had independently formed the intention that Frank should be the provider for our friends: not that we wished to place any particular burden upon him, but his funds were so considerable that two more servants would be no affliction; moreover, not only would Devon be an ornament to his servants' hall, but Bella... Well, as to Bella, there was more of a difficulty, for the skills she possessed were perhaps less frequently in demand in the environs of Cambridge than in those of St James's.

But then, quite suddenly, Sophie and I caught each other's eye, and knew that the same idea had occurred to us both – to the extent that we almost spoke together, our pronouncement being that Frank was to rest assured that as to his birthday, we would supply an entertainment that would long be remembered by his friends.

And what of – what were they called – Somerset and Belle?

Devon and Bella, we responded. Well, we would not claim that our plans for Frank's birthday particularly excluded them; but enjoined him to wait and see.

He now took himself off to Coutts' bank, and happily within the hour Devon appeared with a note of his address in Poland Street, So Ho; and we – having discussed our idea in the interim – made a suggestion to him which produced the effect of complete satisfaction and such gratitude that we were hard put to it to prevent him encouraging us to accept his thanks in corporeal form: which, after the previous day's extraordinary adventures would have laid me in my bed for several days – for to be frank, I could not remember when, within twenty-four hours, I had coupled so vigorously, so variously and with such satisfaction!

Chapter Fourteen

Sophie's Story

There is clearly no advantage in my recapitulating the scenes which took place in Andy's rooms in the Haymarket upon my joining him, except to say that it was pleasant to be reunited with Frank in the manner described. I must rather hasten on to recount the steps I took to ensure that the party he was to hold at Alcovary should be a memorable one, and should celebrate in a proper manner his reaching his majority.

It will I suppose not surprise readers that our minds – Andy's and mine, I mean – should turn immediately in one direction; for what is the passing of a twenty-first birthday but a rite of passage into true manhood? And though Frank was (as I suppose has been perfectly clear) by no means ignorant of the pleasures of adult life, it seemed an excellent idea that he and his fellows should be afforded an opportunity to indulge themselves in a manner more luxurious than had perhaps previously been the case.

How this was to be done, we now discussed.

The simplest idea was to collect together a representative group of handsome girls, to convey them secretly to Alcovary, and to introduce them to Frank and the half-dozen or so of his particular friends; this would no doubt result in a romp of sufficiently enjoyable proportions – and Andy would, I believed, have no difficulty in selecting the young ladies concerned (while the expenses of the escapade would be born by Frank himself, whose purse was quite sufficiently deep).

But after all, as Andy remarked, this was perhaps a slightly unimaginative proposal, which though no doubt enjoyable would scarcely be a tribute to our ingenuity. I then informed him of the idea I had: remembering the expression of wonder which I had remarked upon Frank's face on my suggesting, the previous night, that my two friends might enjoy my person at one and the same time, and his evident surprise at the means employed, might it not be best to make the occasion of his birthday one of education?

From the first, Andy agreed that this was an excellent notion – the only question being how it was to be done. One part of the answer was clear: Devon and Bella must be the main instructors in such lessons as were to be given, for both – through the combination of a natural curiosity and enthusiasm, and the instruction of the Cricklewoods – were as expert in the arts of love as any of our generation we had come across. As to the other participants, the girls at Whister's were (I was assured) almost Bella's equal in the ingenious and enthusiastic purveyance of pleasure, with the added recommendation of their colour, which would be an astonishing matter for the watchers; and Andy proposed to make the attempt to engage them, as a group, for the purpose we discussed.

But how? I enquired – surely Cricklewood would not . . .

Simply, said Andy, upon a monetary basis: Frank was sufficiently wealthy to defray the expenses of such a group as we required, for whatever period the young ladies were needed – and (he added as I opened my mouth to address the very question) there was no reason why Cricklewood should suspect him of having anything to do with Bella's escape from his harem.

The general idea being fixed, we now discussed the minutiae: it would be entertaining, Andy averred, if he were to announce a lecture upon the subject of the relations between the sexes, which should begin at least as though it were as serious a matter as any discussed at the Royal Institution; moreover, it would be pleasant if some costumes could be devised to give the occasion additional interest. Perhaps I would give my mind to that matter, while he would see to the engagement of the young ladies?

I was happy to do so: but how? Though as interested in fashion as the next woman, I was no designer of dresses, and . . .

But wait: I recalled at that instant Mme and M. le Brun – and perhaps, in particular, the latter, who seemed (from his attitude at our last meeting) likely to show an interest in the problem. I therefore took myself off to the Royal Arcade, where Mme le Brun welcomed me with some enthusiasm. Her son, she remarked, was at the moment engaged, but if I would care to take a seat . . .

I did so, but had only been seated for a few moments when the door to the inner room opened, and a handsome young lady appeared, who from the rosy colour of her cheeks and a slight breathlessness which resulted in the rising and falling of an attractive bosom, seemed to have been the subject of peculiar attention by Michel le Brun, who followed her with (as I thought) a somewhat downcast look, but ushered her from the shop with every sign of polite regard.

His face brightened considerably upon seeing me, and as he ushered me into his sanctum he informed his mother that if any client asked for him, he was to be considered as privately engaged for the next hour. She appeared to regard this with equanimity, and settled herself upon her chair with every appearance of a dragon set to guard its cave.

'My dear Mrs Nelham,' Michel remarked, 'I am excessively glad to see you.'

I reciprocated his greeting, with the comment that I hoped he was not too exhausted to give me advice upon a certain topic.

'Not at all,' was his reply, going on to tell me (without my asking) that the Hon. Mrs Panton Fortescue – the young lady who had just left – was a tease of the first order; this did arouse my interest, and on my enquiring further he explained that while she had without demur removed her clothing in order that he might fit a new gown she had bespoken, she had insisted upon dressing herself in it, and when his hand had unfortunately brushed her naked bosom (as he made a proper adjustment to the neckline) she had taken him by the wrist and rebuked him – though, again, not objecting to removing the gown and displaying herself entirely unclothed before him.

'I have a word for such behaviour,' he said – and I must agree that it was curious conduct, for it is only upon the stage, surely, that women may display their bodies to gentlemen without positively inviting their amorous attentions; even in theatrical circles, such an exhibition may be regarded as suggesting that the ladies concerned are available for amorous purposes should the proper financial arrangements be made.

However, I now passed on to business, explaining that my friend Mr Archer and I were organising a party for a selection of young gentlemen, and not hesitating to make clear its style and purpose. I believe that Michel may have supposed at first that he was merely to be an invited guest; but I hastened on to say that I believed that the occasion would benefit from the fitting out of the young ladies who were its chief feature in original dresses – or perhaps 'costumes' – which would aid them in raising the amorous propensities of the male guests (not that, I added, I supposed that they would need such an impetus, but that it would be an additional pleasure to them). I wondered whether – although it was a request which allowed little time – he . . .

He did not wait to hear my request, but producing a little key which hung about his neck upon a silver chain, went to a cupboard, and unlocking a box produced from it a sheaf of papers which he laid upon a table: they were, I saw as he began to display them to me, designs for a number of costumes which might have been made just for my purpose: here, a transparent black gown which fell from shoulders to floor but opening at the front would lay open a lady's body to the amorous view; there, a shirt which was as pretty a thing as any woman might desire – but which ended just at the hips, its frill emphasising what lay beneath . . .

But, I said, though these were admirable, how long would it take to make them up?

He smiled, and asking me to tarry for a moment, left the room – returning after not too long a space with a piece of luggage which, when unlocked, displayed a pile of garments, all muddled together, and of all colours. He had (he explained) made most of the clothing himself, for his own amusement, but as yet had had no opportunity to try whether it was practical – that is, whether the gowns could in fact be worn without discomfort, and to as fine an effect as he had supposed. If I would care to try them, he would be pleased to make any alterations which might be needed, after which they could be mine for as long as I needed them, and without any charge!

I did not demur: at which he delved into the box and produced that first garment whose representation I had seen. In less time than it takes to set these words upon the page, I had unclothed myself and placed it about my body. It was made of the sheerest silk – I suspected that Michel had pilfered a number of lengths of material from some of his wealthier clients, for all the clothes I now saw were made of the rarest and most expensive materials – and the

221

very touch of this upon my body was exhilarating, while Michel himself, from the shining of his eyes, found the prospect as alluring as his imagination could have figured. He stepped forward for a moment, and by simply moving the edges of the garment slightly aside encouraged it to fall open just where the bright bush of my pussy could have a maximum effect when seen against the black of the silk. Stepping back again, he turned me so that I could test the effect for myself, in the mirror which stood nearby. I must confess that while I admire my body no more than the next woman, the picture was an agreeable one.

Next, Michel pressed me to try a dress which was complete except that large circles were cut in its upper part, which laid my breasts open to a caress, while a third aperture would have enabled a gentleman to place his hand (or indeed any other part of his body) in proximity to that other part most coveted by the masculine sort.

I must confess that I was by this time somewhat surprised that Michel had made no familiar gesture, for it was clear from the swelling of his breeches that he was by no means unpleased by the effect made by his clothes, at least when displayed as they were. I can only suppose that while his amorous spirits might have been roused, his interest in seeing how well his garments set off the female form was for the moment paramount.

More and yet more garments were displayed, until finally he lifted from that trunk what seemed a mere scrap of bright scarlet silk – which upon first sight looked merely like a small triangular handkerchief with strings attached to each corner of it.

On my raising an eyebrow, he explained that this was entirely his own invention, and the only piece which had so far actually been worn: it had been designed (he said) for a young bride who, while she understood the necessity to display her body freely before a husband with whom she was only slightly familiar, the marriage having been arranged by her parents, was shy of allowing him the perception of her most intimate part; but (he went on) the garment, if it was possible to describe so diminutive a piece of material in such a way, seemed likely to appeal to gentlemen whose tastes were less for dress than for undress, but who might be titillated by the delaying of complete satisfaction by so minimal a piece of clothing. He had called it (he said) a thong – a word used by farriers to describe a narrow strip of hide or leather.

But how was it to be donned? – I had no notion.

Kneeling before me – my having removed the previous piece of raiment – he placed the triangle of cloth over my most private element, then on my parting my legs passed one of the three cords between them, the other two being carried around my hips, and the three knotted behind. He then rose, and retired, allowing me to see the effect in the mirror – which was a startling and, I confess, pleasing one, as though the hairs of my pussy had been died a particularly bright colour, while the cords (which, I should have remarked, were white) almost vanished against my skin – and indeed, turning, it looked from the back as though I were completely nude.

I smiled, and turned again towards Michel.

Was the garment comfortable? he asked. The lady for whom it had been made had found it slightly irritating, although returning some time after her marriage, admitted that continual wear (and her husband had been so delighted by the thong that he had commissioned as many as twenty others, in various colours) made it entirely bearable.

Moving about, I found that indeed the feeling of the thin cord passed between my legs, so that it sank deeply into the crack of my arse, was slightly uncomfortable.

Perhaps he could alleviate this? said Michel, and turning to a shelf took from it a small pot which contained ointment. Kneeling once more, he invited me to turn, and untying the cords released the garment, took up some ointment upon his forefinger and began to rub it along the cleft between the cheeks of my arse.

This he did with the greatest delicacy and care, and I must confess to finding his attention comforting; when, however, his finger began not only to caress but positively to nudge at the entrance of my arsehole, my emotions began to rise rather than to diminish, and the more thorough his attention became, the more I found it impossible not to bend, and by thrusting out my arse, to invite him to be yet more familiar.

This, he did not hesitate to do – and indeed in a moment I found his finger to be replaced by something less rigid, more flexible, but as determined – for he began to explore with his tongue that aperture shunned by too many lovers.

It would have been unkind of me to allow him to continue such attentions to exhaustion, and in a short period of time, though not unreluctantly, I turned – whereat he made no effort to rise, but merely transferred that energetic and exploratory tongue to my clitoris (as the medical men call it); which he stroked and nudged and licked until I was in no doubt where his attentions were leading – though he at present showed no signs of making love to me in any other way.

He was (though my first experience with him had admirably proved his manhood) one of those men whose pleasure seems to come as much from pleasuring his companion as from satisfying his own amorous hunger. However, I required a more complete satisfaction than even so elegant an attention could allow. Bending over him as he knelt at my feet, I first pulled his shirt from about his waist and raised it over his head, then bending still more was able to undo the waistband of his trousers, whereat the insertion of a hand captured an instrument whose rigidity was uncompromising. Grasping it, I tugged upward, whereat Michel could do no other than stand. Holding him about the shoulders, I now backed until I was able to perch my rump upon the table which stood by the wall, and throwing my thighs as wide apart as may be, clasped the young man so tightly that willy nilly he was unable to avoid his prick entering its proper sheath; whereupon his movements immediately proved that whatever the degree of pleasure he felt in complimenting a lady, his instincts were the proper ones, for soon he was lunging to such an effect that the table was rattling against the wall in a manner which could not but (by the regularity of the sound) advertise the nature of our employment to anyone within earshot.

My pleasure was meanwhile increased by being able to observe, through the mirror, the motions of the young man's backside – that handsome posterior (which I have already described) now glossy with sweat, moving with the freedom, grace and vigour which characterises the cantering of the most comely of steeds.

Excited as he had been by whatever amorous adventures he had already had that morning, by the sight of his garments properly displayed, and by the sighs and groans which I had been unable to restrain while he had been caressing my nether regions, he reached his culmination in a very few minutes – though not before my signalling, by clutching at him with my thighs, that I too was satisfied.

I could allow little time for the niceties which normally follow impassioned encounters; but mopping myself and donning my clothes, complimented him again on his designs, and confirmed that I wished to have the use of them for a day or two – and on the spur of the moment asked whether he might be free to come to Alcovary and act as wardrobe master? – for (I said) the young ladies who I trusted would be engaged by my friend would be of various sizes, and alterations to the clothing might be necessary upon the spot.

His agreement was immediate; I gave him instructions

as to the whereabouts of Alcovary, and appointed the time for him to attend, whereafter we parted with expressions of mutual regard (and I was set upon my way, cheerfully and with equally warm expressions, by Mme le Brun – who I think must be proud of her son's amorous propensities, for she could not but be cognisant of his behaviour).

I now made my way – after the merest pause for a pie and a glass of ale – into So Ho, to the address which had been given us by Devon as that at which he and Bella had established themselves. This was at 9, Poland Street, in an area not unknown for those ladies whose profession is the satisfaction of gentlemen in whatever degree of luxury they require. Indeed, upon the door was tacked an announcement:

MISS BENFIELD
About 19 years old, tall, genteel
and very handsome,
being quite fair, with blue eyes and red hair,
is a very agreeable companion on all occasions
approving herself a devotee of Venus,
a specialist in performing the rites of love
according to the equestrian *order.*
For lessons in riding
which she daily and nightly gives
she expects two or three guineas at least.

It was clear from this notice that my friends had at least established themselves in a house of some distinction, for most ladies in this vicinity charged no more than eight or ten shillings a bout.

The door being locked, I knocked upon it – when a window was thrown open, and the blonde head of a lady appeared, who I supposed to be Miss Benfield herself. Seeing a lady at the door, I fancied that her face fell somewhat; and when she enquired whether I wished to see her upon business, and I responded in the negative, she looked still more disappointed.

On my enquiring for Devon and Bella, she commented that 'the blackies' (as she called them, with perhaps some want of delicacy – though in the accents of gentility) were out; but then, relenting perhaps at my thanks to her for her attentions, asked whether I would care to wait in her rooms, letting down a key upon a piece of string, with which I let myself in.

These I found to be rather more decently furnished than the neighbourhood might have promised; and Miss Benfield herself entirely fulfilled the commitment of her bill, in both gentility and appearance – indeed, being tall and slim, with excellent carriage, she might have been supposed to be a governess or teacher. She was not forthcoming about her antecedents, but that they were of some dignity I cannot doubt. I accepted a glass of wine, and we talked in general terms, my resisting with great difficulty the temptation to ask how such a young lady should have placed herself in the circumstance in which I found her.

After some ten minutes, there was another knock upon the front door; Miss Benfield threw up the window once more, and this time exchanged words with a gentleman. The key once more made its descent into the street, and I was asked if I would mind retiring for a time behind a screen?

I was not especially pleased at the prospect of having to do so; but my inconvenience proved not to be great, for having greeted the gentleman by his Christian name (of Percy) she took him straightaway into the next room, which I took to be the bedroom, and I was able to emerge from my hiding place.

What was I to do? If I left the rooms, I would either have to sit upon the stairs in the dark, or retire into the street – and to be frank, Poland Street is not a likely vicinity in which a young woman can wait, alone, for long before being either verbally or actually assaulted. I sat for a while, attempting to pay no attention to certain muffled noises from the room next door, when a cry of 'Tally-ho!' roused my curiosity to a pitch at which it must be satisfied, even at the cost of some unladylike behaviour – in short, I approached the door and placed my eye to the keyhole.

What I saw should have been no surprise, given the nature of Miss Benfield's bill. In the centre of the room, upon all fours, was a stout gentleman of middle years, who I would describe as unclothed were it not that a leather saddle was thrown across his back, and attached by girth in much the way in which one saddles a horse. The saddle itself was complete, though of course smaller than a conventional one, either having been made for a child or perhaps constructed for the use that it was at present put to.

The steed in question had all the appearance of a stallion excited by a mare, for his prick was fully extended – but it would at present have been inconvenient for him to mount, for in the saddle sat Miss B., also in a state of nature – a state I believe much appreciated by her mount, who could observe himself and her in a full-length mirror. Indeed, the lady was worth observation: she clasped the flanks of her steed with handsomely shaped and muscular thighs, whose smoothness only declared them to be the property of a female, for so strong were they that they could easily have been those of a young soldier. As to her femininity, however, the rest of her body made unequivocal statement, for her breasts were unmistakably those of a woman, bobbing attractively as she bounced in the saddle, reaching behind her with a switch to flick at the bare rump of her client or customer, whose puffs and exclamations were expressive less of pain than of satisfaction.

I had only observed the scene for a moment when the mount gave a great buck, and though it need not have dismounted his rider, Miss B. evidently took the action as a signal, and pretended to be thrown, toppling from her seat to the floor, while her horse raised itself as though upon its hind legs, displaying that organ which while less massive (no doubt) than a true horse's, was still sufficiently large to be either a threat or a promise, depending upon the point of view of the mare.

This mare failed to take fright, and indeed with a very good impersonation of a neigh (for she was now metamorphosed from rider into fellow steed), Miss B. now placed herself upon all fours, and turning her back upon her companion wriggled her bottom in the most pleasant manner, at the same time looking around at him with a smile which could only be an invitation.

The stallion needed no second invitation: neighing himself, he reared up, and grasping his prick with one hoof – or, I should say, hand – planted it firmly in her crupper, which immediately swallowed it, whereupon those motions commenced which most animals have in common when placed in more or less the situation I have described.

At this moment, I heard footsteps upon the stairs outside, and voices which I believe I recognised as those of Bella and Devon; and immediately went to the door – but found that Miss B. had locked it! I was therefore forced to wait until the mating process in the next room had reached its conclusion, when the stallion was unsaddled and had resumed more conventional clothing, and – no doubt having recognised the pleasures of the ride by presenting the equestrienne with a proper tribute of coin – taken his leave.

I then emerged from behind the screen and made my own excuses, thanking the lady for her kind hospitality. On her asking me, with deference, to commend her to any gentlemen friends who I thought might find her services attractive, it occurred to me that her particular expertise might well appeal to any country gentlemen at Frank's party, and there and then invited her to attend it, in a capacity which I believe she understood before I explained it. She was only too happy to agree when I was able to assure her that payment would be generous, and unlikely to consist of any sum less than ten guineas.

At all events, I now took myself upstairs, and reaching the second floor (where, according to Miss B., my friends were resident) did not hesitate to throw open the door and walk in. There being no one in the small sitting room into which I stepped, I walked to the open door beyond – and there indeed found my friends, though not entirely at leisure. A third party was in the room: a plump paterfamilias of some fifty years or so, as I would judge, and portly enough to suggest a certain degree of good living. He was lying upon the bed, with his head towards me; and kneeling astride him was Bella, in such a position that he could exercise his palate by tasting the juices of those parts which most appeal to gentlemen – while behind Bella, I could just see that Devon also knelt, his head bent towards the gentleman's middle parts, and bobbing in a motion suggestive of an action best calculated to give pleasure in the circumstances described.

Bella saw me immediately, and smiled broadly, though placing her fingers to her lips – which were already half open, denoting that she was in receipt of some pleasure through the efforts of the tongue and lips which complimented her – if not from the chubby hands which at the same time played about her breasts.

At that moment, the body of the gentleman gave a bound, and Devon sat up suddenly, his black breast bespattered with a white liquid. Bella immediately climbed from her position; and before the gentleman (whose face was now red) could sit up, I had retired to the outer room, and then to the stairs – for there was no such convenience for concealment as Miss B.'s screen.

The gentleman passed me upon the stairs, with no more than a curt nod – his indifference to me, I presumed, being the result of satiety; and I made my way once more to my friends' room, where I found Devon washing his mouth with wine, and Bella mopping with a towel that part of her body liberally dampened by the saliva of their recent companion. The fact of their being unclothed did not prevent them greeting me with the utmost enthusiasm; though they soon dressed themselves (and indeed the room was sufficiently cool as to be comfortable only when the blood was heated).

On my asking how they did, they responded with enthusiasm: they had had no idea (they said) how easy it was to make money without the convenience of organisation by others. Devon produced a roughly printed handbill which, he said, they had had impressed by the same man as had produced Miss B.'s, who had kindly advised them upon its terms:

> *DARK DELIGHT!*
> *Handsome man, charming woman -*
> *Double pleasure for fatigued gentlemen.*
> *At a charge which normally secures*
> *only the attention of an individual,*
> *discerning men may purchase the regard of a couple*
> *practised in the arts of AMOUR.*
> *9, Poland Street*
> *Two guineas, night or day.*

This had brought them, in one twenty-four hours, no fewer than six clients – they explained; five or them men, one a woman. Their requirements had been various: the lady had certainly been impressed by just that possession which had interested me in Devon, and her interest in Bella had only been in being complimented upon her own figure by another woman (which had been something of a difficulty, for she was ugly as sin, and indeed Bella had found it necessary by subterfuge to keep Devon in a state of excitement by actions of her own, while he attempted to engage the visitor).

As to the five men, one wished only to f*ck Devon while Bella watched, to which neither had objection; a second desired to watch the couple in amorous play while he frigged himself; a third was a mere youngster with no idea of intercourse except with himself, and in search of instruction, which they had been pleased to give him – perhaps, Bella said, in too enthusiastic a manner, for he had been completely bemused by the various combinations of positions and motions which they demonstrated; the fourth, laying himself down upon Bella's body, had invited Devon to lie on top of him, the two, by wriggling their bodies against his, provoking the necessary paroxysm; while the fifth, I had seen in action.

I could not but compliment the pair on their accomplishment, and in so short a time; and wondered whether in view of the success they were having, they could be persuaded to take part in our excursion – but they immediately agreed, partly out of friendship, but partly, I have no doubt, from the promise of some twenty guineas, which was a great deal of money (though no more than, I am convinced, they could have made in London during the time they would spend going to and fro to Hertfordshire).

Arrangements properly made, therefore, I left them; and the following day made my way to Alcovary in the same carriage with Frank (his company being no less welcome during the actual journey than in bed at the Bull Inn at Ware, where we broke it).

Chapter Fifteen

The Adventures of Andy

Although, flushed with my success at retrieving Bella from the harem at Whistler's Club, I had little doubt that I could have succeeded in releasing her colleagues by some more adventurous means, I saw no reason to deny Harry Cricklewood the income from his enterprise by removing the means by which he got it – for although I could not altogether approve of buying young women and applying them to the task Harry laid upon them, neither could I argue that they were particularly unhappy in their present position, for even Jessie had declined my offer of assistance should she wish to leave the club: where (she enquired) could she lay up such sums as were paid her there, even after Harry had taken his share? In any event, a new Bill against slavery, shortly to pass through the House of Common, would make any future endeavours to renew the harem difficult if not impossible of fulfilment.

I therefore concluded that my proper course of action would be to approach Cricklewood formally and come to some mutually agreeable arrangement for the hire of the ladies. It was concluded that we should meet at Whister's to discuss the matter, and it was to those premises that I took myself, on an afternoon two or three days after the last episodes I have described.

I was directed to the private room where I had first set eyes on Bella and her fellows. She, of course, was absent; her friend Jessie was there, however, with the other girls who remained. I believe she suspected the part I had played in Bella's escape; her silence however indicating that she saw it as no part of her duty to betray me to Crinklewood, who sat in an armchair in no very good temper though surrounded by so captivating a clutch of young women, dressed in the usual delightful négligées with which they charmed their visitors. Greetings having been exchanged between us, I could not but ask Crinklewood how he did; whereupon he explained that some villain had eloped with the best filly in the stable – 'You will remember Bella, young Andy,' he said, 'for you had her on your first visit, and will credit it when I say that a great number of friends have been disappointed by her absence, even during a few days.'

I commiserated with his loss, and hoped it would not too much damage the business of the club.

'Not too much, I trust,' said Cricklewood; 'though she was a great favourite with many young bucks, for she was not only willing but accomplished – and more than that, enjoyed the game – and, you know, you may teach a girl all manner of wh*rish tricks, but unless she has a relish for fucking her attentions will be but mechanical, and while they may please, can never delight. Alas, we have some of them among us.'

I would not, I own, care to have expressed these sentiments in the presence of ladies – even those whose living was made from just tricks as Harry alluded to; but Jessie, at this point, winked at me; at which I suspected that Cricklewood had himself never enjoyed her favours, for she certainly seemed to me to be as fond of lechery as any girl I had ever lain with (though at the time of which I write, the total was not great).

I now explained my proposition, to both Cricklewood

and the girls: my offer – or rather Frank's, who had given me a free hand – was of ten guineas to each girl, with an additional twenty to Cricklewood (who of course would also take some – perhaps as much as one half – of the girls' fees). He whistled softly, for the offer amounted to a very considerable outlay; but complimenting me on having a friend prepared to spend so much money on cele-brating his majority, was happy to assent – how better to mark such a birthday, he asked, than to give oneself and one's friends as enjoyable a time as he was sure they would spend with his girls?

He took it for granted, of course, that they would con-sent; indeed, how could they do otherwise? I made an excuse to speak to Jessie afterwards – as Harry thought, by way of commerce; but in fact merely to give her a message from Bella, and to explain that she and they would be meeting shortly at Alcovary, which she was pleased to hear. She was so delighted indeed by the whole idea that she offered me a tumble, gratis; reluctantly, however, I must refuse, for I had a number of business engagements before I could leave London.

This we did, two days before Frank's birthday, crowded into two coaches which I had commissioned for the occasion. Sophie having made her own way separately to Alcovary, I travelled as far as Ware in one of the coaches, and on to the house in the second, after a night spent at the Bull Inn – where (lest the reader should think otherwise) I had planned to sleep alone, and had therefore com-missioned three chambers (four to a bed being no hardship for the girls, all eight of whom could have been happy in the Great Bed, had that still been available at the inn). I should explain that spending a solitary night was not especially to my taste, particularly when such admirable entertainment was available; but I felt that I could not show favouritism as to one girl or the other, and attempting to please eight of them would have been beyond even my youthful powers – though I believe they would not have been disturbed by this, for none of them (needless to say) was in love with me.

However, it seems that they felt bound to me; or else the tedium of the journey was too much for them, so that some form of entertainment became indispensable. At all events, when we had been in the coach for an hour, we became sufficiently warm to be uncomfortable in our outdoor clothes – though against the windows of the coach an east wind threw flurries of hail, turning at last to light snow. The girls made much more difficulty than I believed was necessary about the business of removing their outer clothing. As they wriggled from their coats and jackets, discarding such wrappings as could be removed without too much difficulty, they seemed to me to go out of their way to expose arms, thighs, bosoms and occasionally more to my not unpleased eye: their skirts frequently riding up as a result of their contortions, I was vouchsafed from time to time a glimpse of regions sufficiently enticing to warm any young man's blood.

The girls were far from ignorant of my state, which Denise (Harry had given the girls some curiously unsuitable names, as it seemed to me) was first to discover, placing her hand upon my thigh to steady herself while removing her shawl, and discovering beneath her palm something invariably the result of amorous excitement in one of my sex.

She did not hesitate to advertise the fact, by gestures and winks, whereat the other girls, pretending to be jealous of her cognisance of my size and shape (as they said), insisted on feeling me, first through the wool of my breeches – but then Dolly went so far as to announce that she could not resist a clearer view, unlaced my breeches, and brought out the wares concealed there.

Did I not resist? Can the question seriously be asked? Which of my readers would even have uttered a protest?

– and which of them will be surprised to hear that not only did I make no attempt to prevent Miss Dolly's explorations, but even lifted my rump from my seat sufficiently for her to draw my breeches about my ankles; whereat all four of my alleged admirers took turns to examine what was by now an almost painfully distended prick.

I knew of course that they played with me in more senses than one: though it is not my intention to suggest that I was less well equipped for love than any other young fellow, I was under no delusion that my cock was unusual as to size, or particularly fine as to shape, and it was clear that the expressions of admiration to which the girls gave vent were merely flattery; nevertheless, I once more invite my male readers to consider whether in my situation they would not at the very least have been somewhat pleased to have their prick the centre of such attention – to have had four young ladies outdoing each other in remarking on the softness of its skin, the staunchness of its stand; one gently pulling the foreskin back to reveal the gentle pink hue of the helmet, which called forth more expressions of esteem, another wetting her fingers at her mouth to test, as she said, the smoothness of the skin at the peak, while another admired the thick vein through which a fountain of the liquid of life threatened at any time to project itself, and her friend weighed my cods in the palm of her hand, not neglecting to tickle with the tip of one finger that space just below the root, so sensitive that . . .

But at this point I could contain myself no longer: though I clenched my teeth and bit my tongue, though my entire body went rigid and I knit up the whole of my middle parts in a parcel of muscular resistance, I could only cry out in irritation as despite all my efforts and with the force of a steel spring the apparatus which once set in motion will brook no resistance was released, and gathering at the base of my prick a jet of viscous liquid rushed up the vein, and, happily missing the persons of the young ladies whose attentions had provoked the motion, threw several drops even as high as the roof of the carriage.

Far from being offended, the young ladies positively applauded, and comforted my embarrassment by congratulating me upon the force of the spurt (for, they said, it was the mark of a proper man – a comment which subsequent experience has taught me to doubt). Denise remarked that she knew no young fellow who came so violently, and all of them wickedly conjectured which of them would be the first to experience that force in circumstances more private than those which at present obtained.

They were so cheerful indeed, and so neglectful of the accident which I then regarded as a matter for shame, that I soon recovered my equanimity, and since it was clear that their teasing could not for some time take the same course – at least with any hope of their having the same result – we amused ourselves in talk, two of the girls favouring us with a detailed narrative of their adventures before coming to London, which some day I may recount in future pages.

It will now be understood that it was with some relief that I went to my lonely bed at Ware – not that in a couple of hours my powers had not returned; but as I have already remarked, I shrank from having to make the choice of honouring one girl or the other.

I took my place in the other coach for the second stage of our journey; there was no avoiding it. However, by dint of a combination of mock severity and pleas, I managed to avoid a repetition at least of the culmination of the previous day's teasing, though I must admit that some immodest play took place. The presence of Jessie was an amelioration, for I had words with her before the journey commenced, inviting her to protect me from positive physical attack, in which she was of some assistance, though the talk became extremely bawdy, and in other circumstances might have provoked me to action (though nothing is more offensive than bawdy in the mouth of a young girl under certain circumstances, nothing is more delightfully provocative under others).

To cut the narrative short, we arrived at Alcovary on the afternoon before Frank's birthday, to find the house all a-bustle. The girls were admiring of the place's size and handsomeness, and expressed pleasure at their quarters – which were in a part of the servants' wing not commonly used, for Frank kept a somewhat smaller establishment than his father had done in his time. Sophie was already present, together with a M. le Brun, an agreeable fellow who she immediately took to the girls' quarters together with a mysterious trunk the contents of which I was not permitted to know. Frank himself was somewhat bemused by all the action; used to living alone with a small staff (who were devoted to him) he had had no difficulty in making arrangements for the celebrations of the following day, and now spent the time wandering about and attempting to discover just what we had in hand – without success, for we were determined to surprise him as well as his guests.

With that in mind, I was pleased that I was first to see Devon and Bella arrive, who had travelled down together from town and come in just as dusk was falling; I was able to capture them before Frank suspected their presence, and take them to a comfortable room above the stables, which had been borrowed for the occasion from one of the grooms. There we rehearsed what we had in mind for the following day, and I instructed them to keep themselves to themselves – which was not difficult, for yet more severe weather had set in, and no one in their senses would wish to move out of doors unless forced. Indeed, as the snow whirled about the house that night, we wondered whether any of the guests would be able to travel to Alcovary the following day.

However, only two of Frank's guests failed to appear,

and those two elderly relatives fearful of the chills to be caught in the winter weather. Twenty-five, however, did – a group of respectable neighbours, and five young men of his own age, all from his college at Cambridge University – a lively, vigorous and mirthful group, three of them as wealthy as Frank himself, two the heirs to dukedoms; I had a feeling that Cricklewood would gain considerably from the advertisement of his establishment which would be an inevitable result of the evening's endeavours.

We all sat down at five o'clock to an excellent dinner: a turtle soup, roasted carp, boiled fowl, spatchcocked pheasant, joints of pork and beef, together with plentiful bottles of French champagne wine . . . in short, everything to comfort the belly. We drank toasts to Frank between courses, and at the end of dinner each produced his present – these varying from a set of fine guns to a travelling case containing a round dozen of most mischievously illustrated vulgar books.

Dinner being over, the elderly guests were easily persuaded to retire to the drawing room for a game of piquet, and then no doubt at an early hour called for their carriages and made for their homes: Frank had persuaded his great-aunt Mathilda Franklyn to act as hostess – and indeed as is so often the case, I believe they were all heartily glad to be out of the way of whatever strident enjoyments they believed the youngsters to be ready for – though perhaps they had an imperfect notion of what those enjoyments consisted of.

So, in the first instance, did the others, who I invited to follow me into the saloon, where their entertainment would begin.

The room was most convenient for our purpose: neither too large nor too small, it enabled Frank and his five guests to sit comfortably in a range of chairs set facing the north end of the room, which was curved, and where a little stage only some eighteen inches high had been set, illuminated by candles, around which had been placed mirrors so that the light was evenly spread over it and the bed of cushions which was upon it. I believe that the guests also noticed that similar piles of cushions lay upon the floor in other parts of the room, though no one remarked upon it.

I now stepped upon the stage, and in a serious voice not dissimilar to that employed by lecturers on such topics as philosophy or theology, announced that it was proper, upon a young man reaching his majority, that the fullest information should be given him upon a topic vital to the continuance of the human race: that is, the association between the sexes. (This of course was a false premise where Frank was concerned, for readers of my past volumes will remember that the very first[7] commences with the description of his seduction by Sophie, at the most tender age; it was the occasion, too, on which I myself first encountered the embrace of those arms within whose grasp I am happiest, and to which I return eagerly from whatever other conquests may be mine.)

However, I now begged the fullest and most sober attention of the audience while I discoursed on the subject of the proper course to be followed should any of the young gentlemen before me find themselves in circumstances when close commerce with a person of the opposite sex was unavoidable. First, if I might, I would introduce two persons who would illustrate some of the points which I wished to make.

Now, on to the stage from a door advantageously placed at its side, came Devon and Bella – to a gasp of appreciation from the audience, for they were both in the most complete state of nature, and to anyone who had not set eyes on either a male or female of their colour, produced a most interesting effect – for though in every essential similar to the white races, the unusual appearance of their

[7]*Eros in the Country*

skin, the black of which was tinged almost to purple in the candlelight, was engrossing; while such details as the pertness of Bella's breasts, with their thick, dark nipples (both larger and more prominent than is common among European women) and the provoking jet of Devon's buttocks (to be admired even by the most enthusiastic womaniser amongst us) – to say nothing of his most celebrated feature – could not but interest every observer.

I now mentioned the first essential of an enjoyable commerce between the sexes: that is, the sweetness and cleanliness of the person. At this, I removed a screen behind which was a basin of water, and some soap. As I went on, in lugubrious tones, to explain the advantages of cleanliness not only as a preventive of disease but in sweetening the flesh for those caresses which were most intimate, it soon became clear that (as I had anticipated) no one paid me any attention, but all concentrated upon Devon and Bella, each of whom took a piece of cloth and, wetting it, passed it over their bodies, making the black skins shine yet more and the drops to stand out upon them, shining like jewels upon Bella's breasts, and running down over Devon's belly to sparkle in the jet-black hair at its base (where hung his prick, the size of which even in decline had already provoked whispers redolent not only of admiration but, if I mistook not, of envy).

Next, the couple took each a piece of soap, and began to rub it over their bodies. The result of this was even more provoking: not only did every man present watch with eagerness the way in which Bella's palms glided over her breasts, sides, belly – but observed with delight how the whiteness of the foam threw into new relief the entrancing lines of her person.

Naturally, less attention was paid to Devon, who indeed made no move to follow her example – though the sight of her ministering to herself seemed to affect him almost to the extent seen in the others, for his prick began to nod and rise. But now, Bella turned towards him, and taking the soap from him with a smile, began to rub or massage his body with it, producing great smears of foam under his arms, across his breast; she turned him about, and having smoothed the skin of his shoulders and back, leaving a streak of white upon it, fell to her knees and for some little time paid her attention to the cheeks of his bottom – which, as I have said, were rounder, higher and seemed firmer than those of most white gentlemen of his age. I do not believe that any man present did not wish that he was Devon, as they watched Bella passing her hands over those tight curves, not neglecting to run her fingers down the cleft so that they lay between his thighs, the thumbs passing gently over that aperture most central to the part of his body she was cleansing.

Now, she persuaded him to turn, at which it was seen that his cock had risen to a full stand; and upon Bella beginning to apply the soap to that area, Devon could not repress a broad grin, his white teeth sparkling like the bubbles which soon covered the lower part of his belly, hiding the black bush of hair so that – with an effect which would have been comic were it not so libidinous – the black column was entirely surrounded by them, and seemed almost to float upon a sea of white.

Now, however, it was Devon's turn to assist his friend by spreading the suds over her breasts, sides, back – in the manner in which she had attended him; and similarly paying provokingly complete attention to her quim, his fingers caressing every part of it, even turning aside the lips so that the inside of the portal might be cleansed.

My own narrative had, I must confess, faltered somewhat; and my physical discomfort was as complete as that of any member of the audience – most of whom had moved uncomfortably in their seats, and were conscious of a certain straining within their breeches. But I now directed the pair to a large bath upon the other side of the stage, into which they stepped, whereupon I lifted cans of warm water and poured it over them, then handing them towels with which they dried themselves (and each other); a procedure which provoked some amusement, some portion of which I fear was provoked by the clumsiness of my movements, my prick having bent itself double within my breeches, making any movement uncomfortable.

Newly dried, Bella and Devon now returned to the centre of the stage, where I continued my lecture. Each being cleansed of any grime, and as innocent of perspiration as could be, close proximity must lack (I said) all that distaste which could be provoked by unnecessary odours – and thus caresses could be freely expressed, even towards those parts of the body which . . .

But my mouth dried, and I could not continue; for lying on the bed the couple began to nuzzle each other with the most complete freedom: indeed, I believe that in a moment they had even forgotten that an audience was present, for the liberties they took were without bounds, Bella not only sucking upon Devon's prick with a pleasure almost glowingly conveyed, but taking between her lips each of his cods in turn before trickling her tongue down to the place where a small aperture showed itself, by a pulsing and involuntary opening, to be ready for such a compliment, and not only playing about it but actually entering it.

Devon was as free with his mistress's person, and sufficiently conscious of his viewers to turn her for convenient observation, paid his own tribute to that part of woman most conspicuously admired by us.

Every member of the audience was now riveted to the spectacle before them – and were shortly to be additionally provoked, for now persuading Devon to lie upon his back Bella fixed her lips to that splendid organ of his, and began to revolve her body upon it as though upon a hinge; as she did so, each part of her person in turn came within reach of his tongue, with which he complimented it –

sucking first upon her ears, then kissing her shoulders and the length of an arm, after which a breast was favoured first with a thorough licking – so that the dry black flesh shone again with viscous saliva. Having revolved a full half-circle, Bella now crouched over her lover, her quim (which could also be seen to shine, though with that slippery liquid which anoints those parts where slickness is an advantage) above his face; so that merely by lifting his head he could lap at the full, plushy lips within their furry shield, and – parting those lips with his fingers – reveal a perfect miniature prick, more prominent than in many women, and therefore admired as much by the eyes of the audience as by the tongue of her lover.

Both participants in the ceremony were now clearly ready for the main course which naturally follows so enjoyable a preparation; and gently persuading Bella to rise and kneel upon all fours, placing himself behind her Devon thrust his splendidly grand instrument into its proper place (one great sigh being heard from his observers). And as he did so, on to the stage behind them strode the eight girls I had brought from town, each dressed in one of M. le Brun's creations.

These had been fitted by le Brun (in what Sophie tells me was a scene which gave him no little pleasure) to lay stress upon the particular physical attributes of each: so Dolly, a young person whose bubbies were of a somewhat larger size than – to be frank – was entirely concomitant with her stature, wore what may perhaps be described as a harness of thick white satin, slung about her neck, but then passing below her breasts to lift them and drew them somewhat apart, encouraging the formation of a deep cleft between them which set two such grand hills in peculiar and admirable isolation.

Denise, on the contrary, had somewhat smaller breasts, which le Brun had concealed, almost but not quite completely, by a diaphanous shirt which fell to her waist: below which were a pair of what in France are called *culottes*, the centre of which was cut away to display to admiration a thick bush of jet-black hair, in quantity so great that le Brun had been able to tie blue ribbons in it, to charmingly pleasing effect. Miss Benfield was also present – striding on to the stage with an oath and a crack of a whip, clad in hunting pink: or at least in a pink coat, the rest of the clothing being absent: she raised perhaps the most generous cheer of the evening – but only, I believe, because the ravishing appearance of the other girls had struck the audience almost dumb – as, certainly, did the last to appear: a little girl considered by le Brun to have a figure the most perfectly formed, and who wore only what Sophie later described to me as a 'thong' – a mere scrap of silk which, concealing only her puss, drew attention to it in the most lewd and exquisite manner.

Allowing a few minutes, during which they turned and walked about the stage, pausing in postures which most charmingly displayed their bodies, the girls finally formed a line and bowed to their audience; while Bella and Devon, who had maintained their pose like statues, broke it, and rising stood upon each side of me as I took the centre of the stage.

By now, the audience scarcely knew whether to laugh or cry: the scene was one which was charmingly amusing, yet at the same time – especially to young gentlemen few of whom had had much experience with the opposite sex – provoking to an almost painful degree.

I stepped forward.

'Gentlemen,' I said, 'this display has been not only in honour of our friend Sir Franklin, but is his present to his friends; the young ladies will be happy to relieve those emotions which no doubt have crowded upon you as a result of their delightful display. But I am sure that you will concur when I say that our most honoured guest (though in his own home), Sir Franklin, should be permitted to choose that young lady who shall be the first to allow him to prove his manhood for the first time since the twenty and first anniversary of his birth.'

There was general applause (no doubt for the whole of my announcement, though also approving its last clause); and rising, Frank took a somewhat hesitant step towards the stage. I could see that he was somewhat embarrassed at the choice he must make – no less (for I knew the gentleness of his disposition) at the necessity to suggest that he preferred one girl above the others, than at the fact that (my observation had already disclosed to me) the girl with whom he would most like to play was the only one who already had a partner.

Happily, neither he nor I had to take any steps to resolve the problem, for with his native quickness Devon had also recognised his host's preference, and stepping forward took Bella by the hand, and leading her to Frank, placed her hand in his – at which she leaned forward and pressed a kiss upon his lips.

At that signal, everyone in the room applauded – and Frank was persuaded, under their smiling eyes, to take his companion to one of the cushioned beds about the room, where with gestures not in the least coarse, but on the contrary delicate and concerned, she assisted him from his clothing, whereat she did not have to pretend approval of a prick clearly adequate for any normal intercourse: a duty and a pleasure to which it was almost immediately put.

Having again applauded, the guests in no short time assembled themselves also in couples, and were disposing themselves upon the cushions placed about the room. It may be that there was some competition – that two gentlemen may have set their eyes upon the same girl; but if so, this led to no disagreement, and there were indeed no signs that anyone was disappointed by his partner – as who should be, indeed? – the girls being equally adept at provoking pleasure and satisfying it.

I was pleased to see that in particular Frank was enjoying a most agreeable coupling with Bella: my own experience had proved her a charming companion, and while Frank had begun by simply ploughing her in the most common of all attitudes, as I watched she contrived to roll about so that she was atop him, and to his surprise sat up and began ever so slowly rising and falling upon his captivated cock, while at the same time pinching with her fingers at his tits.

But what of Devon? It would be a shame for any person present in that room to be without comfort. At that moment Sophie took my hand and leading me past a set of cushions upon which M. le Brun was occupied with Dolly, indicated a corner where one slim and somewhat feminine young man crouched over young Denise, his head between her thighs, where (as it appeared from her expression) his tongue was successfully pleasuring her – while kneeling behind him and taking advantage of an attitude which raised and presented his hindquarters in a convenient manner, Devon was fucking him with a careful delicacy calculated to give pleasure without resulting in such damage as could easily be inflicted by so generous a weapon as that he possessed. Catching my eye, he winked and smiled, while the young man, raising his head from his task, flashed us a smile as cheerful as it was approving of his entertainment.

We now crept from the room, and made our way to the upper floor, where in a bedroom we had often shared in childhood, we celebrated our own rites of love, awareness of each other's desires and adeptness in satisfying them providing once more proof – if proof were needed – that if familiarity may sometimes breed contempt, it can also breed that love which is renewed and enriched by each separate communion.

Headline Delta Erotic Survey

In order to provide the kind of books you like to read – and to qualify for a free erotic novel of the Editor's choice – we would appreciate it if you would complete the following survey and send your answers, together with any further comments, to:

> Headline Book Publishing
> FREEPOST (WD 4984)
> London
> NW1 0YR

1. Are you male or female?
2. Age? Under 20 / 20 to 30 / 30 to 40 / 40 to 50 / 50 to 60 / 60 to 70 / over
3. At what age did you leave full-time education?
4. Where do you live? (Main geographical area)
5. Are you a regular erotic book buyer / a regular book buyer in general / both?
6. How much approximately do you spend a year on erotic books / on books in general?
7. How did you come by this book?
7a. If you bought it, did you purchase from:
    a national bookchain / a high street store / a newsagent / a motorway station / an airport / a railway station / other . . .
8. Do you find erotic books easy / hard to come by?
8a. Do you find Headline Delta erotic books easy / hard to come by?
9. Which are the best / worst erotic books you have ever read?
9a. Which are the best / worst Headline Delta erotic books you have ever read?
10. Within the erotic genre there are many periods, subjects and literary styles. Which of the following do you prefer:
10a. (period) historical / Victorian / C20th / contemporary / future?
10b. (subject) nuns / whores & whorehouses / Continental frolics / s&m / vampires / modern realism / escapist fantasy / science fiction?

10c. (styles) hardboiled / humorous / hardcore / ironic / romantic / realistic?

10d. Are there any other ingredients that particularly appeal to you?

11. We try to create a cover appearance that is suitable for each title. Do you consider them to be successful?

12. Would you prefer them to be less explicit / more explicit?

13. We would be interested to hear of your other reading habits. What other types of books do you read?

14. Who are your favourite authors?

15. Which newspapers do you read?

16. Which magazines?

17 Do you have any other comments or suggestions to make?

If you would like to receive a free erotic novel of the Editor's choice (available only to UK residents), together with an up-to-date listing of Headline Delta titles, please supply your name and address. Please allow 28 days for delivery.

Name ....

Address ....

....

....